MARY BY MYSELF

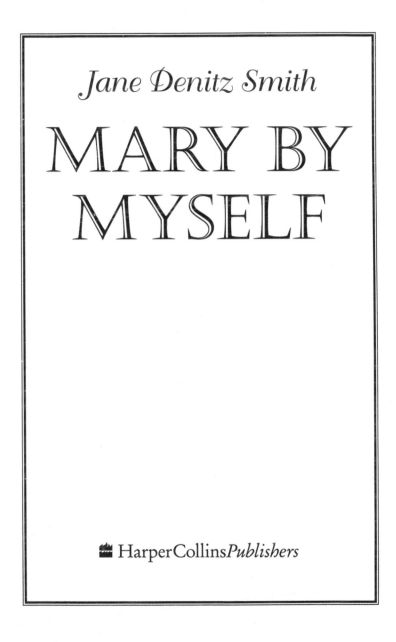

Jane Denitz Smith

MARY BY MYSELF

HarperCollins*Publishers*

Library of Congress Cataloging-in-Publication Data
Smith, Jane Denitz
  Mary by myself / by Jane Denitz Smith.
    p.   cm.
  Summary: While adjusting to new friends and new activities at summer
camp, ten-year-old Mary remembers her infant sister Felicity, who died
suddenly in her sleep several months earlier.
  ISBN 0-06-024517-4. — ISBN 0-06-024518-2 (lib. bdg.)
  [1. Camps—Fiction. 2. Death—Fiction. 3. Sudden infant death
syndrome—Fiction. 4. Sisters—Fiction.]   I. Title.
PZ7.S6497Mar   1994   93-47457
[Fic]—dc20   CIP
                                                                       AC

Typography by Elynn Cohen
1   2   3   4   5   6   7   8   9   10
❖
First Edition

For my parents with love
and to Peter, Who Told Me So

MARY BY MYSELF

Chapter One

I HAD BEEN AN ONLY CHILD for ten years—and had nagged my parents about having a baby for so long— that the summer Felicity was born I would wake up some mornings and wonder if she was real or just a sister who had appeared in my dreams.

Before she was born, I helped my parents prepare her room and was allowed to choose the wallpaper—a yellow-and-white pinstripe to go on the patch of wall under the eaves. When we went to the department store to buy her crib, I fingered the tiny overalls and undershirts, and longed to stock her small bureau with them. But my parents were superstitious, and told me we'd have to wait until after she was born.

My mother went into labor in the middle of the night, and my best friend Adrienne Tannenbaum's mother came to stay with me. She drove me to the hospital right after breakfast. My mother was tired but hungry, and I sat next to her on the hospital bed while she ate an egg salad sandwich. Felicity slept next to us, in a bassinet, and everyone said she looked just like me, except for her ears, which were large, like my father's side of the family.

I held her hand in the back of the car as we drove home two days later. My grandmother was there and had cooked roasted chicken and new potatoes. Felicity slept in her wicker basket in the middle of the table while we ate, and we toasted her arrival with champagne.

Her room was next to mine and down the hall from our parents'. Before her morning nap I would give her her bottle, and lay her gently down in her crib. It was a humid August, and I'd open the window as wide as I could and only cover her with a thin cotton blanket. I would hold on to the bars of her crib and see if I could match my breathing to her short, shallow breaths.

When Felicity was three months old, she could almost hold her head up, and if you dangled a toy in front of her, she could follow it with her eyes. When she was four months old, she liked to sit in her infant seat on the dining-room table and watch while I did my Saturday-morning dusting. Sometimes I'd bundle her up and put her in her carriage for her nap. Though snow dusted the lawn, the sun could still be strong and penetrating.

Felicity cried when she was hungry or tired, but otherwise she was happy just to be sur-rounded by familiar nests of cribs and carriages and arms. Even though she slept most of the day, her tiny body seemed to fill our house like a soft vapor. Every new achievement was an occasion for kisses, long-distance calls to my grandpar-ents. She was connected to us, all day. Even downstairs, after her bedtime, my parents would listen for her cry on the infant monitor—my father called it the umbilical cord—that allowed us to eavesdrop every time Felicity sighed or turned over on her mattress.

We took her everywhere in her infant seat—movies, the mall, out to dinner. And we made plans. We decided we'd go to the far reaches of New England next summer. My parents said they were sure winter would never end, as they spread maps out on the dining room table and guided their fingers along the routes through Massachusetts and Maine and maybe even as far as Nova Scotia.

School mornings were dark, and I wished I could stay home with her and eat French toast with syrup. Sometimes I would miss the bus on purpose, and my mother would sigh and bundle Felicity up in her snowsuit and drive me. When I came home in the afternoon, there she'd be, up from her nap, waiting. There were many icy rains and several heavy snowfalls that winter, and sometimes, after school, my mother would hold Felicity up at the bay window so she could watch while I made angels in the snow, and igloos. "My Present," I called her, for that's what she was like, day after day, all the long and overcast season.

That February afternoon, I came home from school later than usual. The band was rehearsing for the Winter Snowball Concert, and I played clarinet. Even though I wasn't musically inclined, my parents had insisted the year before that I study an instrument. But I still couldn't read music, so I spent most of the practice moving my fingers, pretending I was playing and hoping Mr. Conte, the band director, wouldn't notice.

There was just a thin ribbon of orange light on the horizon by the time the bus dropped me off. The waistband of my new skirt was itching, and I couldn't wait to change into my sweatpants. Our driveway was full of cars. I wondered why my parents hadn't told me were having company on a school night. I opened the front door and smelled perfume and heard voices in the living room. I saw my aunt Margaret and the Tannenbaums.

I stood in the archway of the room and looked for my parents. Only when my aunt moved aside did I see them sitting on the couch, shaking their heads while they were spoken to in low voices.

Then my mother saw me. She held out her arms, and my aunt walked toward me and led me to the couch. My father stared at me, as if he didn't recognize who I was.

Felicity was not there. As suddenly and seamlessly as she had entered our lives, she was gone. From the different voices talking to me, I pieced together the events: Felicity's morning nap; my mother downstairs in the laundry room, putting a white load into the washer; the monitor on, of course, in the kitchen; my mother, downstairs just for a minute, but she's blaming herself; she thinks she heard a peep; she read the paper and had a second cup of coffee; Felicity was sleeping longer than usual; a game show; a phone call; still Felicity slept; it was lunchtime; my mother warmed Felicity's bottle and prepared her apricots so they'd be ready (my father said she acted like a growling baby bear when she first woke up); my mother went upstairs; Felicity was lying on her side; she had kicked the blankets off; my mother opened the blinds to let in the daylight;

Felicity was a light sleeper; Felicity did not move; my mother whispered her name; she yelled it; she shook Felicity but she did not move; she called an ambulance, and they rushed to the hospital, but there was nothing to be done. It happens while they're sleeping, and nobody knows why. All I know is that I gave Felicity a bottle and let her suck on my fingers before I left for school, and by the time I came home, she wasn't there.

Chapter Two

MY NAME IS MARY Vanessa Cole, but when I'm eighteen, I think I'll have it legally changed to Vanessa Mary Cole, which is much more interesting.

We live in a development called Capulet Estates. Our house is ten years old—older than most—so the trees around it seem sturdy compared to their sapling neighbors. There are three styles of houses here: Colonial, Tudor, and Modern. Ours is Colonial, and sometimes, at twilight, when I can't see the green trailer the construction men park in front of the half-completed Tudor across the street, I pretend I'm a girl from the 1800s waiting for my father to ride home in his horse-and-buggy. When he swings his Buick into the driveway and climbs out of the car, looking sweaty and smelling of aftershave, I jump into his arms and say, "Oh, Father, Father, I'm so glad you've arrived safely." Then he pats my head and says something like "It wasn't a picnic on the thruway, pumpkin, but it wasn't *that* bad" as he lowers me, and we walk inside.

At the edge of the development there is a field, and beyond the field is an underpass where you can hear the cars from the highway whizzing overhead. Just beyond the underpass there's the Little League baseball diamond, and way beyond that, there's a steep hill. An oak tree marks the top of the hill, and when I was little, that's where I'd go when I wanted to get away. It's the quietest place I know, and even when it's so hot that no one goes outside unless they have to— even when the only sound is the hum of the air conditioners that line our block with the same regularity as the newly planted trees—a breeze was always blowing in my oak.

My father works late these evenings: He says that carpet sales drop off in the summer, so he has to put in overtime to make up for the losses. My mother talks about going back to work in the fall, just to take her mind off things. But for now, she sits in the backyard most of the day, applying suntan lotion, sipping an iced coffee, and working on the crossword puzzle. Sometimes she'll ask me to bring her a yogurt, or listen for the phone while she closes her eyes, but usually I walk in and out of her line of vision as if I were invisible.

Most days I go to the pool with Adrienne. She has trouble with ear infections and can't spend too much time in the water. She stands on the top step and watches while I practice back dives in the deep end. Then we buy bags of potato chips from the snack bar and eat them while we play cards, or read, or french braid each other's hair. Adrienne's mother sits at the center of a circle of women. We listen as they compare notes about diets and dinner parties. Sometimes they'll look at me and lean forward and their voices will drop. Or they'll say things like "Mary, you be sure to tell your mother we miss her" or "Tell that snobby mother of yours not to be a stranger." Last summer, my mother would have been here too, gossiping and warning me to be careful. Now she says no one can understand what she's going through, and idle chitchat gives her a migraine.

Adrienne and I lie on our stomachs on our beach towels. I know she's waiting for me to talk, but I don't feel like it. As long as I've known Adrienne, she's always made me go first. I have to be the first to feel the water to make sure it's not too cold. When we walk the block between her house and mine, I go first, to make sure the Morrows' big German shepherd isn't off its leash. I order our Slurpees at the 7 Eleven, and test the rocks across the creek to make sure they form a solid bridge.

The sun is beating on my back, and I know that if I don't turn over soon, I'll burn. "Daddy's doing a barbecue tonight, in honor of Terry coming home from camp. Want to come?" she asks. Terry is Adrienne's older brother. He's fourteen and has just spent two weeks at computer camp.

"Sure."

"Mom, Mary's coming for dinner," she calls. Adrienne's mother extends a finger in her girlfriend's direction, telling her to hold her thought.

"Good," she says. "Just don't forget to call your mother, Mary."

"I won't," I say. I reach for my blue jeans and pull a dime out of the pocket, and walk to the pay phone.

I let the phone ring and ring, because I know how long it takes to walk across the backyard, open the screen door, and walk up the stairs to answer.

"Hello?" I hear. My mother is annoyed.

"Hi. It's me, Mary."

"I just fell into a deep sleep the minute you called," she says.

"Sorry."

"So what's up?"

"Adrienne invited me for dinner. Can I go?"

"I never see you."

14

"Yes, you do."

"No, I don't."

"That's not true," I say.

"Honey, I'm too tired to argue. What time will you be home?"

"Eight thirty," I say.

"Have fun," she says.

"And look both ways before you cross the street. Drivers can't see you at dusk."

"I will. I love you, Mom."

"What? I can't hear you. Frank Mills just started his lawn mower."

"'Bye," I say, and hang up. It's silly, I know, but I can tell I'm going to cry, so I walk to the edge of the pool without stopping and dive in.

Chapter Three

I SIT NEXT TO ADRIENNE ON the cold concrete steps that lead from the kitchen door to her backyard. We are watching her father arrange the charcoal inside the Weber grill. He does this with great care, and the lines in his forehead deepen in concentration, as if he were a doctor performing a complicated operation. Without looking up, he says, "Adrienne, more charcoal."

"Where is it, Daddy?" she asks.

"Leaning against the screen door."

Adrienne looks around, but doesn't see the blue bag. I stand up and bring it to him.

"Thanks, kiddo," he says. "We'll be eating in half an hour, I'd say."

Mrs. Tannenbaum slides open the screen door behind us and walks carefully down the stairs carrying a tray filled with plastic utensils and brightly colored paper plates. "This is what summer is about!" she announces. She spins around, showing off her flowered tennis outfit and filling the air with her rosy perfume.

Adrienne and I eat hamburgers and handfuls of chips, and she whispers to me that Terry has a girlfriend—someone he met in computer camp. She knows because she saw her phone number, encircled in a heart, lying on his desk. We have spent a lot of time in Terry's room—though never when he is around. We rummage through his desk drawers and his back issues of *Boys' Life*, like detectives looking for clues. I look at Terry to see if he looks any different, and he does; although maybe it's just that I haven't seen him in such a long time. He is taller, and his hair is short, so you can really see his features.

"I bet he kissed her," Adrienne says.

I look at his face and try to imagine him

kissing this girl. Would he put his arms around her waist, or would she put her arms around his neck, standing on her tiptoes, like in a movie?

"Hey, Mary, catch!" Terry says, and a kickball bounces off my head.

"Keep the ball away from the house," shouts Mr. Tannenbaum. I throw the ball back at Terry, and he throws it, harder, at me. I run barefoot through the dewy grass, and my feet feel as sure-footed as a fox's padded paws. It's hard to see Terry in this fading light, but still I chase him, around the front of the house and back again. He's hiding behind a tree, but he doesn't know I see him, and I sneak up slowly and attack him from behind. He wrestles me to the ground, pinning my arms behind me, and I scream in advance, knowing he's about to tickle me.

"Leave her alone, Terry," says Adrienne.

"But this is war!" Terry says.

Adrienne jumps on Terry's back, and soon we are all wrestling, and then, panting, we lie on our backs and watch the fireflies. I'm between them, and I pretend they're my family; and then I remember it's late, and my own mother and father are probably waiting for me, so I get up.

"Sleep over," says Adrienne, pulling me back down on the wet grass. "We can make caramel popcorn."

I picture my parents alone, in front of the television, wondering where I am. My father's probably looking at his watch, getting ready to call or drive to Adrienne's house to pick me up. When I think of my house, it's dark, except for the light in the living room. Not even the porch light has been turned on. But when I look at Adrienne's house, every window is lit, soft and yellow, like the fireflies' light. I see Mr. and Mrs. Tannenbaum putting dirty dishes in the dishwasher. They're laughing, and I think I hear music.

I go inside to call my house and ask if I can sleep over. My father answers the phone. He says I should just be sure to make myself available tomorrow. He wants to clean the garage and will need my help.

"How are you, Daddy?" I ask.

"How am I supposed to be?" he says. I don't know what he means, so I kiss him good night into the receiver and hang up.

19

———

Adrienne and I lie in bed and look up at the glow-in-the-dark planets and comets and stars she has stuck onto the ceiling. It's hard for me to believe that what I am looking at's not real, when I can see the moon through the window and hear the crickets outside. We hold hands between our twin beds and talk about what it will be like when we move up to junior high school. How will I ever find my way around those giant halls? Will we ever see each other during the day? And what about dances? Do you have to go to those dances? We know a girl just a year ahead of us who already wears a junior high boy's leather jacket. We can't imagine this; it seems so far away. I sing show tunes, softly, and when I look at Adrienne, she's asleep.

The window that leads out to the roof is open. I draw one leg and then the other leg through. I'm standing on the roof looking down at other houses on the block, and the highway, still humming, beyond. I know I have a book of matches inside, in the pocket of my jeans. I look down a lot when I walk, to see if I can find things people have dropped, such as coins or old postcards or matches. I like matches. I like to light them and hold them between my fingers until I can begin to feel the scorch of the flame. Then I blow them out and suck on the carbon tips.

It is a soft and starry night. I get the matches from my pocket and watch Adrienne push a loose strand of hair away from her forehead as she sleeps. Then I climb back out onto the roof. The tar paper is raw against my toes, and I sit down, drawing my nightgown under my feet. One by one, I light the matches, blow them out, suck on their tips, and toss them away. The air is humid, and I think I can smell the scent of every flower sleeping below me.

Suddenly, the front door opens. A flashlight is flicked on. Mr. Tannenbaum's beaming the light up toward the roof. I don't move. The light misses me, and then, on its return arc, it catches the edge of my nightgown.

"Girls?" he says.

"It's me," I whisper.

"I heard footsteps on the roof. Are you trying to scare us half to death? What are you doing out there?"

"I don't know," I say.

"What's that smell?" he asks. He is still shining the flashlight in my eyes, so I can't see his face.

"What smell?"

"I smell something burning."

Adrienne is awake now, leaning out the window.

"I was lighting matches," I say.

"You were trying to burn my house down?"

"No. I just like lighting matches."

"Tell that to my insurance agent when this place goes up in smoke. Get back inside and go to sleep. We'll talk about this in the morning."

We're up by eight, and by the time we go downstairs for breakfast, my parents are there. They look tired, like they stayed out too late at a party the night before. They don't say much. Mostly they just shake their heads, say they're disappointed, and point toward the door.

"And after all your parents have been through. For shame," Mrs. Tannenbaum whispers to me, as I am escorted home again.

Chapter Four

I SPEND MOST OF THE DAY IN my room. Every time I begin to go downstairs, I hear my parents' muffled voices in the kitchen—voices that occasionally rise in an unhappy crescendo and then fall again. I sleep, and I reread my favorite chapters from *Little Women* and wonder why I can't be as serene as Beth, or as boring as Meg.

I hear footsteps on the stairs that stop in front of my door. No one ever knocks before they come into my room, but today I've locked my door. They try to open it, but can't.

"Mary," says my father. "Open the door."

I pretend I'm asleep.

"Mary, I have to get back to the stove before supper burns. Open the door." My mother's voice is edgy.

"Don't push me, Mary, because I'll break it down if I have to." My father is rattling the door knob. I stand up and open the door, and my parents walk in and point to my desk chair. I sit, and they stand in front of me.

"Mary, we're concerned," my father begins.

"That's an understatement," says my mother. "How long have you enjoyed lighting matches? That's what I want to know."

"I thought you wanted *me* to talk," my father says, glaring at her.

"Sorry," she says.

"We've decided to send you to camp."

"Just for August," my mother adds.

"It might be good for you to get away, have a change of scene. Your mother's been making phone calls all day."

"It's kind of late in the game to find an opening. It wasn't easy," she says.

"We found a place." He turns to my mother. "What's it called?"

"Camp Pine Grove. It's in the Poconos."

My father offers me his first smile of the day. "It sounds so nice, I wish I could go there for a vacation."

"It should be nice. It costs enough," says my mother. "Not that that has anything to do with it."

"So what do you think?"

I tie and untie the laces on my sneakers. My mother pushes a strand of hair away from my eyes. "You look like a shaggy dog," she says. "We'll have to get you a haircut before you go anywhere."

"You swim in a lake. And they have archery," my father says, slapping his hand on his thigh as if that puts the icing on the cake, as he says.

I don't speak, not because I really mind the idea of going away to camp, but because I like having both my parents here at the same time, in my bedroom, talking to me.

"Should we do it, pumpkin?" my father asks. "We told the director we'd let her know today. She's got someone else waiting to fill the spot if we don't."

"OK," I say. "I don't care." And I don't.

"'Atta girl," my father says. My mother looks at him. Her eyes widen, signaling relief.

"When do I go?" I ask.

"In two days," they say. "Day after tomorrow."

At the mall that afternoon we shop for camp clothes. My mother has brought along the checklist the director gave her over the phone. I need hiking boots, a mess kit, a soap dish, insect repellent, a flashlight. We buy new T-shirts, and warm pajamas. I can't believe everything piling up on the counter is for me.

We have lunch at Hi-Fi Pizza, and my parents hold hands across the table. A lady is pulling a baby carriage up the front steps of the restaurant. She has packages under her arms, and the baby is fussy. My father stands up, opens the door, and helps her push the carriage over the top step. The woman thanks him, and my father leans down, toward the baby.

"How old?" he asks.

"Three months," she says. "He's my first. I'm still getting the hang of this."

My father returns to the table, where my

mother is busily wiping crumbs off the surface with her napkin and throwing trash away. He puts his hand on top of hers, to stop her from cleaning.

"That's their job," he says. "Let's go home. What do you say?"

We smile at the lady and her baby, open the door, and step into the sunlight and heat.

Chapter Five

I'VE BEEN AT CAMP PINE
Grove for three days. It is rest hour, and
I'm lying on my bunk, trying to write
Adrienne a letter. She called me on the
phone before I left to tell me that she was still my
best friend, but I know it will take longer for her
parents to forgive me.

There's three of us in our enormous tent,
which is pitched on top of a platform and cinder
blocks above the ground. The walls are thick
canvas that we roll up in the morning to let the
sunlight in, and roll down at night to keep the
mosquitoes out.

Celeste sleeps in the cot next to mine, and Laura has moved her cot, which is covered with a puffy, flowered coverlet, to the farthest corner of the room. Laura is small and thin. Her hair is nearly white, and you can't see her eyes because they are covered by bangs. But her cheeks are as pink as ballerina tights. She sits on her bed most of the time, self-contained as a beetle that curls up inside its shell as soon as you touch it. She reads whenever she has the chance, and every day so far, she's gotten huge care packages in the mail that she opens and puts in the middle of the floor. She never touches any of it, not even the KitKats.

Laura wears only a black, oversized man's T-shirt to bed. But no matter how many layers of clothes I put on—socks, sweatpants over my flannel pajamas—I still wake up frozen in one position and having to go to the latrine. So I climb out of my sleeping bag nest, turn on my flashlight, and walk down the wooded path to the outhouse. By the time I return to my cabin I am wide-eyed and awake, and it takes me nearly until morning to fall asleep again.

Last night when I woke I up, I shined my flashlight at the ceiling so that I could see without waking anyone else. I looked at each of these girls—strangers, still—who slept in the same room that I did at night. I felt protective, like a pioneer woman in the wilderness, defending her babes against intruders.

But where was Laura? Laura was not there. Maybe I would pass her, coming from the latrine. But I didn't. Where had she gone? Did she run away? Should I report that she was missing? I waited up for Laura, but she never came back. I must have fallen asleep, because when the wake-up call came over the loud speaker, I imagined it was the voice of the lifeguard at the pool, telling me not to dive off the shallow end. And there was Laura, sitting on the edge of her made-up bed, fully dressed and reading. Laura was here. I looked at her face as if it would offer me an explanation, but she looked at me and said Hi without smiling.

Tonight, I wake up again. But it's a warmer night, and I don't need the bathroom. I reach for my flashlight, and it falls on the floor. Someone turns over in her sleep, but no one else moves. I press the button and shine it at the bottom edge of Laura's bed. She's not there, but by morning she's once again slipped inside her sleeping bag. She is more tired than usual, and only gets up when Marjorie, the head counselor, passes through for third wake-up rounds.

I like the routines of each day: wake-up and chores, bunk inspection and then breakfast in the big mess hall, dodgeball or kickball until the midmorning sun gets too strong. Then we might sit under a tree while one of the counselors demonstrates knot tying, or how to build a fire that will stay lit with only one match.

We have lunch at noon, and then an hour of rest, and then a long hike, maybe through the woods, and in late afternoon, a swim in the lake. No matter how hot I've been all day, or how much I have looked forward to this, the first plunge into the cold water always leaves me breathless and dizzy. No swimming pool could ever make cold this bottomless. Some girls spend half the swim period or more just getting wet. They paint the surface of the water with their toes and screech whenever there's a splash nearby. They fix their bathing caps, maybe so they won't get an ear infection, and smooth the edges of their beach towels.

I run and dive in and swim out as far as I can, or at least beyond the line of other swimmers. Then I float on my back and look at the small dome of sky and the circle of pine trees around the lake. Sometimes the lifeguard has to blow her whistle two or three times before I hear her, and swim back to shore to join my group.

We have dinner, and after dinner we sing songs. Then there's a movie or a campfire. Our counselors tell ghost stories, and sometimes we make S'mores. I'm always hungry here, and in the dark, if no one's looking, I'll take more than my share of marshmallows.

Though I'm not particularly close to any of the girls yet, I quickly discover that Celeste Johnson, who shares my cabin, is the girl no one likes. She wears too much bug repellent and always complains about the cold and needs to go to the infirmary to get shots for her allergies. If we get demerits during inspection, it's usually because Celeste has shoved her dirty laundry under her bed again or forgot to do a work job. But I lent her my poncho the second day of camp, when it was raining and she couldn't find hers, and ever since then, she thinks I'm her best friend. Even though I try to sit with the other girls at meals, Celeste always manages to find a place next to or across from me. The more I ignore her, the closer she seems to stick to me.

Only Laura doesn't mind eating alone. Only Laura doesn't *seem* to mind. I watch her a lot, when she's not looking. She always finds a seat at the end of the table, with at least one place setting between her and the rest of us. She likes to wear black, even when the temperature is 90 degrees, and she reads during the entire meal. The first couple of days of camp, the head counselor, Marjorie, told her that part of the camp experience was socializing, but Laura just looked at her as though she were crazy, and turned back to her book. The other girls whisper about her behind her back, saying that her hair looks like a rat's nest because she never combs it, and she wears black all the time because she is evil. But still, whenever Laura will put one of her almost daily care packages in the middle of the floor, every one of these same girls will swoop down and help themselves to mini Hershey's bars and Peppermint Patties and never say thank you.

By the end of the first week, I am still sitting with these same girls, but I'm watching Laura's corner of the table. I dress in the morning to please her: hair uncombed, my most faded T-shirts. And I color over my white tennis sneakers with a black Magic Marker.

I haven't said more than hello to Laura; she makes me feel shy. And I notice she's missing one afternoon during swimming period. At dinner our counselors announce that Laura has hurt her ankle on her way to the latrine, and will be on crutches for a few days. She won't be able to put much weight on her ankle and needs someone to bring her her meals. No one volunteers—not one of those girls who devoured the contents of her care packages—and so I raise my hand.

Chapter Six

I WALK SLOWLY BACK TO our tent, carrying Laura's tray of macaroni and cheese and bug juice. A letter from my parents is on top of the tray:

Dear Mary,
Say hello to Camp Pine Grove from me! Dad is out now, buying a new sprinkler at the hardware store, and I am just about to go to the market and buy some chopped chuck for supper. It's been hot here, but soon enough, the cold weather will come. Might as well enjoy it while we can.

Don't forget to use your bug repellent. Mosquitoes carry diseases. We miss you. The house is so quiet that sometimes I turn on the TV just for company. Dad tells me we're throwing money away keeping our membership at the pool if I never plan on using it again. Oh well, that's not your problem.

We miss you and send you 1,000,000 kisses. Can't wait until Parents' Weekend. And I know you're busy, Mary, but just drop a postcard and let me know how you're doing. We worry.

Love,
Mom

It makes me a little homesick, hearing my mother tell me how much she misses me; but I know that if I called her on the phone, she would probably just sound aggravated and say that I was calling at a bad time. I put down Laura's tray and fold my mother's letter into the smallest square possible and stuff it into the back pocket of my jeans.

Laura is writing in a notebook when I arrive with her tray. I put it on her night table and stand beside her bed, watching.

"Yes?" she says, looking up. "Thanks."

"You're welcome," I say. Laura spears some macaroni and cheese with her fork and puts it in her mouth. Then she keeps writing. "Do you need anything else?" I ask.

"No."

"I like to write, too," I say. "Mostly poems, but sometimes stories, for my school's literary magazine."

Laura doesn't answer. She picks her tooth with her nail, and continues.

"What do you like to write for fun?" I ask.

Laura rolls her eyes, impatiently. "This isn't fun," she say. "This is work." I look over her shoulder, but her handwriting is nearly illegible. "I'm taking notes."

"For what?"

"For my book."

"That sounds like fun."

"It isn't supposed to be fun." She sounds offended. "Like I said, it's my work."

"Sorry," I say. "How was I supposed to know?"

"How long do you have to bring me my meals?"

"I don't know."

"Well, thanks for the macaroni. You can go now," Laura says.

I stand in the doorway and say, "No one else even *wanted* to bring you your stupid meals. I just thought you might like to know that."

"So."

"I was the only one who volunteered."

Laura writes on the rubber tip of one of her high-tops with a ballpoint pen. She shrugs her shoulders and says, "Am I supposed to care?"

"I don't know what you're supposed to do, Laura," I say, and I start down the steps of the platform.

"Mary?"

"What?" I am listening to her, but I don't turn around.

"Who's going to bring me my dinner?"

"I don't know," I say.

"Will you?" she asks.

"I don't know," I say, but I'm only playing a game. I know I'll bring Laura her dinner, if that's what she wants. I've already fallen under her spell.

"Just tell the cook no meat," she says. "I'm a vegetarian. OK?"

"I don't know," I repeat, but I'm heading down the wooded path toward the mess hall to deliver Laura's instructions to the kitchen staff.

Chapter Seven

BY THE END OF THE WEEK, Laura's ankle has improved enough for her to walk, although she still isn't allowed to put too much weight on it.

I've brought her her meals, and she, in return, has let me be her friend. We never share secrets, but we do things together, like sneak out of the tent during rest hour and gather plants in the woods. She can identify all kinds of wildflowers, and we cut them and hang them upside down over our cots so they can dry. Laura names the different varieties of thistles, and I watch her as she pulls the purple blossom off its thorny stem, grinds it between two smooth stones, and places it in a plastic sandwich bag, neatly labeled. I am learning, too, for instance, that in the marshy land around the lake we can find lady's slippers; and in the meadows there are more black-eyed Susans than we could ever gather.

I no longer sit with the same girls at lunch, and letters from my family or Adrienne don't hold much interest. Laura and I do everything together. Marjorie talks to us about branching out and making other friends, and I have seen the other girls laugh at us behind our backs. But I don't care about anything anymore, except me and Laura.

Now that Laura and I spend so much time together, I no longer wake up in the middle of the night to see if she is sleeping or has left the tent. I dress warmly and curl up with my legs tucked against my chest like a baby's. I face the wall, away from the others, and sleep until the wake-up announcement.

One night, I go to bed with the sound of a slow rain tapping against the canvas tent. The wind blows through the tall pines, and I close my eyes and imagine my mother, father, and I are at the ocean. I am sitting close to the water's edge with my father, and we are digging a moat around our sand castle. My mother, her stomach just beginning to bulge with the fullness that will be Felicity, waves to us as she applies more sunblock. I know that evening we'll shower, and I'll put on my new sundress and sit on the chair outside our room, on the balcony of our motel, waiting for my parents to come. They look beautiful, and each puts an arm around me as we walk down the boardwalk to a restaurant for a lobster dinner.

Someone is shaking me by the shoulders and whispering my name in my ear. I open my eyes and there is Laura, fully dressed. "Come with me," she says, and, not fully awake, I climb out of bed and reach for my sneakers and my thickest sweater. We walk down the steps of the tent platform. The rain has stopped, but droplets of water from low-lying branches brush against my face. The moon has risen over the trees, and lights our path so clearly that Laura never even bothers to turn on the flashlight that she holds in her hand. We walk past the infirmary and the director's cottage, past the mess hall and the pond, across the open field with the flagpole in the center. We are at the edge of the woods now. Laura points to a faintly worn path into the forest, and I duck and flail my arms so that the brambles don't scratch my face. We don't speak. I step into pools of mud and pull my feet out. My sneakers are sopped, but it doesn't matter. Maybe it's the darkness that makes it seem as though this journey will never end. I'm panting, trying to keep up with Laura, who crashes through, far ahead of me.

Finally she stops. I can see a little clearing just ahead. She turns to me and says, "This has to be our secret. You have to swear you'll never tell."

"I swear," I say.

"We have to take an oath." She reaches for a strand of my hair and yanks. I put my hand up to my head and look at her in amazement. Then she pulls a piece of her own hair off. She holds the two strands in front her and reaches into her pocket for a book of matches. She hands the matches to me.

"Ignite them," she says, and I touch the flame to our hair, and it sizzles, filling the air with a strange and musty odor.

"Now we're sisters," she says, and we walk a little farther.

There's a house in the clearing, almost so small that at first it looks like a playhouse. But it is made out of stone. Laura opens the heavy wooden door and we walk inside. The house has only one room, with a cement floor and a large stone fireplace. Kindling and thicker branches are gathered in a corner, and the room smells of damp ashes.

"What is it?" I say. "How did you find it?"

Laura runs her finger over the one remaining frame in the room's single window. "It's a hunter's lodge. Isn't it beautiful?"

"I guess," I say.

"It was the first or second afternoon, right after camp started. I was supposed to be at arts and crafts, or something stupid like that. I lied and said I had a headache, so they let me stay in the tent. But I decided to see if I could take a walk and get lost, which is something I like to do. Anyway, I followed that path into the woods and this is where it led me. Like Hansel and Gretel."

I had never heard Laura say so much at once. "Is this where you come in the middle of the night?" I ask. Laura looks at me, pretending not to understand. "When you leave the cabin in the middle of the night," I repeat.

"You're dreaming," she says.

"I shine a flashlight on your bed sometimes, and you're not there."

"So what are you doing up in the middle of the night? Spying on me?"

"Sometimes I get cold. It makes me have to go to the bathroom. Is that a crime?"

"I get up. I walk."

"Where?"

"What are you? My mother?" She laughs, and shakes her head.

"I worry about you. I thought we were sisters."

"No."

"Have a piece of bubble gum." I pull one out of my front pocket and throw it at her. "It's really yours, anyway. I stole it from your care package."

She thanks me, and begins sweeping the floor.

Chapter Eight

EVERY TIME WE COME TO our Crimson Lodge—which is what we name it because of the reddish color of the tiles on the roof—whether it's during rest period or in the middle of the night, Laura and I first have to do our chores. We sweep away the leaves and twigs that blow in through the open window. I take the cup that held my toothbrush and bring it to our lodge to fill with fresh wildflowers. And Laura no longer gives her care packages away. We carry them back to our little house and fill the cupboard above the sink that no longer works.

We're working on voodoo dolls. Laura's doll looks like her, and mine sort of looks like me. She is making hers out of twigs held together by string and painted black, like the clothes she wears. I make my likeness out of an old sock stuffed with grass, so that I have a swollen waist and tiny head. I look more like a snowman than a girl, but I carve two brown eyes out of wood and glue them on, so at least part of it resembles me. The dolls really seal our friendship, Laura says, announcing that if I betray her or she betrays me, we have the right to torture each other's dolls.

I'm eating Cracker Jack while I'm working, when I ask Laura where the care packages come from. At first she doesn't want to talk about it. But I press, and she tells me that her real mother lives in New Mexico, but that her new stepmother tries to win her over by sending her these huge boxes of treats.

"Is she nice?" I ask.

"She's not my mother and she wants to be. It's really obnoxious."

"Is she nice to you?"

"She buys me things. She tries to take me out for lunch, but I don't let her. And makes me read her poetry."

"She's a poet?"

"She thinks she is. She teaches literature at the community college, but she tells everyone she's really a poet. She keeps telling me I'm a poet, too."

"What's her name?"

"Tania. Isn't that revolting?"

I think she sounds wonderful.

"And she hates Eve, which is almost unforgivable." Laura seems to assume that I know exactly what she's talking about.

"Who's Eve?" I ask.

"My cat. But Tania," she says, sarcastically, "has a slight allergy to cats, and can't tolerate Eve jumping on her bed. Once I saw her peel Eve off her lap and throw her halfway across the kitchen. Eve almost cracked her head on the cupboard. I told my father that if she hurts Eve, I'm going to sue her. He thought I was joking. They sent me here so they could go on some theater tour of London. Whoopee." She looks at her watch. "We have to go now," she says.

We're at the edge of the woods now, back on camp property. Though the air's still cool and damp, and the outline of the moon hovers in the sky, I can tell by the way the mist is rising off the field that it is going to be a hot day. We tiptoe into the tent and I lie down, quiet, and try to count how many different kinds of birdcalls I hear. I fall asleep just as the camp director plays a recording of a trumpet call over the loudspeaker. I groan like the other girls, and begin to laugh, but then I remember that Laura wouldn't laugh—she'd just roll her eyes—so I stop myself and pull shorts and a T-shirt out of my trunk.

By midafternoon, the sound of thunder can be heard in the distance, in the mountains beyond the lake. At the first flash of lightning, the lifeguard blows his whistle, and we all run on shore, grab our towels, and hurry back to our campsite. But the rain is already falling—hard and steady. We're given permission to stay here until dinner or go to the arts and crafts barn. I'm tired from last night's trip to our lodge in the woods, and so I stay. Laura stays, too, and is lying on her stomach, writing. I reread a postcard from my mother and father that begs me to send news and tells me how much they are looking forward to seeing me on Parents' Weekend, at the end of this week.

There is a weight on the end of my bed, and I look up. Celeste is sitting there, smiling at me. She's eating a candy bar from the camp canteen, and the chocolate in her mouth makes her look toothless. I have hardly spoken to Celeste since I lent her my poncho that rainy afternoon, right after camp had started. She had tried, it's true, but by then Laura had taken me to the lodge, and she didn't seem to like it when I talked to anyone else.

"Hi," she says. "Want a bite?"

"No thanks," I say, trying to look busy and avoiding looking at Laura, at the other end of the cabin.

"My mother wanted to send me to a camp for overweight kids this summer, but I promised her I'd try to cut down," Celeste says. "I treat myself to one a day. My sisters are skinny, wouldn't you know it, but my father just tells me there's that much more of me to love."

"Yeah?" I say, softly. I don't want to act too interested in conversation—not with Laura so close by.

"Oh well," she says. "At least I have good eyes. Everybody else in my family either has glasses or contact lenses."

She's not overweight, actually. She's soft, but not overweight. And she wears baggy clothes that don't do much for her figure, as my mother would say. But she has a nice face, rosy and freckled, and even though I pretend to be busy right now I don't mind her sitting on the end of my bed, keeping me company.

Celeste walks back to her trunk and brings me an envelope full of photographs. Her family. Sitting around a picnic table. "We kids go from six years old to twenty," she says, "and I'm right in the middle."

I take the picture from her hand and study it. "How many of you are there?"

"Five. Two younger sisters. Two older brothers. It's crazy. Not to mention all my brothers' friends who freeload off of us all the time. Of course the house is a mess because even if you do your chores, somebody comes along two seconds later, and makes corn chip crumbs on the couch, or Benny—"

"Who's Benny?"

"Our cocker spaniel. Or Benny has an accident on the carpet."

Celeste swings her legs, kicking the metal bed frame with a steady motion. "Do you have a picture of your house?"

I shake my head. "It's big and kind of new, and it's near my school."

"You're lucky," says Celeste. "We're too close for the bus, but it's still a pretty long walk. We found a good shortcut, though. So what do you have?"

I don't know what she's talking about.

"Brothers? Sisters? Both? Neither?"

No one's asked me this question, not even Laura, I suddenly realize.

"I have a sister," I hear myself saying. The wind is howling in my ears. My voice is small; I am at the other end of the cabin, whispering this to Celeste through a Dixie cup telephone.

"What's her name?" Celeste asks.

"Felicity. She's just a baby."

"A baby sister. You're so lucky. I love babies."

I hear myself telling Celeste that I have a picture of Felicity, and I find it, inside the little metal safe deposit box where I keep all my valuables. Felicity is propped up between my legs on my parents' bed. I am smiling at the camera, and she is facing me, reaching for the features on my face. She's wearing a terry cloth sleeper, and if I look closely, I can see a formula stain under her chin.

"Let me see," says Celeste. "What a cutie."

"You'll meet her on Parents' Weekend."

"I'll eat her up alive," says Celeste. "You must miss her."

"I miss her," I say, but then Laura sits up and tells us to go somewhere else if we want to talk, so Celeste goes back to her cot, and I sit on the steps of the tent platform, watching the rain.

Chapter Nine

LAURA SAYS CELESTE IS shallow and insipid. I'm not sure what that means, but it doesn't sound good. Laura also says that she won't sit with me in the dining room if I choose to sit with Celeste, because she'd rather not engage in any conversation at all than in trivial conversation about family and school. Sometimes I think I can be divided down the middle and separated into two halves. There's the Celeste half, that likes to sit around playing Old Maid and eating Hershey's bars on a rainy afternoon, and doesn't seem to care whether or not Laura ever gives her the time of day. And there's the Laura half, a black-clothed shadow, that only seems to come alive under moonlight, or under the half-light of the woods, like a toad.

And there's also Adrienne's world, back at home. She writes to tell me she's cut her hair just above chin length, kind of a bob. Her parents aren't mad at me anymore, just worried. And she likes some boy named Ben, who's already in junior high and barely notices her, except when she's in the pool and he sneak attacks by grabbing her ankles or dunking her from behind.

The counselors have divided us into teams, to tackle some of the duties of Parents' Weekend. I am on the bedtime snacks committee, with a small group of girls that doesn't include Laura or Celeste. This is fine with me. I am happy to let a girl named Ellie tell me what to do. She asks me whether I want to take charge of trail mix or fruit fondue, and I tell her it doesn't matter.

"Good," she says. "Mary has the right attitude," and I am surprised by how pleased her compliment makes me feel.

We gather on the steps of the counselors' tent,

before lunch, so each committee can report its progress. Suddenly Marjorie appears. "Where's Laura?" she asks.

"She's bizarre," I hear, and the door's been opened.

"She's a snob." "I try to be nice to her but she gives me the weirdest looks. It gives me the creeps." "Maybe she got lost." "Maybe they'll kick her out."

For a moment, I am loyal to Laura, and almost defend her. But I don't.

Marjorie looks at me. "Do you know where Laura is, Mary?" she asks.

I shrug my shoulders.

"Is there any place you can think of?" she continues.

"I've been with my committee most of the morning," I say.

The counselors huddle together, and we can't hear what they are saying.

"We'll wait until after lunch," Marjorie says. "Mess hall in a half hour," she adds. The girls stand up to leave. Marjorie comes over to me and puts her arm across my shoulders.

"You're closest to her, Mary. If you can think

of anything, it's important that you let me know."

"I will," I say.

"Because this is no laughing matter," she continues.

"I promise," I say.

At lunch, I sit next to Celeste, and eat my chicken croquettes and mushroom sauce with real appetite. Laura says institutional food stinks—and especially chicken croquettes—so the last time they were served, I pushed them to the side of my plate. But I like this food, and I am always hungry. So I eat my croquettes and even have a second helping of butterscotch pudding.

By midafternoon, Laura still hasn't returned. The director of the camp has been told. I can see her at the edge of our dodgeball game, talking to Marjorie and the other counselors. I can't lose today. I throw the ball and never miss. We go swimming and, for the first time, I don't keep anyone company on the sandy shore, but swim out to the diving platform and practice my cannonballs.

At dinner, I overhear the counselors debating

whether or not to call her parents or the police.

I know where Laura is; I have always known.

I eat my macaroni and cheese and apple crisp and slip away from the mess hall. It is song time, and a counselor from one of the younger units is sitting on a stool in front of the tables, tuning her guitar. Outside, I hear the first chorus of "Donkey Riding." I run down the stone path in the woods and catch myself from falling over some roots. I fly past the infirmary and the director's cabin. I cross the wide field and am at the edge of the woods.

With one look behind me, I separate the branches of the trees and follow the trail to the cabin. I can see the red sun lowering between the trees. Tomorrow will be even hotter. I knock on the door of Crimson Lodge, but no one answers. Laura is lying down on a rusty cot. Her eyes are red.

"You were crying," I say. I go toward her, ready to give her a hug. But she sits up straight, hands across her chest.

"I think I'm allergic to pollen," she says.

"What are you reading?" I point to a letter and

envelope beside her.

"My mother," she says. "More lies. What do I expect?"

"What do you mean?" I ask.

"I don't want to talk about it," she says, so icily that I can't move from where I'm standing. Then, in a softer voice, she says, "I knew you'd come. I'm starving. What did you bring?"

"Nothing."

"Thanks a lot."

"They're worried, Laura."

"They are?"

"You'd better come now, before they call your parents or the police. Marjorie's talking about calling the police."

"Good."

"What have you been doing all day?"

"Reading. Writing. I've kept myself busy. And you—did you have a fun day playing with all the girls?"

I don't know which way to turn. Which Mary should I be? Instead, I don't say anything, except "It's time to go, Laura."

She stands up, and to my surprise, follows me.

On the way back to camp, Laura makes me promise I won't tell anyone about the secret cabin—our lodge—and I agree. So we make up a story. We'll tell Marjorie that Laura took a walk and got lost and is sorry we were scared. Back at camp, Marjorie hugs Laura before she reprimands her and tells her how much we've all missed her. Then she thanks me for my cooperation, and asks Laura to follow her to the director's cabin, so they can speak to her privately. I go back to the tent and get ready for bed.

Laura comes back to the tent after lights-out and shines her flashlight in my eyes.

"They were really worried about me," she says. "Isn't that stupid?"

"Stupid?"

"I was fine." She pauses. "Everybody knew I was missing. The whole camp. That's what they told me."

"That's true." She's enjoying this, I think to myself. She ran away on purpose, just to see if anybody would know she was gone.

"I wondered where you were. You could have looked for me a little earlier."

"I was busy." I want to be alone now. I want to go away and think about Laura and the way she makes me feel. "But you're back now, and that's all that counts."

"Yes, unfortunately."

She takes off her sneakers and crawls beneath the fancy pink quilt that doesn't seem to suit her at all. She looks tiny.

I think of what my mother always said, and whisper, "Good night, sleep tight, don't let the bed bugs bite."

"That's stupid," Laura says, but she doesn't sound as if she means it.

Chapter Ten

I T IS THE NIGHT BEFORE Parents' Weekend. Even though you can usually count on the evenings being cool, tonight it's just as humid as it was during swimming lessons at noon. I get into bed with my flannel pajamas on, but quickly strip down to just a T-shirt and underpants. I will only do this between my sheets, because I don't want anyone to see my body.

Long after it seems as though everyone else is asleep, I turn my pillow over and over again, pushing my hair off my face and resting my cheek on the cool side. My legs dangle off the side of my cot, and then I put them on top of the bedspread, but I feel too exposed, like someone is watching me, Adrienne's brother Terry, maybe, and he'll pounce on me and tickle me, and I won't want to laugh, but I will have to.

I sweat and feel as though I can't breathe. I stand up and walk to the steps of the tent, pulling the canvas flap behind me. A layer of dew now covers the grass, and though the temperature has not dropped, it's cool enough out here so that my skin now feels clammy. I go back in and climb into bed, and in my dream I remember.

I remember that it's January, and Felicity and my parents and I are driving to my grandmother's house, in Metuchen, New Jersey. My father has spent the last twenty minutes defrosting a thick layer of ice from the car windows. Though my mother thinks we should cancel this trip because of road conditions, my father tells her to stop being ridiculous. His mother is expecting us—cooking brisket and boiled potatoes—and he doesn't want to disappoint her.

They ask me to sit in the back, so that I can

keep Felicity entertained. But before I climb into the seat, I grab a fistful of snow and close my mitten around it. I want to see how long it will take before the ice begins to melt. My father has turned the radio on, but the car's heater and the smell of wet wool make us sleepy. Just a few miles from our house, my mother presses her head against the window glass, and is asleep. Felicity gnaws on the tail of her lamb and makes a swipe for my mouth. But in a few minutes, she, too, closes her eyes.

I open my fist and look at my snowball. It has almost dissolved, but small balls of ice cling to my mittens. My fingers are wet and raw, and I take them off and suck on the water, which tastes something like gravel, or a mixture of dirt and leaves.

My father drives, with one hand on the wheel and the other on the back of my mother's seat. He turns around and winks at me, and suggests that I take a nap, too, since we have a long drive in front of us. But even though I'm sleepy, I have to stay awake. Who will watch out for *him* if I, too, slip into sleep? Maybe there's a curve in the road that he won't see because he's turned his head to check on his children, and maybe we'll cascade over the embankment and lie in a snow-drift, where no one will hear our muffled cries for help. So I close my eyes and open them every few seconds, looking at the pine trees that line either side of the road.

Felicity sighs in her sleep, and I pat her leg, just to let her know that someone is close by. She is breathing in short little sniffs, as if she is about to cry, and wrinkling her forehead. Her eyes dart back and forth under her eyelids, and I know she is in the middle of a dream. I think it was Adrienne who told me that it's dangerous to wake someone in the middle of a dream, and I don't. But I hold two fingers under her nostrils, so close I can feel each breath. Bit by tiny bit I raise my fingers until they are covering each opening. She moans in her sleep, and turns her head in the opposite direction. I'm horrified by what I have done, or what I could do if I wanted to. I secretly vow that I will be as kind to her as I possibly can. I won't get annoyed when she drools banana all over the clean outfit I've just put on. I'll rub her back when she has a hard time settling down for a nap.

When I wake up and look at the clock that rests on my trunk, only a half hour has gone by. I curl up in a ball and think about something that doesn't have anything to do with feelings, like a sky or a white wall. Eventually, I fall asleep.

Chapter Eleven

I T IS SATURDAY MORNING, and we are cleaning our tent before the counselors come around for inspection. We know that today they will look under our beds as well as on our shelves, so Celeste and even Laura are on their knees pulling out mildewed socks and empty soda cans. My routine doesn't change today. I'm a tidy housekeeper. I line my shoes up vertically under my bed, and rearrange an overturned book on my shelf. I made my bed when I first woke up, and the blanket is as taut, the tucks as symmetrical, as they could possibly be.

We're supposed to dress a little differently to-day: white shirts and dark-colored shorts or pants. Laura, of course, refuses. She wears all black, even though she knows someone will probably ask her to change. Celeste offers to braid my hair, and from across the room, I see Laura looking at me and rolling her eyes. I thank her anyway, and tell her I just want a pony tail today. Celeste turns around and notices Laura watching me.

"You don't have to do what she tells you, you know," she says.

"I don't."

"Yes, you do. But it doesn't matter. I'll still be your friend."

"Forget it. Don't bother."

"Come on, Mary. I was just joking."

I can't back down now. Celeste looks hurt. I'm sorry, but also relieved. I remember once, in the spring, when Adrienne told me that this boy, Robbie Parsons, liked me. Robbie had been my friend since first grade, and at first it seemed ridiculous that he could think of me in any way other than as a sister. But then he started sending me notes, and asking me if his mother could drive us to a Saturday movie matinee. I didn't know how to say no, so I made myself hate him—his teeth were slightly yellow, his finger-nails were dirty. And Celeste? She was plump and friendless and said mean things to me.

She puts her hand on my shoulder and is ready to cry. "You promised me I could meet Felicity."

Felicity. I even sacrifice Felicity to Laura's friendship. "She's not coming," I say. "So it's not even an issue. She has a cold."

"Oh. But I told my mother all about you. She said she wants to meet you."

"Mary—" Laura is calling me.

"Drop it, Celeste. Take a hint. Leave me alone." I've seen other girls be this mean, but I've never been good at meanness. I'm horrified by this black seed taking root inside me, but I'm also thrilled. I've started something that I don't know how to stop. "You buttoned your shirt wrong, Celeste," I say, and leave her standing there, looking down at her blouse.

After lunch, we don't have a rest time. We're

allowed to sit in the grass next to the parking area and work on our arts and crafts projects—whittling miniature totem poles—while we wait for our parents to arrive.

Laura and I lean against the back of the maintenance man's rusty yellow pick-up truck. Cars are already starting to move up the driveway. We watch the families tumble out.

"Bad bleach job," Laura says, pointing to one woman's hair. "She would have been better off not doing it on her own."

"Bad news," I say in agreement, though secretly I am sure I wouldn't have noticed if she hadn't pointed it out to me.

"And check out that guy's belt," she goes on. "White. Yuck." I am almost positive my father owns a white belt. I pray he doesn't wear it.

The bleached-blond mother hands the girl a present which the girl opens. It is a necklace, I think, because I see the mother gently turn the girl around by her shoulders so she can clasp the gift around her neck.

I feel as though I'm watching through a telescope. Or at the movies, watching what goes on in front of us, but not a part of it.

Celeste runs to meet her family's station wagon. I can't make out the people inside, but I see arms waving frantically through the glass. Even before the car stops, it seems as though people are piling out, and she's swallowed by arms.

"They're going to crush her. Which wouldn't be the end of the world." Laura chews on the end of her hair and watches. "Better watch out. They might get you too," she says.

"What do you mean?" I say, without looking at her.

"Isn't she your mascot? She might bring them over to meet you and they might crush you to death."

I don't know what to say. I am not able to think in terms of whole sentences, or even words. All I am is sensations today, like the taste of sherbet, or colors, like black and red.

By midafternoon, the parking lot is nearly full. Laura is sure her father and stepmother have forgotten and says she's relieved. I know my parents are coming, but am used to them arriving late.

And then Laura sees her father's red convertible from a distance. First she rolls her eyes and says, "Oh great," as it approaches, but then she watches in complete silence. The car stops and two people get out: a tall man, with thick, graying hair. Trim, as my mother would say, and wearing a blue and white striped shirt and khaki trousers. He goes around to the other side of the car and opens the door. A woman gets out. She is beautiful. Her thick red hair sweeps over her forehead and down her back in one braid. She has on a gingham jumper and black cowboy boots. This must be Laura's stepmother, the poet. I can't stop looking at her.

I expect Laura to walk toward them and stand, with her hands at her sides, while they kiss her hello. She hasn't told me much about them, but none of it has been good. Instead, she runs toward them, and her father catches her in his arms and swings her around as if she were a little girl. I am standing at attention in the grass now, waiting for Laura to bring them over to meet me. I'll be polite, but not too friendly—Laura always tells me I'm too outgoing. But she doesn't even look at me. The three of them are walking toward the lake, with Laura in the center. Her arms are around both of their waists. I don't understand this, or why my eyes begin to smart against my will, but then I see my parents' car, and run toward it, as fast as I can.

Chapter Twelve

Y FATHER PULLS IN to one of the last parking spaces available and opens the door. He pauses for a few seconds, eyes unfocused, and then he steps out. The first thing I see is that my mother is not with him. The second is that he's wearing his white belt. He kisses me on the forehead. The heat has made his aftershave, which I usually like, especially strong.

"You're late," I say.

"Don't ask," he answers.

"Mom. Where's Mom?"

"She couldn't make it. She had to go to Grandma's."

"Is Grandma sick?"

"No."

I don't want to talk about this anymore. I change the subject. "The woodlore demonstrations have already started."

"Well, let's go," he says. "But first I need a bathroom." We walk toward my unit. He seems tired and older. Probably no one else would notice, but I can see, for a second, what he 'll look like in the future.

He goes to the latrine, in his coat and tie, and leather Oxfords. He looks small and confused, the way I felt on the first day of camp. I wonder if he peers down the hole after he goes to the bathroom, into the darkness, the way I always do. I worry about him.

We walk to the woodlore demonstration, but all that's left is fire-building. My father tries to look interested, but I know that for him, this is torture. He likes to stay in motels and eat in restaurants when we are on vacation.

"I'm starving," he says. "When do you people

eat around here?" he whispers into my ear.

"Six. Ham and sweet potatoes."

"Oh."

"It's a special dinner." He is disappointed, but trying to be a good sport. He hates ham, and I think he actually may be allergic to sweet potatoes.

"How about I take you out?" he says.

"I don't know if I'm allowed. I'll have to ask." It has been so long, it seems, since I have left the gate of the camp.

"Where's your counselor? I'll ask."

I see Marjorie talking energetically to a small cluster of families. We walk over to her and she takes my father's hand, and introduces herself. She tells him what a great girl I am to have around, and how much I've grown in the past weeks. I look at her the way I would look at a stranger, or a TV screen. I have no idea what she's talking about. My father asks if we can have some family time alone and promises to bring me back in time for evening activities. For a second, Marjorie looks skeptical, as if she thinks she's supposed to, and then smiles and says, "Sure. Why not?"

We walk back to the car. I don't see Laura or her father or her stepmother, but I do see Celeste and her family. She sees me too, and waves, hesitantly. I pretend I don't see, and slip my arm through my father's.

We drive to a restaurant called The Cellar Door, which he has seen a couple of miles back, on his way to the camp. Everything seems new and especially luxurious: the white tablecloths, the thick amber water glasses, the basket of rolls of different varieties. I go to the Ladies' Room and wash my hands twice with Yardley English Lavender soap. There's a dryer instead of paper towels, and I shake off the excess water and rub my hands together in the warm air. When I am through, my hands feel smaller, and more delicate.

I sit down at our table in an oversized captain's chair. My father has already ordered a drink, and the lines around his eyes are smoothing so that he is starting to look younger and more familiar to me. Without my mother to warn me not to lose my appetite, I eat as many little rolls and butter as I want, and finish my soda even before the dinner has arrived.

"So." My father leans back in his chair. He has asked the waitress to bring him another drink while we are deciding what to order. "How goes it?"

"Fine." I am shy without my mother.

"Are you making nice friends?"

"A few."

"Take advantage of it. It's an opportunity."

"I will." I search my mind for small talk. I ask him how his job is, even though I'm still not entirely sure what it is he does.

I order a tremendous amount of food, more than I know I will ever be able to eat: clam chowder, chicken pot pie, creamed spinach. I order because I like these things, and not because they necessarily go together. My father has a steak and mashed potatoes. Green beans are the vegetable of the day. He hates green beans and asks for a double of potatoes instead. Without my mother to remind him of cholesterol levels, he peels the paper off three pats of butter and lays them delicately on top of the potatoes, before burying them with his spoon.

"I'll tell your mother you look fine. She was

worried about you," he says.

"Why was she worried?"

"She didn't think you brought enough warm clothes."

"I know she thinks I enjoy being cold, but I don't."

"Don't be smart. She worries about you."

The waitress fills my water glass. I am full, but I continue to eat my creamed spinach. "How long is she staying at Grandma's house?" I ask.

"You'll have to ask her," he says, though not really to me.

"Why?"

"She's stir-crazy. She needed a change of scene."

"Why?"

"She's trying to figure things out. She will."

"Will she be there when I get home?"

"Most likely."

"*Most likely?*"

"What do you want me to say, Mary?"

"I don't know."

"She'll be there. Don't worry." He reaches across the table and squeezes my hand. "We've toyed with the idea of moving. An apartment, maybe." I hate apartment buildings, except the ones in the city. "Less trouble to maintain. I want to make less trouble for your mother."

"But I like this house." I dig my fork into the tablecloth. My father pulls it out of my hand.

"We don't need all that space," he says. "When you pay the mortgage, you can live wherever you want."

"But it's our house. My room—I like my room."

"It's a seller's market," my father says. "Three bedrooms could do well."

"And what about Felicity's room?"

My father looks at me as if I've said a curse word. "Yes?"

Of course Felicity doesn't need a room anymore. But how will I remember her if I can't walk into her room and close my eyes and imagine? "I miss her. That's all," I say.

"It's killing your mother," he says. "It's supposed to get easier as time passes, for Christ's sake. She's making me lose my mind."

I know now why my mother has gone to my

grandmother's house. I want to be there, too. My father is still talking, and I wish he would stop.

"I have feelings, too, you know? Where's there room for my feelings? It stinks. What can I say? Where's the damn waitress?"

I am older than my father now. I am larger than life, like the balloons in the Thanksgiving parade on TV.

"Do you want dessert?" The waitress is standing behind my chair.

"What do you have for dessert?" he asks.

She looks at the list on the back of her pad. "Strawberry shortcake, lemon sherbet, strawberry ice cream, chocolate layer cake." I shake my head no. My father orders the layer cake.

We sip our water, and the only thing my father says until the waitress returns is "It'll work out, I guess. It always does." He's a big man, though not overweight, but since he's been here he looks deflated, like he's been punctured with a pin.

He slices his fork into his layer cake without pausing, and presses the back of it against the plate until all the crumbs are gone. Normally, I'd ask him for a bite, and he'd laugh and roll his eyes and say, "I told you you should have ordered one of your own," but tonight I just sit and watch.

It's time to return to camp, and I'm relieved when we pass through the wooden gate at the bottom of the driveway. I don't like being out there. I like my little cot and night table. Here, everything has its place.

My father walks me to the mess hall, where the Singing Jamboree has already begun. He kisses my cheek and says he won't stay, if that's OK with me; he's tired from the long drive, and wants to find his motel and get a good night's sleep before tomorrow's activities.

I turn around to say good-bye, and there is Laura. I have forgotten about her, though I still feel some edge of annoyance, some sense of having been betrayed—something to do with her family?—that I can't put my finger on. She is wearing all black, of course, and an oversized straw hat.

"Well, hello, Mary," she says to me. "I wondered where you were."

"My father took me out to dinner."

thinking?" She notices that I'm quiet, lying on my back.

"Who do you live with? I was wondering where you go when camp is over."

"It's not like I have a lot of choices," she says.

"Well, there's your mother—"

"My mother sent me another letter today. Did I tell you that?" She scans her night table for it, then gives up. "She's looking for a bigger apartment, one for both of us, but she says the rents in Santa Fe are outrageous so I just have to be patient. She tells me she loves me more than life itself. Did I tell you that?"

"Your father loves you, doesn't he?" I say.

"My mother's been looking for a place big enough for the two of us for over a year. It can't be that hard, can it?"

"Maybe she's busy," I say.

"That's what my father keeps telling me. Of course, he's no prize parent either. Did I tell you Tania's moving in with us?" She nibbles the skin around her thumbnail. "It's a crazy family. You're lucky. Your family's normal."

I picture my mother, sitting in the backyard applying suntan lotion. My father mows the lawn on weekends and comes home every week day at exactly six o'clock. We have barbecues and fireworks on the Fourth of July. I get new shoes for school—maybe loafers this year—and try, for about a week, to keep them free of scuff marks. My parents are invited to dinner parties, and I know, now that I am entering junior high, that there will be parties besides birthdays, and going to the movies with a boy will not be the same as it used to be. But there's another picture, too, of a room no one will open, and my father, driving by himself to Parents' Weekend. We're not normal, but I don't tell any of this to Laura.

The next morning my father arrives just after breakfast. He has shaved and is no longer wearing a suit. He is smiling and full of energy, and tells me that he slept like a rock. There is a nature walk this morning, for all the parents in my unit, and then a special lunch one of the committees is preparing over a campfire.

We stand at the head of the line, and he jokes with another father about how roughing it doesn't build character, just a bad back. We enter the woods, and in a few minutes, the conversation stops. We're concentrating on the hike, which begins with a long, steep hill before it levels off. There's some more joking about heart attacks and lawsuits, but mostly all you hear is adults breathing in deeply and women trying to look cheerful as they navigate the rocks and stumps in dressy shoes.

"I didn't come all this way to be tortured," my father says. And then the hill levels off, and we leave the cover of underbrush behind.

I'm familiar with this trail, for it leads past Crimson Lodge, which you can see if you know where to look, just behind a row of birches. I notice that the front door has been left open, and am about to close it, when Celeste taps me on the shoulder.

"Hi," she says.

"Hi."

"What are you doing?" She wipes sweat off her forehead with the back of her hand.

"Catching my breath."

"I'll wait for you," she says, sitting on a fallen log.

"Don't bother," I say. "I'll be a while."

"I don't mind."

"But I want to be alone."

"Oh." She stands and starts to leave, but I see her turn around just as I step off the path and close Crimson Lodge's door.

We are in an open meadow now, and we take a break to drink water from our canteens and lie in the sun. There are wildflowers up here—daisies and Queen Anne's lace—and I make myself a crown. My father lies on his back and looks at the clouds. It's a high summer sky, but up here the colors seem more vivid and the air is clearer. Something is shifting; there will be many other steamy days, but fall is coming. We climb back down, into the woods again, and my father scrapes his nose on a low-hanging branch. It's bleeding, but he insists that he is fine. We reach the campsite in half the time it's taken us to climb, and wash our faces and go to the campfire circle for lunch.

The theme is open-hearth cooking, and there is bread that is so hard I have to dissolve it in my mouth before I can swallow. And there is soup and baked beans, and an Indian pudding for dessert.

By late afternoon, the families begin to leave. I walk my father to the car. He thanks me for a great time, and tells me to have fun.

"I'll pick you up next weekend, pumpkin," he says.

"Maybe Mom'll be back from Grandma's by then," I say, but it is really a question.

"Maybe. We'll see."

"Tell her I miss her."

"I will."

I want to hug him hard, but am scared I'll start to cry, so I pat him on the back and kind of shake his hand. I see him wave good-bye until he is out of sight, invisible, through the gates of the camp.

Chapter Fourteen

LAURA NEVER ASKS ME about my mother or my sister. With Laura, I don't travel through time. I am simple and flat, like a cartoon rabbit run over by a steamroller. There is only the present. Nothing else matters. And I like it this way. It makes everything so much simpler.

"What's that?" she says.

"Nothing. A postcard from my mother." We are on our way to volleyball practice, and the mail has just been handed out.

"Can I see it?"

"It's stupid," I say, and I mean it. She tells me

she is having a nice rest at my grandmother's, and is looking forward to seeing me when camp ends. I fold the postcard in half and put it away in the back pocket of my jeans. Out of the corner of my eye, I see Celeste. Her face is red with the effort of trying to keep up with the others. Every time her eye catches mine, she raises her eyes, which makes her forehead crinkle.

I've stopped torturing myself about whether or not I should be nice to Celeste. It is too difficult to try to take care of her and Laura; they are just too different. Laura has had something to do with this decision. She's given me her favorite black T-shirt and told me that I won't be allowed to use Crimson Lodge anymore if I have anything to do with Celeste—it's too risky, because I might mention the cabin in the woods by accident, and then we'd be discovered.

I have not been there in several days. In fact, I don't really like it, because the air is damp and there's no corner to make me comfortable. But I like to know it's there, like a secret, and so I agree.

We play games behind Celeste's back, games I

would never play without Laura's encouragement, and I'm amazed how easy it is for me to be cruel.

We imitate Celeste's bouncy walk, or we'll sit in the mess hall and ask her to pass something in voices so soft that she couldn't possibly hear, and then Laura'll screech, "What's the matter, Celeste? Are you deaf or something?" and Celeste will blush and pass the butter, or the salt and pepper shakers.

I never look her in the eye. Only once, by mistake, and she excused herself and ran into the bathroom.

This morning we cast spells on Celeste in the privacy of our lodge. Laura peels some bark off of a tree, and tells me to gather some twigs. She attaches these twigs to the bark body by crisscrossing twine. With her pocketknife, she carves a face, and glues on leaves to resemble hair.

"This is our Celeste voodoo doll," she says, "and it must never leave the lodge. Ever." She squints as she looks at me, as if she is not sure I am to be trusted.

The more I look at this doll, the more it resembles Celeste. Its eye holes seem to glare at me no matter where I stand in the room.

"Now, have you ever cast a spell with a likeness?" I shake my head. "I didn't think you had. Now watch what I do, so you'll know the next time." She dangles the doll by the tips of its stick arms and runs around the room, shouting "One, two, three!" with each circle. Then she places the doll on the floor in the center of the room.

"Any ideas what you'd like to have happen to her?" she asks me.

"Something small," I say. Laura looks disappointed. "Something small, but something that everybody sees," I continue. This seems to make her feel better.

"Let's have her break her arm," says Laura.

"That's not small."

"Well, it's not a *permanent* injury. Do you have any ideas?"

"She's been practicing her diving," I say. "How about a belly flop?"

Laura likes this idea. She is shaking her head. "Good," she says, and commands, "Fall down on the floor three times, in front of the likeness, and yell the subject's name."

"Why me?" I say. "Why don't we do it to-gether?"

"Because it's your idea. The casting of the spell has to come from you."

"Why don't we do it together?" I wonder why I have to be the one who will look stupid.

Laura sighs, tolerant, and says, as if she is speaking to a small child: "I already told you why. If you don't want to, we can forget it."

Laura is annoyed with me. I'd rather look stu-pid than have Laura be annoyed with me.

"OK," I say. I walk into the center of the circle and look down at this doll. Three times I bend my knees and fall to the ground. Each time I say Celeste's name, Laura directs, "Louder! Louder! Louder!" When I am through, I brush myself off and stand beside her.

"That was pretty good," she says, "but it could have been louder. I hope it works." She picks up the Celeste doll and puts her on the mantelpiece, and I follow her out the door.

We watch Celeste's every move that after-noon, and she knows we are watching: Celeste, tripping over a stump on a nature walk; Celeste, leaving the residue of a chocolate bar all over her mouth. She watches us watching her, and I'm secretly thrilled every time she messes up. Once Marjorie catches my eye, and shakes her head in disapproval when she sees me laughing at Celeste. I'm ashamed, but I don't know how to stop. We watch Celeste on the diving platform, adjusting her bathing cap and holding her hands together, preparing to dive. The swim instructor is next to her and places her hand on Celeste's neck, in order to position her head correctly. There is no way Celeste can fail, and secretly, I am glad. But at the last minute, the instructor lets go and Celeste lifts her neck up, so her face is parallel to the water. She lands on her stomach, and, before we can see her, we see waves of water splash on the diving platform. She swims frantically to the shore, and when she gets there, she is out of breath and crying, surrounded by a group of girls.

"Make me puke," says Laura, smiling, and she whispers, "It worked. Nice job."

Late Monday night, we sneak to the lodge. I

don't want to go, because I know I will be tired the next day, but Laura insists. "It's important," she says.

"How important?"

"Really important."

So I put on my sweatshirt over my nightgown and grab my flashlight and follow her into the woods. My sneakers are wet, and I know they will take the better part of the next day to dry, but I follow her. She has matches and makes a fire in Crimson Lodge's fireplace. But either the wood is damp or the flue is not open, because the entire place fills up with dense smoke. We throw dirt over the flames and open the door to air the cabin out.

Even though my eyes are smarting, I follow her and sit in the corner. She pulls out a pack of bubble gum and gives me a piece.

"So tell me," I say. "Tell me what's important."

"What's important?"

"You said you brought me here to tell me something important."

"Oh." She blows an enormous bubble and

sticks her finger through it. "I was just joking."

"Just joking?" I am angry. If she were Celeste, I would tell her I was angry, but instead, I can't think of any words, and I just stare at her.

"Have a sense of humor," she says. "I knew it was the only way I'd get you to come."

I lean against the wall with my eyes closed, and pretend I am asleep. Laura asks me if I have any pets.

"A dog," I say. "A cocker spaniel named Ginger."

"Figures," she replies, and I want to ask her what she means, but once again, I let it go.

"Actually, I brought you here because I wanted to tell you about this bird. I had a bird once. A canary named Skipper. I was supposed to be responsible for him. Clean his cage, talk to him, you know. But every time I put my hand into Skipper's cage, he would go for my finger, and it really hurt. So you know what I did?" I guess I nod my head, because she continues. "I stopped feeding him."

"What?"

"I starved him." My eyes are open now, and

Laura looks straight into them and continues. "He got weaker and weaker, and my father couldn't understand why he wasn't flying around and chirping any more, so he called the vet. The vet said to bring him in, and I figured he'd know right away what the problem was and I'd be in trouble, so I placed a little dish of food in Skipper's cage."

I am relieved. Everything is going to be all right.

"Of course, Skipper ate it right up. He was starving. So I put another dish in and he ate that, too. I kept feeding Skipper all day, and he never stopped. The next morning I heard a little scratching sound inside the cage. I looked, and you know what? There was Skipper lying on the floor, breathing heavily. He breathed and he breathed, and then, kaput! That was it! He didn't move. I dug a little hole in the neighbor's flowerbed and buried him. My father was worried that I was upset and offered to replace him, but I told him not to bother."

"Why'd you do that?"

"I don't know," she says. "It was fun."

"Fun?"

"I didn't really starve him anyway. He just skipped a few meals."

I don't say anything, as usual. But this time my silence seems to make Laura talk more.

"You take everything so seriously, Mary. I guess you never stepped on an ant."

"Not on purpose," I say.

She stands and brushes herself off. "Besides, it was just a story."

"What?"

"I made it up. It never really happened. If I had a bird, which I wouldn't want to anyway, do you think I would name it Skipper?"

I follow her out of Crimson Lodge like a sleepwalker and hear her say, "You take everything so seriously. Do you really think I could starve a canary to death, if I even had one, which I didn't?"

Chapter Fifteen

I DON'T SLEEP WELL THAT night. I am thinking about Laura, who can make up a horrible story at some poor bird's expense. The next morning, I avoid her, and just before lunch, she takes my hand and pulls me aside. "You're my best friend here, aren't you?" she whispers. I don't want to agree, but of course I do. "Here's my plan," she says, whispering in my ear.

We leave the mess hall early, after Tuesday lunch, and sneak back to the tent, where we drag Celeste's trunk outside and push it underneath the tent platform. It was Laura's idea, but I know that if we get caught, I will be just as much to blame as she is. The trunk is heavy and leaves marks on the wooden floor, but we work quickly because any second we will hear the voices of the others, coming down the path.

We walk in separately, so we won't look suspicious. I even smile at Celeste when she looks at me, and she smiles back—a kind of relieved smile.

It's not until we go swimming later that day that she even notices it's missing.

"My trunk," she says. "What happened to my trunk?" Everyone looks, including Laura and me. Eventually, she goes to the counselors' tent, in tears, and Marjorie comes back and asks us who is responsible for this, because it's really not funny. I know she is looking at me, but I make myself feel invisible by looking at a spot on the wall, just beyond her head.

Celeste is crying now, and other girls from our unit have brought clothing from their own trunks and offered it to her. I hand her my sweatshirt.

"Thanks," she says, and for a minute I almost

believe that I had nothing to do with this.

"We should move it back," I whisper to Laura.

"And why should we do that?"

Because it's not fair, I think. And "Because we're going to get caught," I say.

"No, we won't."

"She'll come back and find her trunk exactly where it was before. It'll be really weird."

"Maybe. OK. That might be fun," she says. "We'll play it your way." We stay behind while the rest of the girls go to the canteen. Moving the trunk up the stairs is more difficult, and Laura isn't much of a help. But we slide it across the floor and run to join the others.

"It's back," Celeste announces.

"Who moved it back?" someone asks. "What do you think, Celeste?" But Celeste doesn't seem to care. She returns all the clothes she has borrowed, including my sweatshirt, and spreads her canteen purchases out on her bed before choosing.

Chapter Sixteen

THAT NIGHT, LAURA decides it's time to perform a seance. For days, she's been talking to me about how we'll conjure up the spirit of the Other World. Even though the idea doesn't particularly thrill me, I listen to her plans and know that I have no choice.

I fall asleep easily, and am shaking with cold when she wakes me up at midnight. The kerosene lantern in the counselors' tent is still lit; we can hear their laughter and the low sound of music, so we don't turn on our flashlights until we are well out of sight.

It is a moonless night, and the branches

scratch my cheek, even though I crouch low as we walk in the woods. Laura walks quickly. I hear branches breaking far ahead of me, and I call for her to slow down, but either she doesn't hear me or she thinks I should take care of myself, for her footsteps don't stop.

When I reach Crimson Lodge, the door is already open, and I can see candlelight flickering through the broken window panes.

"Where did you get those candles?" I ask her. They are everywhere: on the mantelpiece, in each corner, and in a circle around the floor.

"I stole them from the kitchen when the staff wasn't looking." I don't say anything. "You don't have a problem with that, do you?" she says.

She gestures for me to sit, and I do, next to her. "No, across from me," she says, placing a candle between us. She places her fingertips just above the flame, and for a second I think she really does have powers that would allow her to touch fire without doing herself any harm. "Who to conjure, who to conjure," she says, and I ask her what she means.

"Who do you want to bring back from the Spirit World?" she asks.

"Anybody?"

"Anybody. Or any spirit, I mean," she giggles.

"Famous people?"

"Why not?" Laura lifts up the candle and turns it over, dripping hot wax into the palm of her hand.

"We could both pick somebody," I suggest.

"OK. I'll take Joan of Arc. I always liked her. Who do you want?"

"George Washington."

"That's boring."

"Then the Three Stooges." My father and I always watch the Three Stooges on cable.

"I hate the Three Stooges," she says, "but whatever you want. It's your choice," she says. "OK. Now there has to be complete silence. Do you understand?" I nod my head.

"Three Stooges, Three Stooges, by the light of this flame we welcome you."

Silence.

"We are here, ready to assist your spirits as they make the treacherous journey from the

Other World to this dimension." I am chilled, and I draw my arms across my chest to stay warm.

"We are patient. We can wait." For a long time, Laura sits cross-legged, concentrating on the flame in front of her. She looks like she is in a trance. I stand up.

"Where are you going?" she asks.

"I have to go to the bathroom."

"What?"

"I have to go to the bathroom. I'll be right back. You go on without me."

"Forget it," she says, throwing her hands up into the air. "The spell is broken. Go to the bathroom. Take your time."

"Sorry," I say, but I do have to go, so I step outside, finish, and come back in. "I'm sorry, Laura. I didn't know spirits were that sensitive."

"Well, what did you think?"

"We could try again," I say. "What about Joan of Arc?"

"Forget it. Why would Joan of Arc want to hang out with us, anyway?"

"It's just a game," I say.

Laura blows out the candle, and the center of the room is dark. I can't see the features of her face anymore—just the shape of her body on the floor, and the flickering shadows the other candles cast on the cold stone walls and dirt floor of the lodge.

"Then let's leave."

"No," I say. "What about the Three Stooges?"

"If you think this is just a big joke, then let's go. I have better things to do with my time."

I'm sorry," I repeat. "I didn't realize you took this so seriously."

"Well, I do," she says.

"Can we try again?"

"I don't care."

"Please, Laura." Once again, I am begging Laura's forgiveness, apologizing for my behavior, assuring her that she's right.

"If you insist." She relights the candle, and stares once again. I do exactly what she is doing. I wait for a long time, and am just about to ask her if there is something I should be doing, when she says, "Spirit world, spirit world, summon the Three Stooges and let them know that we await and welcome their presence."

I picture Larry bopping Curly on the head while he dances on top of the flames and almost laugh again.

"Step into the warmth of our light," Laura says, "and give us a sign. Any sign."

We wait and wait, and the only thing out of the ordinary that takes place is that the moon suddenly rises over the tops of the pine trees and shines in through the lodge's window.

"That's it," Laura says.

"What's it?"

"That light. The moonlight. That's our sign. It worked." Her eyes look glazed, like marbles. She pushes her hair back from her face. "The room is hospitable. Let's try again. Let's hold hands across the flame. It will strengthen the power of the spell." She reaches out for my hands, and I pull away. I have never touched Laura before— not a casual pat on the shoulder, or a friendly arm around her waist, like I do with Adrienne. It's almost as though there is a magic circle drawn around Laura that makes her dangerous to touch.

"Take my hands," she commands. "I'm not

going to bite, for God's sake." I place my hands in hers. I have never looked at them before and expect them to be cool and smooth. But I am surprised. They are sweaty and rough, and I can see, even by the light of the candle, that though the nails are a reasonable length, the cuticles are all bitten.

With my hands in hers, she says, "Now. Who should we summon?"

I shrug my shoulders.

"I think it should be someone we know. Someone who's been important to us, someone we miss. Like a grandparent."

"Let's do one of your grandparents," I say.

"I never knew them. They died before I was born."

"Oh."

"I once knew a boy who was hit by a car. He was in the other fifth grade."

"So let's do him." This is taking too long. I'm going to be a mess tomorrow. Laura won't let go of my hands.

"But the problem is, I didn't know him very well. Besides, I don't think I'd be the person he'd make the trip from the Other World to see. He didn't like me very much. But you," she says, squinting as if she knows a secret, "there must be someone you know. Think."

"Felicity." I think: If I wanted to, I could remember every eyelash, every crinkle on the bottom of her feet.

"Who's Felicity?"

"My sister. Felicity."

"Your sister?" Laura repeats, loudly. Her voice howls in my ears and pushes away my memories. "She died?"

"It was sudden. It happened while she was sleeping. It happens sometimes and no one knows why, but—" I am rattling off the same report that I remember, that somebody told me that day so long ago when I walked home from school. I remember the smell of perfume, too, but I'm not sure why.

Laura cuts me off. "Wow." I have pleased her. "Perfect."

She walks outside and returns with a twig, which she hands to me. "Carve her name into the floor." I do as I'm asked. By now the moon lights up the whole room as if it is midday. I watch Laura and follow her instructions carefully, as if she really is capable of conjuring up the spirit of my sister.

"Say her name. Three times."

I do as I'm told.

"Stare into the flame without blinking until your eyes fill with tears."

I stare.

She is talking to Felicity, summoning her from the Other Side, telling her I am here. "Do you have that picture of her?" she asks. I shake my head no. "Too bad. Too bad you don't have some personal object. That would really help."

I reach behind my head for the clasp on the necklace with the gold heart pendant. My grandmother gave me this necklace for my sixth birthday, and Felicity liked to swat at the heart with her fists. Even though it was my necklace, I always told myself that I would give it to her for a birthday present when *she* turned six. The necklace slides into the palm of my hand. Laura reaches for it.

"Good," she says. She dangles the heart over the flame. "What are you doing?" I reach across the candle and try to grab it from her, but she moves her hand too quickly. "The object needs to make contact with the flame," she says.

"Why?" I ask.

"Trust me," she says. "I'm almost done." She dangles it and dips it into the flame, and when she hands it back to me, the heart is softer and slightly out of shape, and the back of it is scorched.

"You ruined it," I say.

"I didn't ruin anything," she answers. "You wanted me to bring your sister back, didn't you?" I'm just doing what you asked me to do."

Of course she is right. We wait. I hear a tree branch crash, in some faraway part of the forest, and my throat tightens. Clouds pass over the moon, and the room darkens, and still we wait.

"She's not ready to make the journey," Laura says. She licks the tip of her index finger, and is ready to place it over the flame, putting it out.

"Let's wait a little longer," I plead.

"We'll try again another time. I'm cold. I want to go back."

"Just a few more minutes." I know this is a game, and Laura's losing interest, like she always does, even though it was her idea in the first place. But I don't want to lose that flame. Whether I see her or not, she is here, I am missing her. "I'm going," Laura says, standing up. "Are you coming?" I don't want to walk through the woods alone, but I don't want to leave Felicity, either. "Listen," Laura says, "I hear something. Maybe it's a spirit." She cups her hands over her mouth and burps, long and low. There was a time when I would have been impressed, would have even practiced my own burps so they could resonate like hers, but not tonight. I stand and follow her. "Don't forget the candle," she says. I bend down and blow the flame out. The spell is broken. I put out the other candles, and follow her through the woods with my eyes closed to see if I can find my way, just by sound alone.

Chapter Seventeen

IN THE MORNING, I DON'T get out of bed. My throat feels raw, and my head is fuzzy. I'm hot and cold, and all I want to do is sleep. By noon, I still don't feel better—I try to get out of bed, but am so dizzy I have to hold on to the bed frame for support—and Marjorie sends me to the infirmary to see the camp nurse.

She wears white and has white hair and looks skeptical when Marjorie explains my symptoms. But my temperature, though just over 100, is high enough to convince her that I am not faking. I lie down on the cool white sheets of the cot and cover myself with a blanket. All afternoon, I fall in and out of sleep and dreams that I can't remember. I hear voices, too, in the front room, and even though I'm usually a light sleeper, these voices are pleasant, like a faraway radio when you're lying on the beach. The nurse puts a thermometer in my mouth, and the smell of the alcohol reminds of the black vinyl that covered my Barbie lunch box when I was in the first grade. I also remember places we visited when I was a baby, the speckled linoleum that covered the floor in my nursery.

I sleep, and when I wake up, the sun is no longer shining directly on the white walls of this room. It is cooler now, and the infirmary has taken on the green tinge of the pines outside the front door. I am cooler, too, and waking up. When I open my eyes, I see Celeste standing at the foot of my bed.

"The nurse told me I could wait," she says, "now that your fever's broken."

"Hi," I say.

"I came to see how you were."

"Thanks. That's nice."

"So how are you?"

"Better. Much better." The nurse comes into the room with a tray. Suddenly, I'm starving. There are two slices of buttered toast and ginger ale, and red Jell-O. I nibble the toast slowly, to make it last.

"That's good. Everybody's asking about you. We had to make you a giant get-well card in arts and crafts."

"Thank you."

"You're welcome."

She looks at the clock on the wall. "I have to go. I promised I'd be back in fifteen minutes. But before I go, can I ask you something?"

"Ask away," I say, propping pillows up under me.

"I was wondering, Mary, why you didn't tell me the truth?"

I don't know what she is referring to, but there is a hard black brick sitting on my chest right now, making it difficult for me to breathe.

"What do you mean?" I ask. I am frantically trying to recall everything I did to Celeste—the voodoo doll, hiding her trunk, spells by the pond.

"You told me you had a sister." I don't know what she is talking about.

"You told me you had a sister. You showed me her picture, didn't you?"

"I did have a sister." I am still waiting for her to get to the point. Celeste looks at me patiently, as if I am a small child.

"You made me think she was alive. You told me she'd be coming to Parents' Weekend. Laura told me you lied to her too. You let her think you had a sister, and then last night you told her that your sister died."

"I do have a sister," I say. Even Celeste has turned against me.

"Laura says she hates liars."

"Is that what Laura says? Who cares what Laura says?" I'm starting to cry. I will stay in this infirmary until my parents come to pick me up. I'll hold my breath until my heart stops beating.

"You could've told me the truth, Mary," Celeste says softly. "I would have been your friend. I have to go now. Get some rest, OK?"

I spend the night in the infirmary, and the next day my fever is gone. It is Thursday, and I have one more full day until it'll be time to go home.

The nurse sends me back to my unit. I climb the steps to my tent, but nobody's there. It's swimming hour, so I put on my suit and walk to the lakefront. I can see the girls in the distance, standing on the sandy edge of the water, or doing cannonballs off the diving platform. As I walk closer, I look for Laura, but don't see her.

That is because she is surrounded by a group of girls—girls we never spoke to before, girls whose names I'm not even sure of, girls we used to laugh at and make up imaginary tortures for. I spread my towel and sit on it by myself.

I have only been gone for one day. What have I done to make this happen? How can things change so quickly?

And yet. And yet there is a small corner of me, so small I am not even sure it is there, that is relieved, that would rather be alone than have to be like Laura. So I go to the arts and crafts barn by myself, and make a collage from different patterns of fabric. Laura spills glue on it and enthusiastically tells me she is sorry.

I eat by myself—one chair separating me from

my closest neighbor—and listen to the after-dinner announcements about the final bonfire as if I'm listening to a news report.

I hear the camp director reminding us to invite our families to a final lunch on Saturday, before we go home. Without looking up, I see a piece of paper that has been passed to the front of my plate. I unfold it in my lap and read, "Looking forward to meeting Felicity at lunch. Love, Laura. P. S. Crimson Lodge is off-limits. You are no longer welcome there." I look at her, but she's facing the director. I shred the note and bury it in tuna casserole.

I find a stick and roast marshmallows with the others, and then I brush my teeth and get ready for bed. But I am busy making plans. Laura steps around me in the tent as if I were contagious, but I no longer care, and I avoid Celeste, who tries to catch my eye. I lie on my back, fully awake, and wait until the breathing in the cabin is regular with sleep. I am not cold tonight as I climb out of bed and slip between the closed back flaps.

The front door to the arts and crafts barn is

open, and I scan the walls with my flashlight to find what I am looking for. There is a box for me to put my supplies in. I still have a long way to walk, so I choose what I need with care.

As soon as I arrive at Crimson Lodge I begin to work, squeezing red poster paint out of its plastic container onto the floors and wall, until there is none left. Then I walk along the perimeter of the cabin so I don't get paint on the soles of my shoes. And finally, I pull a book of matches out of my pocket.

The Laura doll sits on the mantelpiece, in between the Celeste doll and the Mary doll. I remove it and hold it by its hair. I light the match and wait for the flame to get so close to my fingertip that I can almost feel the scorching heat. Then I blow it out and am about to light another, when I notice a shadow at the window. I hear the snapping of branches moving closer toward the front door. I know I'm imagining these sounds. This is the first time I've come to the cabin alone at night, without Laura's voice to distract me. But still, the sounds—probably trees in the distance, or maybe a fox or a coyote—continue.

We walked past the cabin."

"I remember."

"I guess the door had blown open from the wind. You closed the door. I knew the place had to be special if you were bothering to close the front door. But that doesn't explain why you went there tonight."

"I hate her," I say.

"I know."

"She told me I was lying. She told me she didn't even believe Felicity ever existed." Celeste puts her arm around my shoulders and shakes her head. "She made everybody hate me."

"I don't hate you."

"Everybody else does."

"That's not true. And besides, why do you care?" I sit for a long time, staring straight ahead. I understand now why Laura hated Celeste, and why I couldn't stand to be around her either. It wasn't because she was overweight, and wore furry slippers whenever she walked around the tent. And it wasn't because she smiled at me and tried to be friendly, no matter how mean I was. We hated Celeste because no matter what we

There is nowhere to hide in this room, and no furniture to crawl under or closet to enter. So I shove the Laura doll under my arm, open the door, and run. I stumble over branches and wonder if I've missed the curve on the path that leads from forest to field, and suddenly, I am out in the open, running across wet grass, faster and faster, back to my tent. I think I'm dreaming, and then I see Celeste, sitting on the front steps.

"What are you doing here?" I whisper, in my most irritated Laura voice.

"I was waiting for you," she says. "I knew you were upset, and when I heard you leave the tent, I couldn't go back to sleep, so I waited."

"What are you, my mother or something?" I say, walking past her.

"No. If someone was saying terrible things about my sister, it'd make me upset, too."

"I'm not upset."

"OK," says Celeste.

"Besides, why shouldn't you believe Laura?" I say. "Everybody else seems to."

"Not everybody. Not me."

"Why not?"

"Because you showed me Felicity's picture."

"But Laura's right." I am standing now, facing Celeste. "My sister never was coming to Parents' Weekend. I don't have a sister." I am whispering but I feel as though my voice is about to explode into a shout.

"But the photograph—"

"It's old. A year old," I say.

"Oh."

"I had a sister. I don't have a sister anymore. So Laura's right. Case closed."

"Then why are you so upset?" Celeste says.

"Because I am. OK?"

"Do you remember Felicity?"

It is odd to hear someone else call her by name; it's been so long. "Of course I do," I say.

"Do you remember what she smelled like? Do you remember her favorite doll? Do you remember changing her poops?" I smile a little, even though I don't want to, and nod my head.

"Then you didn't lie," says Celeste. "Felicity's still real."

"But Laura says—"

"Laura's jealous. Laura's trying to make Felic-

ity go away. But she won't, because you re[member] ber her. Long live Felicity," she says.

"Long live Felicity," I repeat.

"So where were you, in the middle o[f the] night?" asks Celeste.

"Our cabin. Crimson Lodge. This place i[n the] woods. Laura found it."

"I figured."

"You knew about it?"

"Yes."

"But how?"

"I always knew. Right from the start."

"How?" I repeat.

"I'd hear you leave the tent, late at nigh[t]. Sometimes you talked about it. And sometim[es] I'd hear you come back."

"Did we make a lot of noise?" I wondered who else knew that we were missing.

"Not really. I'm a light sleeper. Once I even tried to follow you, but I'm kind of afraid of the dark."

"But how did you know that's where we went?"

"When we took the hike on Parents' Weekend.

said to her, or how we tortured her, or how much we hurt her feelings, Celeste still didn't try to be one of us.

"I miss Felicity."

Celeste only says, "I know." I can feel my nose becoming prickly and know that I am close to crying. And then I tell Celeste everything I remember. Felicity—a little seed in the corner of my memory—starts to sprout the more I talk. She grows and grows, and by the time I finish, she is here, in this room, not by the power of a seance, but by the strength of my memories.

It is late, and we stand and stretch. But before we go inside the tent, Celeste notices the Laura doll that I have placed next to me. "What's that?" she says.

"It's a likeness."

"A what?"

"You know. For spells." I picture the Celeste and Mary dolls, side-by-side on the mantelpiece. "We used to cast spells on people."

"Can I see it?" says Celeste. She takes the doll by its twig hands and makes it dance. One of the twigs falls off. I take it from her hands.

"What are you doing with it?"

I take Celeste around to the back of the tent, behind a grove of trees. I light the match. The wood is dry, and it lights quickly: first the hair of leaves, and then the bark. The Laura doll sizzles and shrinks. We stamp out the remaining embers in the dirt, and go to bed.

Chapter Eighteen

I T'S FRIDAY, THE LAST DAY before we will be going home. The entire camp spends the morning collecting firewood for the final bonfire that evening. The smallest girls gather the kindling—twigs and little branches—and the older units haul whole trees that have fallen to the center of the field and saw them into smaller pieces.

There is goulash for lunch, and nobody complains about the food today. We all come back for seconds and pour more bug juice into our cups even before we have finished what is already there.

In the afternoon, after rest hour, we go swimming one last time in the lake, and then the rest of the day is ours, to return clothes we've borrowed and pack our trunks. I think I'm alone in the tent and am down on my knees, reaching under my bed for a misplaced sock, when I see two black high-tops standing next to me. I take my time, but she waits patiently, and I slide back out and brush the dirt off my stomach. She is dangling something in my face. It's my voodoo doll. The snowman with the twig eyes.

"So?" she says.

"So what?" I reply.

"So why'd you do it, Mary?" For an instant, I don't know what she is referring to. She sticks a pin into the snowman's stomach, and I feel that old, familiar rock in my chest.

"Do what?" I say, and then I remember the cabin, and the red poster paint.

"You know what I mean. Crimson Lodge. Why'd you ruin Crimson Lodge?" She holds my doll by its feet and swings it around and around. "And now," she says, "it's time to decapitate you." She pulls a scissors out of her back pocket and puts the blades around the snowman's neck. She is smiling.

And then I remember what Laura has said about my sister, and how quickly she left me alone, and made the others take sides against me. I say, "Crimson Lodge wasn't your cabin, Laura. It was our cabin. At least that's what you always told me."

"I found it."

"You said it was ours. You called it our getaway."

"You ruined it. You poured paint on the floor. And it got all over my sneakers, too." She shows me the soles of her feet. "Don't think I'm not going to make you pay for them, either."

"How do you know I did that?" I say. I am surprised by my voice. It sounds far away, and clear as a wind chime.

"Who else would do such a stupid thing?" Laura asks. "Besides, I don't really understand why you would be so angry, anyway."

"Maybe because I hate you," I hear myself saying, my voice still steady and strong.

"What did I ever do to you?" She is backing

away from me, and her voice rises defensively.

"Felicity. You used my sister to get back at me. You said I was a liar."

"I was only joking. Can't you take a joke?"

"No, I guess I can't," I say.

"Then you and Celeste deserve each other," she says.

"I guess we do."

"I could get you in a lot of trouble if I tell Marjorie that you stole art supplies and ruined a building."

"She'd be pretty thrilled to hear how much time you also spent roaming around in the middle of the night."

"I don't care."

"So tell her, Laura," I say. I am tired now and I want Laura to go away. "Whatever makes you happy. Just leave me alone."

When a rag torch dipped in kerosene touches the tip of the bonfire, the wood instantly catches. Even though there are rocks marking the edge, I think everyone jumps back a foot or two. I sit cross-legged next to Celeste, our knees touching.

We sing songs, and when one of the counselors tells a ghost story about a young girl who gets lost in the woods and comes upon a headless hunter in a cabin nearby, we both look around for Laura, but can't find her. Hershey's bars are passed around, and I eat mine slowly, seeing how long I can make it last. At the end of the evening, as the counselors pour buckets of dirt on the fire to make it go out, I hear some of the girls crying. Celeste and I promise we'll write all year, and maybe even get together for a long weekend over Christmas vacation. I give her a present before I go to sleep. It's the Celeste doll, wrapped in a paper towel from the latrine and tied with a shoelace. I don't bother to brush my teeth before I go to bed. I look at Laura, scowling as she sits on top of her covers. I can hear music coming through her headphones. It must be hard to be Laura, I think, as I turn over and tumble into sleep.

Chapter Nineteen

THEY ARE BOTH THERE, and they are there by noon, unlike Parents' Weekend, when I waited with Laura until late afternoon for my father to arrive.

Even though it has only been four weeks, I feel like I haven't seen my mother for a lifetime. I never thought the smell of her perfume was so important to me, but as she hugs me, its smell is so familiar, like the color of her hair, or the sound of her voice. We walk around camp, since she has never seen it before, and I show her my tent, even though all that is in it is a half-empty bottle of shampoo and a plastic garbage bag lying on top of a mattress.

We eat in the mess hall, and I guess I eat too much—a grilled cheese with bacon, french fries, and a milkshake—because I feel a little queasy when we drive home. My mother makes me put my head between my knees, which helps.

It's early evening when we pull into our driveway. Before I went to camp, lawn furniture and hedges, the neighbors' house, and the edge of the sidewalk all seemed to blend together, fuzzy but part of the same picture. But now my house stands out to me, like it's lit by a different, brighter street lamp. I follow my father as he opens the front door, and run up to my bedroom. It smells of Lemon Pledge. My bed is neatly made, with stuffed animals lined up against the headboard according to size. There are new curtains on the windows—yellow gingham—that I have wanted for a long time, and a new diary with a tiny key on my desk.

I wish my room could stay like this forever—orderly, with everything in its place. But I know that, no matter how much I try, in a few days, there will be dirty T-shirts thrown in a corner, and cookie crumbs on the rug. I turn around and see my parents at the doorway, watching me.

"Thank you," I say.

"You're welcome," they reply. "Welcome home." My father hands me a phone message from Adrienne. She wants me to call as soon as I get home. I start to leave, but my mother says, "Come see the rest of the house."

My father follows her. When his hand rests on the small of her back, her fingers, just for a second, almost by accident, touch his. I follow them into their room, and they show me a new black chrome floor lamp they have bought, and new sheets and bedspread in a brown-and-black pattern. We walk down the hall. They have installed a brass towel rack in the bathroom, and tell me their plans to re-wallpaper the room. "Something more dramatic," my mother says. I follow them to the end of the hall, to Felicity's room. My father opens the door casually, as if were just a TV room, or a linen closet.

The crib is gone. In its place are two twin beds with a night table in the middle. A framed poster of an oversized petunia hangs on the wall. There is a bookshelf next to a desk with a word processor sitting on top of it.

"It's kind of a combination guest room and study," my mother explains. "It's something your father and I have always needed."

"But this is Felicity's room," I say.

"Listen, pumpkin, nothing can stay the same," my father says.

"Try and be understanding," says my mother.

I open the closet door. "What did you do with everything?" I ask.

"Well, we gave a lot of it away," my mother says, looking at my father. "To families in need."

"We did housekeeping everywhere," says my father. "It's something we've should have done a long time ago."

"But in *here*," I say. "Couldn't you wait until I got home?" I hear my voice, louder and shriller.

"Don't yell at your mother," my father says. "She doesn't deserve this." They are standing behind one of the twin beds; I am miles away, it seems, opposite them, behind the other.

"I don't deserve to be talked to that way,"

my mother adds. "Not after what I've been through."

My father softens his voice. "You've had a very nice summer." He steps toward me. I cannot move. "Try to be understanding," my father says. "What did you want this room to be? Some kind of a museum? A shrine?"

"But there're no pictures. You took down the Babar poster."

"Yes," says my mother. "I couldn't live with it. Not with a shrine." I am frightened. Though she lowers her voice she is hissing, and her eyes stare at me, small and black. "I. Me. What do you think of that? You're eleven years old. You're a part of this family. Now start acting like it."

"I am?" I hiss back.

"What's that supposed to mean?"

"I don't feel like a part of this stupid family!" I am yelling now.

"So go over to Adrienne's house, if you think everything's hunky-dory over there, miss."

"Don't start," my father says softly.

"No, I mean it," my mother continues. "If she wants everything lovely and nice, then she's barking up the wrong tree."

"Whoever said anything about Adrienne?" I ask.

"She wants everything lovely and nice," my mother says, turning to my father. I leave as she says, "Sometimes things are crappy. Aren't they?"

I slam the front door and run down the street, toward Adrienne's house. The street lights are starting to come on. I can smell wood burning in a fireplace, and small clusters of leaves, on the tips of the trees, are starting to change.

They're home; I see a shadow in front of the living room window, and the lights in Adrienne's room are on. I throw a rock up to her window to get her attention. She waves, and gestures for me to wait. Seconds later, she opens the front door and runs down the walk to meet me.

"I've missed you," she says. "I called. Didn't you get my message? Come in. I want to show you something. How was camp? Why didn't you write me more?"

She takes my arm and pulls me inside. Her

mother is lying on the couch, and she stands up to greet me. Her father is sitting on an easy chair in front of the TV, and he holds up the hand that's not holding a drink.

"It's the play-offs," Adrienne whispers. "No one's allowed to speak."

For a second I wonder if he is still angry at me for lighting matches on the roof of his house, but then the game breaks to a commercial, and he stands up and gives me a hug.

"Well, well, well," he says, "the prodigal daughter has come home." I'm not sure what a prodigal daughter is, but it doesn't sound bad. "Adrienne here's been champing at the bit all month. Saw your parents last week at the McGinnis wedding. Your mother looked terrific. They couldn't stop talking about how much they missed you. Isn't that right?"

"Terrific," Mrs. Tannenbaum says. The game has come on again; Adrienne's father sits back down in his chair.

The phone rings. I don't want my parents to know I'm here. I want them to worry. But it's just a friend calling for Terry, who's working late, scooping ice cream. I lie on my stomach, on Adrienne's bed. She asks me how I liked camp, but I don't know how to answer. Suddenly, I'm very tired, and I wonder what I am doing here.

"One more week," she says.

"One more week until what?"

"School. One more week until school. Did you get your homeroom assignment?"

"I don't know."

"I got Mr. Adams. Thank God."

"Thank God," I repeat. I can barely remember who Mr. Adams is.

"*And* my mother took me shopping yesterday. *And* I like someone. *And* I'm getting a new haircut tomorrow. Something short. Want to come?" As she talks, she takes her new purchases—an oversized black sweater with geometric patterns, a large canvas bag, black leggings—out of her closet, and lays them around me.

"Maybe," I say, and I turn over on my side.

"Why are you so quiet?" she asks.

"I'm sorry, Adrienne. I shouldn't have come," I say, and stand up, and start toward the door. I can't go home, but I shouldn't be here.

"Do you want to sleep over?"

"I just got back, Adrienne."

"Oh yeah. Well, maybe tomorrow."

"Maybe."

"Are you mad at me?"

"Of course not," I say, and I give her a hug. "I just shouldn't have come. I'm tired."

"Call me in the morning."

"I will," I promise, and I leave.

It's dark now, and I walk on the grass next to the road. My sneakers are wet, and squeaking with every step. The rest of me is cold, too. I should be wearing a sweatshirt, but part of me is hoping I will get a cold, or maybe even pneumonia. I swallow, and think my throat is already a little bit sore.

Each house is full of light, and, as in the fourth-grade diorama I made of a Mexican village, the windows show little scenes that I stop to watch, from behind a manicured hedge or tree. At one house, I see a couple playing cards. At another, a woman stands as she talks on the telephone. The cord is twisted around her waist.

I pretend I am a little orphan girl who is imagining which home she'd like to live in, if she could choose.

I walk on the curb as fast as I can without losing my balance. I don't know where I am going. All the streets look alike. There are no tall trees, except at the edge of the development, because they have all been cut down to make room for the new houses. It's quiet, except for a car approaching behind me. The car flashes its headlights, and I turn around. It's the Buick. There are houses all around me, and so close together that there is nowhere to run, so I keep walking straight ahead without looking. The car slows, and I can hear the automatic window being lowered. My mother sticks her head back in the window and says, "Get inside, Mary. It's too late for you to be out."

I shake my head and continue walking.

"Get inside," she says. "I'm not playing games."

"Leave me alone," I say.

"I will not."

"Why?" I say. "You hate me."

"I don't hate you."

"Yes, you do," I say. I am crying now, and I wipe my nose on my arm.

"Get in the car and we'll talk."

"No."

"Stop walking, Mary. I can't hear a word you're saying."

I stop. "No," I repeat. I can't look at her, except out of the corner of my eye. I see her reach over to the passenger side and open its door.

"Get in, Mary," she says.

I'm cold and tired and hungry. I still don't look at her, but I walk around and climb into the front seat. I sit with my body pressed against the front door, as far away from her as I can get, with my arms folded across my chest.

"Your father didn't come," she says, "because he thought this was just between us. In case you were wondering. Which doesn't thrill me, Mary, because my night vision leaves something to be desired."

"I don't care," I mumble.

"What?"

"I said I don't care."

"Well fine. That's fine." She drives up and down the development's newly paved roads. "Is there something you want to tell me?"

"No," I say.

"Because clearly you're angry at me. Clearly I've done something wrong."

I shake my head.

"I know you're mad at me because I never made it to Parents' Weekend." She drives with both hands on the steering wheel and looks small behind the wheel of my father's car.

"I don't care."

"I couldn't, Mary. I had to get away."

"You promised you'd come."

"I know."

"You wrote me a letter and said you couldn't wait."

"I know. I'm sorry. What can I tell you? All I can hope is that you try and understand."

"But you promised—"

"Can we stop talking about it. Please. I apologized. What else do you want me to do? I'm getting a migraine."

"Sorry," I say.

My mother slows the car down and looks at me. "Take the sarcastic tone out of your voice, please," she says to me.

But I can't stop now. "You changed her room."

"What now?"

"Felicity's room. You changed it all around."

"Here we go again."

"Why?"

"So shoot me," she says.

"You never loved her." I turn, not even for a second, to see her face. I know I am hurting her, but I don't want to stop.

"What?" she says.

"You never loved her. If you did, you wouldn't have ruined her room." I am hurting her. It feels good to hurt her.

My parents tell me that the only time they hit me was when I was three years old and ran into the street just as a truck was coming. I don't see her reach over. It isn't until I feel the sting on my cheek that I realize she has slapped me. I take a deep breath and wait for her to yell and tell me how cruel I am. She pulls the car over to the side

144

of the road and puts on the brakes. Then she drapes herself over the steering wheel and buries her head in her arms. She is crying. She is speaking, too, but I can't make out what she is saying.

She cries forever, it seems, and I don't know what to do, so I pat her on the shoulder. She faces me and throws her arms around me. Now I am crying, too. In the streetlight's glare, we catch each other's eyes. Her mascara is running down her cheeks, and my nose is dripping. "We're a fine pair," she says, and we both begin to laugh.

We don't talk as we drive home, and when we arrive, my father is waiting at the front door. I see him look at my mother, puzzled. She takes my hand and we go to the kitchen. My father follows, and we watch her take ice cream out of the freezer and chocolate sauce out of the cupboard. I find three bowls and spoons, and we each make enormous sundaes.

Later, my mother tucks me into bed. "I saved this for you," she says, and she hands me Felicity's lamb. "I'm sorry, Mary," my mother adds. "I should have waited. But it was too hard."

"OK," I say.

"We'll talk in the morning," she says, kissing me good night.

"OK," I repeat.

"Good night, my darling, my big girl," she says, and she turns out the light.

Chapter Twenty

AT THE START OF LABOR Day weekend, my parents wake me gently. Even though I have been in a deep sleep, I get up immediately and put on the blue jeans and sweatshirt that are waiting at the foot of my bed. I can smell coffee downstairs, and bagels, and as I wash my face in the bathroom before going downstairs, I can see that the sky, though black and starry overhead, is brightening in the east.

We eat silently in the kitchen, or, when we do talk, we speak in hushed voices, as if we are afraid of waking someone. My father goes outside to check the car, and I help my mother clear the table, and run upstairs to be sure I haven't forgotten anything. I also make my bed, because I like to make sure everything is in order before I go away.

By seven o'clock, the holiday traffic is making the interstate fairly crowded, but we have been traveling for three hours now, and are starting to see signs for the Jersey shore exits, and advertisements for casinos, and fudge, and salt water taffy, so I know we are close.

This sudden vacation was my mother's idea, and my father immediately called a bunch of motels before finding one that had a room available. I'll have to sleep on a portable cot at the foot of their bed, but I don't mind.

There are no trees along the highway—only low, scrubby bushes growing in the sandy soil. But suddenly I see inlets and condominiums, and we turn off our air-conditioning and open the windows. Mostly, I smell exhaust fumes, but sometimes there is a whiff of salt air.

We ask directions at a gas station for Breakwater Street, and find the motel. My father registers in the lobby, which is painted a green that looks like sea foam. I sit on a vinyl couch with my mother and rub my fingers across a heavy glass ashtray on a coffee table. My father holds up the key as if it is a prize, and we walk up a set of outside stairs to a room on the balcony, overlooking a pool and, beyond, the beach.

Inside, I pull back the heavy red draperies to let the light in. The room is not fancy, but, says my mother, at least it's clean. We don't even bother to unpack. We just change into our bathing suits, stuff some towels into a beach bag, take two beach chairs out of the car, and head for the ocean. We walk up a cement ramp, and across the boardwalk. I sit on top of the cool metal railing, and look, in both directions, at the thick wooden planks that stretch and curve as far as I can see. Maybe we'll rent bikes in the early morning, before breakfast, and I can practice riding with no hands.

The water is warm at this time of year, and my father and I dive right without even hesitating. My mother, too, eventually gets herself wet, and we three bob up and down, always looking out to sea for any large, incoming waves.

My father and I use our hands to build a sand castle with a moat, and long passageways that lead to the water. By the time we are ready to leave, the tide is coming in, and the water is already softening its edges.

Later, we take turns showering and dress for dinner. There is a seafood restaurant my parents want to try that is a twenty-minute walk down the boardwalk. I sprinkle myself with baby powder, and put on a sundress. We are thinking about lobsters and crab cakes, and corn on the cob. My parents walk ahead of me, with their arms around each other's waist. I pretend I don't know them, that I am judging them on first impressions only. They are nice-looking people, I think. People I would like to know.

My mother pulls a camera out of her purse, and my father and I groan.

"Honey, the reservations," my father says, looking at his watch.

"This'll only take a minute," she says, adjusting the light meter. "Perfect," she says. "Now smile!" My father and I lean against the railing and smile. Then my father takes a picture of me and my mother, and then I suggest taking one of just the two of them. She is putting her camera away, when an old man in a straw hat walks over to us. "How about a shot of the three of you?" he says. "Such a handsome family."

My mother says that would be wonderful, and shows the man where to look, and what button to push. We stand against the railing again, this time with me in the middle. The first picture doesn't work; the little red light doesn't go off. So we try again. This time, we don't move until we hear the click that tells us the picture has been taken.

The man hands the camera to my parents, who thank him, and he walks away. I'll keep this picture in my scrapbook, this photo of us three. And maybe, if we have a really good time, we will come back next year, and the year after that, and the year after that. And each year we'll have a picture taken, in exactly the same spot. We'll grow a little older, but basically, everything will stay the same.

My parents tell me there will come a time

when I won't want to go away on vacations with them—when I'll roll my eyes and make excuses. I look in the mirror, and sometimes I think I can see that girl they are speaking of. But she is still in the distance, as far away as the end of the boardwalk where the beach starts to narrow, and the water begins to lap underneath. I won't think about this now, because today, even though the light is shifting, even though the season officially ends in two more days, right now, it's still summer, and that's good enough for me.

KALEIDOSCOPE CITY

Honey and Dust

All Kinds of Magic

KALEIDOSCOPE CITY

A Year in Varanasi

Piers Moore Ede

B L O O M S B U R Y

NEW YORK · LONDON · NEW DELHI · SYDNEY

Bloomsbury USA
An imprint of Bloomsbury Publishing Plc

1385 Broadway
New York
NY 10018
USA

50 Bedford Square
London
WC1B 3DP
UK

www.bloomsbury.com

BLOOMSBURY and the Diana logo are trademarks of Bloomsbury Publishing Plc

First published in Great Britain 2015
First US edition 2015

Some of this material has previously been published as "Crossing Place: A Year in Varanasi"
as part of the Global Oneness Project.

Extracts on pages 1, 13, and 183 from *Banaras: City of Light* by Diana Eck, copyright © 1982
by Diana L. Eck. Used by permission of Alfred A. Knopf, an imprint of the Knopf Doubleday
Publishing Group, a division of Random House LLC. All rights reserved.

Extracts on pages 31 and 33 from *Ramayana* by William Buck, copyright © 1989 by the Regents
of the University of California. Republished by permission of the University of California Press.

Extract on page 161 from *The Great Pilgrimage: From Here to Here* by Osho,
copyright © Osho International Foundation. Reproduced by permission of
Osho International Foundation, www.OSHO.com

Every reasonable effort has been made to trace copyright holders of material reproduced in this book,
but if any have been inadvertently overlooked the publishers would be glad to hear from them.

No responsibility for loss caused to any individual or organization acting on or refraining from
action as a result of the material in this publication can be accepted by Bloomsbury or the author.

ISBN: HB: 978-1-60819-868-9
PB: 978-1-62040-557-4
ePub: 978-1-62040-558-1

LIBRARY OF CONGRESS CATALOGING-IN-PUBLICATION DATA HAS BEEN APPLIED FOR.

2 4 6 8 10 9 7 5 3 1

Typeset by Hewer Text UK Ltd, Edinburgh
Printed and bound in the U.S.A. by Thomson-Shore Inc., Dexter, Michigan

To find out more about our authors and books visit www.bloomsbury.com.
Here you will find extracts, author interviews, details of forthcoming events,
and the option to sign up for our newsletters.

Bloomsbury books may be purchased for business or promotional use.
For information on bulk purchases please contact Macmillan Corporate
and Premium Sales Department at specialmarkets@macmillan.com.

For Lucy, this one's for you

Contents

Introduction   I

Instant Moksha   9
Searching for Rama in Ramnagar   31
Sex for Sale   51
The Mice in the Mithai Shop   79
The Ganga   97
The Warp and the Weft   121
The City of Ten Thousand Widows   145
Harmony, Rhythm and Order   161
Afterword   183

Select Glossary   187
Notes   195
Select Bibliography   199
Acknowledgements   201
Index   203

Introduction

Kashi is the whole world they say. Everything on
earth that is powerful and auspicious is here, in this
microcosm. All of the sacred places of India and all of
her sacred waters are here. All of the Gods reside here,
attracted by the brilliance of the City of Light. All of
the eight directions of the compass originated here,
receiving jurisdiction over the sectors of the universe.
And all of time is here, for the lords of the heavenly
bodies which govern time are grounded in Kashi.
– Diana Eck, *Banaras: City of Light*

Perhaps for all of us there is a country, and within that a single
place, in which some essential element of the world is illumi-
nated for the first time. Sitting down on a park bench in a
beam of sunlight, or lost in the cacophony of a spice market,
it comes to us that we have never been this vibrantly, persua-
sively alive. Our heart centre – as the Indian yogis like to call
it – is aflame with the wonder of all things.

I first came to Varanasi when I was twenty-five, en route for
Nepal through northern India, and with very little idea about

the city other than it was supposed to be interesting, and that it made a convenient resting place for a few days before I continued my journey. India had already begun to work her magic on me, but it was in Varanasi (known as Kashi in the scriptures, or more recently *Banaras*) that the full possibility of what India might be seemed to announce itself. Here was a vast experiment in human cohabitation that had been going on for five thousand years: a river city containing every facet of humanity, every creed, colour, caste, both astonishing beauty and the most harrowing ugliness and desolation. Here was the madness of India, as well as its wisdom, the sublime poetry of its spiritual traditions and the dirty imbalance of corruption. Here were Hindus, Muslims, Buddhists, Christians, Jains and Sikhs, as well as infinite sects pre-dating any of these major traditions, but which persisted happily within the larger whole. All of it combined as the city itself: one entity, a composite of spirit and form.

Until then I had supposed India was essentially unfathomable: it was too fast, too swiftly changing to yield to any categorisation. In Varanasi, however, I found a city whose spirit seemed to denote the whole. On that first trip, even from my fairly cursory explorations, it seemed abundantly clear that there was something unique about the place, an energetic quality, a feeling that spoke in the body long before it appeared as thought. There was an intensity to the alleys and the dust, which was part of the makeup of the citizens themselves, the most passionate, lively people I'd ever encountered. Even after leaving it behind, the resonance of Banaras kept returning to me like some haunting snatch of music. I wanted to hear that music again, let it play upon my ears for a while, until it revealed its secrets.

The following winter I returned for a month, and the winter after that for three months. At first, my reasons for being there remained unclear to me – I studied yoga and meditation, walked for hours, spent long days reading at the library Krishnamurti had set up at Raj Ghat, sometimes taking a boat ride home, a blissful hour in which the whole sweep of the river front would pass before me. I was in my mid-thirties, still restless. Why I should find answers here was anyone's guess, and yet a certain intuition kept my ear to the ground. As with the thousands of pilgrims who arrived here on any given day, I was hoping the city herself would respond.

Finally, the opportunity came to return for a longer period, perhaps a year. Here now, at last, I felt I might cease to be an outsider and penetrate to the city's heart. I returned during the last burning days of summer, the Ganga lower than I had ever seen it owing to a poor monsoon, the heat shimmering off the flat plains of Uttar Pradesh at over 40 degrees. With one small bag of clothes, no camera, and the germ of an idea to write about my experiences, I went to Assi Ghat, which has long been the haunt of foreign residents. The word 'ghat' refers to the flights of stone steps descending the banks of the Ganga into water: there are nearly a hundred in Varanasi, with Assi the southernmost. Because of this, it has retained an open village-like feel, bucolic at its edges, until very recently.

Looking back over my notes from those first days, I notice the shock and exhaustion of my re-entry: dust-red eyes from whizzing rickshaw rides, ears resounding with the blasts of incessant car horns, mind spinning with the velocity of it all, which somehow, I don't know how, I'd forgotten. As any quantum physicist will tell you, all we are is energy, but in

Varanasi that energy seems more highly charged: spinning faster, amplified somehow so that basic human tasks such as simply going to buy rice become shattering experiences of navigating two-hour traffic jams, throwing oneself against the side of an alley to avoid being crushed by a roaring Tata motorbike, or weaving between unruly cattle in the course of crossing the street. The crush of human numbers, the crumbling medieval architecture built upon and compressed by concrete structures, the hissing charge of frayed electric wires used as ropes by monkey troupes, the appalling pollution and a thousand other environmental factors combine to make the city an alchemist's crucible, transmuting all who live there. Should you, after returning home across the city, wipe your face with a white cloth it will be stained black from the traffic fumes. Your lungs burn, your eyes stream, your stomach purges, and yet despite all this your spirit soars.

Within a week or so I'd found a place to live: two rooms at the top of a supremely ugly custard-yellow concrete building right on the edge of the river. My landlord, Khado Yadav, lived with his wife, son and grandchildren on the ground floor, along with a legion of mice who would scuttle about, searching for fallen crumbs, while the family watched soap operas on television. During one of our first conversations, while Mr Yadav examined my potential as a likely tenant from his armchair, I gained a useful lesson by observing how the family simply let the mice be, utterly unconcerned by their presence. This was the key, perhaps, to surviving the city: an equanimous acceptance – for a foreigner, easier said than done.

After the necessary haggling over the rent, Mr Yadav, a little creaky in his early seventies, and wearing a dal-stained white vest and lungi, showed me my quarters – two rooms with bare concrete floors, and with only mesh windows, painted several generations before with a cobalt-blue now flaking paint. An iron key that might have unlocked a castle door clicked open the padlock. The only piece of furniture of note was a bed, built in the Indian style of wooden planks. In short, the place was perfect: cheap to inhabit, authentically Spartan, and with a view from one side over the Ganga herself. I could use the family's own bucket shower for washing, and if things needed to be dried, there was the rooftop – he pointed a digit vertically – which I was welcome to make use of.

I moved in soon after, purchasing the essentials of a gas ring, a few pans, a cast-iron *tava* – a convex disc-shaped griddle – for cooking chapattis, and a mosquito net. I arranged my single shelf with a few scholarly tomes on the city, a metal beaker for drinking water, notebook and pens, a postcard image of the great saint Sri Ramana Maharshi, as well as certain concessions to modernity, such as my laptop. As I lay down on my bed that first night, the warm wind streaming in through the rusted window mesh, I could hear rhesus macaques and tussling crows on the neighbouring roof. The months stretched ahead like an open promise, the river flowed past my window carrying the first night-time oil lamps, floating prayers cast out into the twilight.

My landlord, I discovered, was a former army officer, who had spent forty-five years manning checkpoints in a variety of inhospitable locations across India. Now in his retirement, he was devoting his life to spiritual matters and could be heard vociferously reciting the scriptures at first light. In him

I gained an early consultant on all things Banarasi, and would often leave in the morning with a hand-drawn map – slivers of paper torn along a Helix ruler.

Bearing these military diagrams, I began my exploration of the city. Close to the Ganga, the *galis*, lanes, seemed little changed from the time of the Buddha, thronged with white- and orange-clad pilgrims stepping gingerly over the cowpats on their way for a morning dip. These tapered streets had a poetry about them that filled me with wonder. Every crevice held the potential for unexpected bursts of life: a blood-red Hanuman statue no bigger than a human hand, a dog suck- ling eight blind puppies, verses from the mystic poet Kabir scrawled in chalk, already dissolving.

Though almost everything ever written about the contem- porary city seems to use the word 'chaos', I found an unexpected serenity in these narrow *galis* – some of them too slender even to allow two people to walk abreast. In the early morning especially, before the first blare and rumble of motorcycle engines, one can close one's eyes and imagine a lost world, some biblical city opened through the fabric of time. The powers of ritual and myth still endure there, and it is just this presence that animates the ancient stonework, rendering it more than an inhabited museum but rather a living organism: humans going about their business of trying to survive, their thoughts half on this world, half on the next.

Varanasi is divided into eight wards. Within these there are the *mohallas* – a word translating as something like parish – whose makeups differ widely in language and population, so that there are Bengali mohallas, South Indian, Nepali and so forth, as well as mohallas grouped by caste or occupation.

Each with its shrine, mosque or temple, the mohallas are microcosms of the larger city: miniature villages whose residents form extended families and have their own headmen given to the adjudication of minor disputes. In the open space of the mohallas, women will dye fabric or thresh grain, and during weddings or festivals the whole community will join together in stringing up lanterns and coloured lights, banners and decorations. At the important times of the year – *Ramlila* (a devotional play) or *Muharram* (the first month of the Islamic calendar) – the residents of neighbouring mohallas compete with each other for the quality of their performances and decorations, a friendly rivalry that links the communities together. Walking these mohallas, getting lost, and almost always finding a profound hospitality and kindness, was a key way I got to know the city.

This was Varanasi, the fabled City of Light: its scriptural name 'Kashi' means, literally, 'luminous' in Sanskrit. Certainly it was dazzling, but to my eyes it was more like a kaleidoscope: full of symmetry and colour, but also operating on the principle of multiple reflection. Everything I saw cast perspective on something else, almost every viewpoint I heard could be countered or, at the least, seen as incomprehensible by someone a few streets away. As I explored, certain themes of the city – the interplay between life and death, the industries of silk-weaving and sweet-making, the drama and music that make Varanasi both a stage and a soundtrack, a human city as well as divine – began to emerge. Corruption, endemic poverty and the lingering prejudices of the caste system were part of that, as was a substantial heroin trade and the human trafficking of sex workers by ruthless cartels.

And yet, despite this, the simplicity of life in the old medieval alleys, the poetry of the city's rituals and beliefs, seemed to
me to represent the best of India, the best, perhaps, of the
human condition. There was a straightforward friendliness to
the people there, a jocular sense of humour. Above the basic
hunger for survival was a sense of our place in a much larger
order alluded to in a thousand subtle phrases and offerings. All
of this was the language of Banaras, its own private patois. It
seemed like a language I'd been waiting to learn my whole life.

Instant Moksha

Virtue does not grow easily in Banaras. And vice
has no better place. For all come here to burn.
– Raja Rao, *On the Ganga Ghat*

Death is ever-present in the Holy City. To visit here without
encountering it is impossible. Sipping chai in the narrow *galis*
of the old quarter, one hears the distant sounds of chanting:
'Ram Nam Satya Hai, Ram Nam Satya Hai', literally 'The
name of God is Truth'. A minute later, six men bearing a
corpse on a bamboo ladder come into view, walking purpose-
fully towards the river. Bound in white muslin, the corpse
may be decorated with silver tinsel, or a garland of orange
marigolds. It moves, in funereal stillness, towards the cremation ground, and the world beyond.

One or two of the chai drinkers may look up. Most will
barely raise a glance from their newspapers, or falter in their
recounting of the latest test-match scores. Bodies pass through
these alleyways with as great a frequency as cattle or goats,
and there is no cause for alarm.

Drawing closer to the cremation ghat itself, one confronts

an even starker view. Here, in plain sight, corpses smoulder among carefully stacked piles of wood, and the air is filled with the smell of burning. Among the mourners, tears are very rare. Rather, there is a calm acceptance of what is, and the surety that a relative has ended their journey at the most auspicious place in the Hindu world. 'If only a bone of a person shall touch the water of the Ganga,' says the *Mahabharata*, 'that person shall dwell, honoured, in heaven.'

Woven tightly into the fabric of Varanasi is its association with death. For the visitor to the city, especially from the West, the ubiquity of death here can seem shocking, and one of India's greatest contrasts with our own deeply private traditions. Like so many travellers, I went to see the cremation ghats on my first visit, eager for this rite of passage into the city. I rose at five o'clock one morning and strolled down to the waterfront, where I engaged the services of a boatman. Mist pooled over the river, and the air rang with the plaintive cawing of crows. The boatman was an aged fellow who drew the oars through the water with a look of excruciating effort. Veins stood out on his forearms like cords of wire.

As we drew close to Manikarnika, most esteemed among the city's burning ghats, I could make out the orange glow of a funeral pyre on the shoreline and, blinking a little, noticed the corpse on fire, smelled the smoke in the air. A skyline of soot-darkened temples formed the backdrop, and I was to wonder how much of that carbon deposit was formed of the dust of human bodies, risen on the wind and pushed back into the very structure of the city. Amalgamations of history, cities are constructed of the dead as much as the living, Varanasi perhaps most of all.

In that early morning silence, I felt the tremulous thrill of one who is standing at a threshold, beyond which there is unease, the end of what is known. Everything about this place was alien to me – its rituals, belief systems, the unending flow of people moving with such purpose. We sat under the wide open sky. On the shoreline people moved in a measured clockwork. They seemed part of a timeless fabric, moving according to patterns laid down long ago.

The boatman said nothing. He was used, perhaps, to the introspection this scene provoked in his passengers. He kept the wooden craft pointing at the shore by twisting the blade of the oar in the murky water so that the force worked back against the current. Into the great emptiness came the sudden clang of temple bells, the low tones of Vedic chanting. White birds dipped over the river, and from an alleyway behind the ghat I watched a Japanese tourist emerge excitedly, camera poised, then visibly quail as he took in the scene. He removed a white mask from his pocket and snapped it over his face, like a surgeon preparing for the operating theatre.

'Everything ends in this place,' said my boatman on that first morning, watching the smoke rise. His voice was almost a whisper. 'But also everything is beginning. Bodies end their journey here and return to spirit. This is what we have always been, of course, but while living we forget this. Working here, as I do, I daily try to remember. We are not this body, we are not this mind.'

I let the words sink in, considering what it would be like to really believe what he was suggesting. If death ceases to become a conclusion, but merely a crossing place from one world to the next, then the human form, so tangible and solid, might simply be a costume to wear for a time then discard like an old suit of clothes. I looked down at my fingers with a newfound suspicion, imagining myself, at some future time, burning on one of these ghats, and this world dropping away.

To comprehend the ancient association between Varanasi and death, one must look back several millennia. No one knows exactly how old Varanasi is, but it may be as much as five thousand years, Some say it is the world's oldest inhabited city, its present shape reaching back to the sixth century BC in a continuous tradition. For much of this period the city has lain at the heart of the faith we now call Hinduism, standing as the place of creation, and representing the whole of the universe in a single symbolic circle, a mandala. The Hindu tradition, in fact, emerged along the Gangetic plain, the focus shifting from ritual sacrifice to the worship of gods.

According to this tradition, still practised by the majority of the world's one billion-plus Hindus, the cosmos is composed of a cycle of death and rebirth called 'samsara'. This notion underpins the entire Hindu faith, and is the basis for understanding religious life here. In human terms, the ultimate goal of this life is not paradise, as in the Abrahamic traditions, but liberation from this never-ending wheel. Called 'moksha' in the Sanskrit texts, this 'liberation' means to merge with Brahman, the Ultimate Reality itself, never to be reborn.

Moksha, however, is considered so lofty a goal in Hinduism that none but the strictest ascetics would expect to find it during one human span. Rather, through the accruing of good karma, or merit, one may simply hope for an auspicious rebirth, and in the case of an impious life expect an incarnation lower down the chain, perhaps in the animal or plant realms. The Hindu view of time is vast: most are content to let things happen at their own pace. Yogis and sadhus (religious ascetics) are revered here because they've left everything behind in a quest to break free of samsara once and for all. But for the Hindu householder, spiritual life – with all its colourful worship of Ganesha, Vishnu and Shiva – accepts the likelihood of rebirth as an unfolding in the slow procession towards this final revelation.

Into this picture, the mythology of Varanasi adds an all-important twist, for it is said that if one should draw one's last breath anywhere in the city, the entire cycle of death and rebirth can be sidestepped: moksha is granted regardless of one's current place in samsara. For some Hindus, this is little more than a superstition: while they accept the city as sacrosanct, its ability to act as kind of spiritual get-out-of-jail-free card remains moot. For the vast majority, however, this belief is absolutely accurate, and thus the city's greatest power. Death here becomes free of terror, and a gateway into the realm of the immortals. A folk saying – still muttered by pilgrims – reads 'Kashyam maranam muktih' – 'Death in Kashi is liberation'.

It is a bright morning in November when I arrive at Harishchandra Ghat, the second of Varanasi's two sacred cremation grounds. By the rules of Indian caste, in which social classes are defined according to thousands of hereditary groups, these burning ghats are managed by a people known as the Dom Raja. They are a subset of the larger Dom caste that includes scavengers, weavers of ropes and baskets, magicians and jugglers.

I'm here to meet one of their elders, a man named Gupta Choudhary, who I hope will provide a unique perspective on the subject of death in the holy city. Receiving me in a small open-fronted structure (a sort of lean-to wooden shed built onto the side of Bhairav temple), he smooths out a bamboo mat for me to sit on. A sober-looking man, he wears a plain white kurta (collarless tunic), two bright streaks of crimson and white across his forehead. He has large ears, from which coal-black tufts of hair protrude to an impressive distance. Studying me with open amusement, he lets out a boom of laughter that shatters any preconceptions I may have about the Dom. It's the laugh of someone absolutely at ease with life, full-throated and infectious. Vitality exudes from him – surprising, perhaps, in this place of death.

Sitting before an open fire, and observed with interest by several of the younger Dom, Gupta tells me about his life at the cremation ground. He has the confidence of a tribal elder, a man assured of his place in the scheme of things. From this vista, I notice the ugly concrete structure housing the recently introduced electric crematorium, as well as a drift of smoke from the more traditional pyres at the water's edge. The open space beside the river provides the arena for the burning of bodies, which are spaced in an ordered fashion on their pyres. It's another normal day for these men, who crack jokes and puff small clay chillums of marijuana, while the business of death unfolds. Far out in the current, a fisherman throws his net into the brackish water, while from a distant temple a harmonium hums a soft monotone.

'It is true that to understand death in this city you must know the Dom Raja,' Gupta begins in his rasping, baritone voice. 'We know things that no others know about this city, our view is unique. But to understand the Dom Raja you must first know the story of King Harishchandra, for whom this ghat is named. Every Hindu knows this story.'

Accepting one of the small pipes, Gupta brings it to his lips thoughtfully and takes a long pull.

'In the epoch of Satya Yuga, when this world was ruled by the gods, there was a just and perfect king named Harishchandra. When the gods heard of this man, they were suspicious that anyone could be so honest and decided to give him a test. Let's see if he will be so good if we take away all he has, they said!

'The gods selected a sage called Vishwamitra to tell Harishchandra he had given away his kingdom in a dream. Even when he heard this, the king did not become angry! He took the news, gathered up his wife Taramati and son and took to the road. They wandered in the wind and rain for many days, until finally they reached the holy city of Kashi.

'When they got here, Harishchandra could find no work and his family grew close to starvation. With no option left to him, Harishchandra was forced to sell himself into slavery, at this very cremation ground.'

Gupta taps the ground beneath us to illustrate that this piece of Hindu legend occurred in the very area in which we sat.

'Becoming a slave was not trouble enough for Harishchandra. Soon after, his son was killed by a naga [a poisonous snake] while collecting flowers. And when the boy's mother, Taramati, brought the body to the cremation ground, the king failed to recognise her, seeing her as just a poor beggar woman. Noticing that she had no money for the cremation, Harishchandra told her she must sell her golden *mangalasutra* – the necklace worn by Indian wives as a symbol of marriage – to pay for the cremation. She agreed, and when she removed the final part of it from her body, the gods appeared in a blaze of light. King Harishchandra had passed the test, and was praised for his steadfastness.'

Gupta pauses to extract a splinter of wood from the fire. He blows out the flame at one end, taps it carefully to remove any ash, then holds the glowing tip to the pipe bowl, sucking gently to coax a few more puffs from the chillum. 'With his son now miraculously returned to life,' Gupta continues, 'Harishchandra was offered his place in heaven. But he refused. Why should I be granted entry to heaven, he said, unless every one of my subjects also are allowed inside? At this, the gods realised that truly this man was without flaw, and they accepted.'

'It is for this reason,' chimes in one of Gupta's cousins, from whose tonsured head a short plait protrudes, 'that all Hindus, no matter what their deeds, may obtain salvation in this place. Harishchandra did this for us.'

'And also that we Dom, to this day, use the honorific "Raja",' adds Gupta proudly, 'after our ancient association with the king. We who work at this cremation ground see ourselves as his descendants.' He grins. 'We are also kings.'

I turn to gaze out over the scene at the edge of the ghat, where a group of male mourners cluster around an unlit funeral pyre. The body, mummified in its layers of muslin, rests with its head to the north, the feet to the south and, since the deceased was a Brahmin, clasps a piece of gold in its palm. Along a human chain from the river, sacred Ganga water is passed in a copper vessel to the eldest son, who pours it around the stacked wood, walking with careful steps over the mud. Conducting the scene, a white-clad Brahmin priest prepares the final prayers that will allow the soul to merge with the Universe.

Closer to where we sit, two emaciated cows bask on their haunches, and a group of young boys play *gend balla*, cricket, hollering from time to time as a wicket tumbles. There's something extraordinary about this interplay of life and death, the groups of mourners enacting their rituals beside everyday pursuits – the passing boats, domestic animals, dark spires of smoke rising into a pale sky. I turn to watch the mourners once again, wondering if, perhaps, they work in modern office blocks in some distant city, wielding tablets and mobile phones, but have brought their father's body to Banaras for the cremation. There is nothing in this scene to situate it in the twenty-first century. They are doing their duty, I think to myself. And these duties are also forming their social identity.

'The special *jati* [caste characteristic] of our family is to give the *tilak* [mark on the forehead] to the dead bodies, and tend to the sacred fire,' says Gupta, noticing me watching the funeral. 'By doing this work, the dead benefit.'

The bodies don't seem to smell unpleasant, I remark, even if normal wood alone is used.

Gupta smiles, apparently pleased at my observation. 'This means we have done our job well, actually. We use ghee for this purpose, which also raises the temperature of the pyre significantly. Wood is not really hot enough by itself to really break down a human body. And then a mixture of many other things: sesame seeds, barley, balsam resin, camphor, *haldi* [turmeric powder], saffron. All these add fragrance. Blending them is an art. The richest people use a lot of sandalwood.'

I ask Gupta about his childhood. Was it not strange to be around death, even as a boy? Did the bodies never frighten him? Didn't the prospect of spending his life amongst mourners depress him? I think of the funeral I attended myself as a child; it was a bleak occasion, beset by a cold wind and full of the sound of weeping. Even the memory makes me shiver, and yet while there is sadness at this cremation ground, it doesn't feel morose.

'You Western people fear death so much,' Gupta says sympathetically, 'but you fear it because you do not *know* it. For you, death is the counterpoint to life. It is something final, something bad. But for us Hindu people we see death as the counterpoint to birth.' He shrugged. 'So even as a boy, I was never fearful of it. After school I would just come down here to help. I would stoke the fires, and watch the bodies burning. Actually, this was enjoyable for me. This was my family business, my work and my caste. One thing we learn very young in the Dom Raja is to accept what will come to us all. How can we not when we see the bodies turning to ash, and hear the cracking of the skulls as the fire does its work? In this city of death it is our dharma to stand at the central point.'

This talk of caste leads me to ask Gupta about his views of caste discrimination in India. Despite Gandhi's attempts to reform the caste system, their social position remains deeply marginalised. During the mid-1990s, the right-wing Hindu Bharatiya Janata Party embarked upon a campaign drive to demonstrate its solidarity with the lowest castes. In a publicised stunt, the BJP insisted that several of its leaders share a breakfast with the Dom Raja. The prospect, however, was too much for a number of the BJP Brahmins, who waved away the 'polluted' food.

'Yes, it does sometimes upset me,' concedes Gupta. 'Caste remains supremely important here. Some of these fellows go to cleanse themselves if they accidentally touch us in the street. On another level, I accept this as the way of the world. Besides' – he grins mischievously – 'king or peasant, Brahmin or untouchable all pass through this cremation ground in the end.'

Over the next few weeks, I stop by the burning ghat whenever the opportunity unfolds. Gupta seems pleased to see me, and takes time to explain the intricacies of his workplace, with its towering piles of timber and billowing smoke, but also a general sense of order and discipline. Sobriety is the overwhelming atmosphere here, rather than any trace of melancholy. This is a serious business, though not one to be sad over. What's important is that things are done properly. The dead must be honoured, no detail forgotten. These rituals provide a framework in which the mourning can unfold: both a safety net and a musical score. In this performance, the Dom Raja are the most unobtrusive conductors, going about their business without ever drawing attention to themselves.

Running my eyes along the one hundred or so ghats that make up the waterfront of Varanasi, it seems that all of life has its assigned place on these stone steps leading down to the river. Some are used for bathing, others for laundry, washing buffalo, puja (worship, ceremonial offering), and this one for the business of death. The smells are of woodsmoke, buffalo dung, urine and jasmine flowers. The sounds are of rustling kites and lowing cattle, crackling wood and prayer.

'We honour many gods here,' Gupta tells me one day, smearing my forehead with sacred ash. 'But for the Dom, one is perhaps the most important. Agni, the god of fire. He makes our work here possible and we worship him accordingly with a special reverence. It is said there are five elements in the universe: fire, water, air, earth and ether. When death comes, the fire element in the human body goes out. For the soul to achieve moksha, it must be returned by way of the cremation fire, and in this way the natural order of things is balanced. Every fire on this ghat is lit from a dhuni (sacred fireplace) that has been burning continuously here since Satya Yuga. It is not for anyone to bring their own matchbox!'

We approach the eternal fire, smouldering in a small temple to one side of the ghat. Varanasi has risen and fallen over thousands of years, I think to myself. Perhaps this fire is the only thing which has remained constant over all these millennia.

'Fire has a cleansing capacity,' continues Gupta, lighting a splint, 'which is why the bodies of children are never burnt. They're already clean, you see: their souls are pure. In those cases we merely take them to the centre of the river, attach a large boulder to them with rope, then tip them into Ganga. The Holy Mother will carry them home. Sadhus are not burnt for the same reason.'

'I've noticed many sadhus at the cremation ground,' I remark. 'Does this place have some special sacred significance for them?'

Gupta tilts his head and a flicker of amusement crosses his craggy face. 'For most sadhus, the cremation ground is an inauspicious place that they keep clear of. However, there is one type of sadhu for whom the opposite holds true. We call them Aghoris. Do you know about these fellows? They are a special type of sadhu, for whom the cremation ground is a kind of meditation hall. Some people are very afraid of them, but if you don't object I can introduce you to one. Come back tomorrow and you will see that their perspective on death is a little different, to say the least.'

I had heard of Aghor sadhus, and even seen a few from a distance during my time in India, but the prospect of speaking with one was enticing. Of all the myriad religious subgroups here, they're the most feared, and perhaps the least understood. To meet one here in Varanasi seemed especially appropriate, actually, for in their aspiration to reach moksha, they seemed to encapsulate something elemental about the city: a primal spiritual hunger, a fierce determination to break through some essential barrier of this earthly realm. Aghoris flock to Varanasi, I learned, first because of the city's traditional associations, but also because one of their number, Baba Kinaram, achieved sainthood here, and the prestigious title of *Aghoreshwar*. Aghoris from all over India flock here to honour their ancestor.

I return the next morning, a little nervous, but ready for my encounter. Jagged clouds race across the sky above, and a cool breeze ruffles the surface of the Ganga into muddy brown wavelets. At the cremation ground, Gupta waves cheerily as I draw into view, then falls back into conversation with the man I'm here to meet, who turns out to be one of the most striking-looking individuals I've ever encountered, even among the strange coterie of Indian holy men. His clothes appear to be made from the stretched hide of a leopard, and beneath his flowing beard he wears a necklace of miniature skulls carved from bone. His gaunt face is smeared in white ash, which, contrasted against the flowing dreadlocks, gives him a somewhat sinister appearance. His eyes are the palest dots of black liquid, his lips a faint smear. Offering him the customary namaste, I sit down beside the dhuni and watch him from the corner of my eye. He exudes a ferocious energy.

Gupta, however, seems nonplussed by the Aghori, explaining to him in his usual upbeat manner my wish to learn something of his way of life.

'*Mai Aghor Nath hoon*,' he begins at length in a surprisingly soft voice. 'I am an Aghori, a tantric sadhu. For us, the *smashan* [cremation ground] is our home, and we like to be nowhere else. I neither fear death, nor seek life. Across the world, storms come and people die, but the human being cannot accept this. For us, liberation is not possible until we accept this primary fact of life, and so we live around death for as long as it takes until this lesson has been learned. All that is important is to escape samsara, and we do whatever it takes to achieve this in as short a time as possible. Because of this, the cremation pyre is the ultimate reality for us – a constant reminder that everyone has to die.'

I watch this extraordinary man across the fire, with his erect torso, and a physical presence that seems unusually self-contained. He packs himself a chillum and inhales a vast quantity of smoke, expelling twin plumes from his nostrils like a dragon. Unlike most sadhus, for whom humour seems a constant companion, the Aghori exhibits a mirthless solemnity. With his left hand he counts the beads of a rosary made from rudraksha seeds (*Elaeocarpus ganitrus*, the olive nut, a broad-leaved evergreen tree). The clicking continues rhythmically, like a metronome counting out our conversation.

'How long have you been on this path?' I ask.

'Twenty-six years. I came from a village in Chandauli called Harsu. I was from a good family, a Brahmin family, and as a child I would spend my life in the forest. But even then I became attracted by spiritual things. There's a temple of Durga in the forest there called Mandeshwari. The story is that two girls went into this forest to cut wood for their parents. Two men came to chase them, but rather than be molested they took sati [ritual suicide by burning], in order to protect their honour. Afterwards a temple was built there.

'As a child I would take the cows to the edge of this forest to graze them in that place. One day, while the cows were drinking from the river, I saw this baba [holy man] who was coming towards me. As he approached, I saw that his two teeth were broken and his eyes were filled with tears. He put a garland of flowers around my neck and said that from today I am his disciple. That was the beginning of my life as an Aghori.'

'You didn't question him at all?'

'No.' The Aghori closed his eyes, revealing his white lids, smeared with ash. 'My heart said yes. When you encounter a true saint, you know this feeling.'

'Didn't you go home,' I ask, 'to tell your parents your decision?'

He taps the ash from his pipe against the edge of the fire. 'Yes, I went home and put the cows back in their stall. I felt sad to be leaving them behind. I bought one bucket from the market to put my possessions in and, with the garland still around my neck, went to tell my parents what I was going to do. They were crying but they understood my mind was made up. The baba had told me that for the first part of my training I must take a retreat, far from any other person. I knew a mountain some miles away, whose summit was about a half-kilometre up, and decided to go there to begin my meditation. I had one copy of Tulsidas's *Ramayana* with me, which I used to study also. That was my companion in those first months.'

I picture him up there − a teenager perhaps − alone in some dank cave. How is it possible for someone so young to take such a forceful course of action? How could the parents allow it, and how could a young man bear the austerities such a life would entail? India seems to allow for such behaviour like nowhere else on earth, I think.

'And how did you come to Varanasi?' I ask at length.

His thin lips spread into a yellow-toothed smile at last. 'I came here for salvation, of course. Kashi is the place for salvation. After so many years in retreat, the urge came upon me to make my final journey. That was in the year 2000, and I knew, once I'd arrived within the borders of this holy city, I would never leave again. I can't explain by myself how I feel here, and I would say that even thousands of gods and goddesses could not either. The goodness of this place is beyond all description. This is Shiva's city, and ever since I came here this elation has stayed with me. I have given my life entirely to Him.'

'What can you tell me about Baba Kinaram?'

The sadhu presses his palms together at the sound of the name. 'Baba Kinaram was one of our greatest, a true yogi,' he says. 'Many centuries ago he attained the state of supreme purity and excellence in the Girnar mountains of Gujarat, then devoted his life to the service of others here in Banaras. I knew of him from a young age because he too was born in Chandauli. Even as a child, my parents would tell me stories of his miracles. He could call dead animals back to life, and restore the sight of the blind. Once he was visiting a jail and there saw weak people who had to grind flour. So he touched all the grinding stones with a stick and they moved on their own. All this becomes possible when you turn towards Shiva.'

A little nervously, I turn to perhaps the most difficult aspect of Aghori life to broach: their ascetic practices, famed and feared in equal measure. For many Hindus, Aghoris are figures of nightmare: an assumption that many Aghoris find useful, in fact, because it allows them to practise their austerities without disturbance. I had heard extraordinary rumours about the types of practices Aghoris undertook.

'Can you speak about your practices?' I ask. 'Is it true the things they say?'

'There is a great ignorance about our way of life,' he begins. 'People tell stories about us, but they do not realise why we live this way. I will try to explain. In India there are two paths towards moksha, a path of light and a path of darkness. The easier path is the path of light, but it can be a slow one. So we

Aghoris take the dark path towards liberation, also called the "Left-Hand Path". That means we have to do some difficult things, things that can seem strange and disturbing for those who do not understand. It is best for you not to worry about them,' he muttered, turning back to the fire.

We fell quiet for a time; I wondered if I had pushed him too far. I watched him from the corner of my eye as discreetly as I could. Behind the ash and the ferocious costume there was a slender man in his mid-thirties. In another life perhaps he would have worked for the Bank of India, shuffling rupees and bringing up two small children, henpecked by his wife. As it was, he was a true outsider, without kin or caste. All he had was his path, his determination to break through the veil. Unexpectedly, he began to speak again.

'Without training, our austerities could kill a man,' he whispered, 'while others would die merely from fright. The aim is to embrace death so completely that one loses all dread of it, and therefore transcends it. Most of our actions as human beings are through some attempt to perpetuate our ego. But we choose to give this up voluntarily, thus merging with Brahman.'

'I admire you,' I said honestly. 'You have set aside all the foolishness of the world.'

'I simply see the world as God,' he said. 'All of the world, without excluding anything. For this reason, we seek out those things we fear, those things which the mind has told us are not God. For us it is nothing strange to spend a night sitting upon a corpse. For us it is an altar, I have done this many times. Gradually, one leaves fear behind entirely. That is liberation!'

He watches me steadily. 'What you are afraid of has power over you. For this reason *anything* of which we have fear must be embraced. Some of us choose to eat the flesh of these corpses, others to eat excrement. Sometimes we cook our food on the embers of cremation pyres, or drink water from a cup that is a human skull. There are many other things, some I cannot talk of. This knowledge takes us beyond the Eight Snares of Existence: lust, anger, greed, delusion, envy, shame, disgust and fear, which bind all beings.'

I ask how many Aghoris there are in India.

'A thousand, perhaps fifteen hundred,' he says. 'But unlike the sadhus, we do not associate with one another. Only the relationship with the guru is important.'

'I think I would find eating human flesh very difficult,' I say.

'Many of you foreigners eat animals, do you not? Well then, what is it you eat but dead matter, devoid of the life force that once animated it? The only difference is in your mind, and this concept is your own prison.

'This is not your calling,' he adds, without judgement. 'For me there will be no rest until moksha is attained. In this I follow the path of Lord Shiva himself, the greatest Aghora. From him we learned that if all indeed is Brahman, one must not spurn anything. If he created everything, then everything must be perfect. If we deny the sacredness of any object, we are moving away from moksha, and we will continue to be reborn.'

Certainly, almost every aspect of life and death is on display in the Holy City. Like all Indian cities it's overpopulated now, and the medieval alleyways groan under a multiplicity of life

far beyond their natural holding capacity. Cows and tinkling
bicycles make way for the latest Maruti people carriers, while
the spicy *chaat* (savoury snacks) stalls and traditional street
food compete for sales with McDonald's and Domino's Pizza,
emissaries from the New World.

The business of death, too, stands at the threshold of modernity and inevitable change. Only the most desperate resort to
the government crematorium, Gupta confides, for while no
one knows for sure whether the gods may be any less pleased
by electricity, it makes no sense to gamble on the matter. More
bodies than ever, he adds, are ending up in the river without
having been cremated at all. Traditionally, it is only children,
holy men or the victims of snakebite who forgo the cleansing
flames of the burning ghat, but with the city now so overcrowded, some simply carry the body to the river, find a
convenient point and cast it in. Many horrified tourists, afloat
on the river for a view of the waterfront, find themselves agape
at the sight of a distended human corpse. All of this adds, too,
to the rising pollution of the Ganga, whose waters only the
most devout would now consider pure.

'These things are not good,' Gupta mutters, with the
furrowed brow of a man who sees the world leaving its
well-ordered lines. 'Tradition should be maintained. Rituals
should be performed correctly. Otherwise, how will the dead
achieve their salvation? The Ganga must also be kept clean.
How can we consider her a god and yet pour this poison
into her?'

Gupta may be justified in his concerns, for Varanasi – like
the nation of which it is part – stands in the flux of overwhelming change. The population of Uttar Pradesh is now

greater than that of Pakistan, the sixth most populous country in the world. Competition for jobs and land is mounting here, while the city continues to grow like a sponge in water. At the heart of India's change lies an unmistakable shift away from moksha as the central goal of life, towards that of material prosperity. It's a shift from a cosmic view of time towards a highly personalised one: it is *this* life that matters, one's own success and pleasure now. How religion will fare when this great levelling is over is anyone's guess.

'The gods made this city so that we can get moksha,' says Gupta, with a thoughtful wag of his head. 'But people in this city are now facing so much pressure for survival that they are thinking of other things instead. They forget that Shiva made a promise to us that no one shall go hungry here. Even his wife Parvati tried to test him on this. She took a louse from his hair and hid it in a matchbox, thinking that before too long the louse would be hungry, without any possibility of finding food. But when she opened the matchbox the next morning, a single grain of rice was there. Shiva does not forget those who look to him, you see. And it is his wish that we should find salvation.'

'Do you think the Dom Raja will still be cremating the bodies here in another hundred years?' I ask Gupta.

'Of course,' he says. 'We will always be here. India may be changing but there will always be bodies to burn. You may say this is the job security of being a Dom Raja.'

Searching for Rama in Ramnagar

> Oh Saunaka my friend, whoever tells
> Ramayana to others becomes free.
> — William Buck, *Ramayana*

It is a sultry late summer evening, the lingering heat quickening the trade of the fan sellers. I wield one myself, a rudimentary *pankha* made of woven bamboo that offers the feeblest respite from the humidity. Even the black crows perching on the gulmohar branches seem groggy from the heat: they caw grumpily, waiting for the cool of nightfall. For most of the several thousand in this field, however, anticipation overcomes the heat. Within a few minutes, the *Ramlila* play will commence, a crucial mark on the year's devotional calendar. This is not mere entertainment, but a play that retells the greatest story of the Hindu faith: the story of Rama, seventh avatar of the god Vishnu, king of the ancient city of Ayodhya, and one of the most popular gods in Hinduism. His story is India's Iliad: an epic journey of courage and heroism, central to Hindu identity. While differing versions play out all over north India, principally at Ayodhya, Vrindavan, Almora,

Satna and Madhubani, it's the performance here at Ramnagar, surrounding the Maharaja's palace, that has come to be
seen as the epicentre of north Indian religious folk drama, not
least because the play continues for thirty consecutive nights
rather than the more general ten. It is both entertainment and
a devotional act, not to mention an astonishing feat of stage
production.

Sitting pensively, I take in a scene that is among the most
remarkable I've ever witnessed in India. Under a wide and
purpling sky, at the centre of a dusty field that teems with
people, stands a makeshift stage lit by candles and old-
fashioned braziers. Smells of woodsmoke, camphor and rose
petals fill the air. To one side, two enormous elephants offer
the Maharaja and his retinue front-row seats that no one is
likely to step in front of. The rest of the audience sit cross-
legged on blankets and palm-leaf mats, awaiting the first
familiar lines. I can see no telephone lines, no cars; all is hushed.

There is an excited, expectant energy here. Families have
come with picnics, dressed in their smartest kurtas and saris.
Old friends greet each other and share a chillum pipe, cele-
bratory snacks are passed around in tiffin boxes: samosas,
puffed rice with spices, nuts and curry leaves. Many of the
older generation have brought their copies of the *Ramayana*
too, so as to follow each line as it is spoken. I notice copies
wrapped in parcels of silk being reverently opened up and
perused. The audience is not here to discover, but to remember. Since childhood, these stories have entered the marrow
of their bones, so that the Lila plays offer the heady mix of
familiarity and wonder, as these old friends are discovered
anew. It's the affection these people have for the pantheon of

Hindu gods that imbues the play with its meaning, and soon these much loved characters will come to life. A man on my left, wearing a faded turban of cerulean blue, selects a page from his *Ramayana* at random. He moves his lips as he reads the words under his breath, a finger tracing the script across the paper.

> *Who is that courageous one, who controlled his ire, who is brilliant, non-jealous and whom even the gods do fear, when provoked to war. . .*

When he has finished, and turns his attention once more to the stage, I lean forward to catch his eye and ask him how many years he has been attending the Lila plays.

'More than fifty,' he says, after spending some time in calculation. 'Since I was a small boy I have not missed a night!'

'And why do you come?'

'Quite simply, this is bhakti [devotion],' he says, holding a finger aloft. 'We do not come to see actors, we come to see the gods themselves.'

Just then the first low drumroll stills the crowd and, craning my neck to make out the small stage, I see that the play is about to begin.

Arriving in Varanasi almost a year before, I'd quickly been recommended the Lila plays as something unmissable, and highly revealing of local culture. People spoke of them as a link to the ancient world, a means of understanding one of the defining myths of Hinduism. Professor Ananda Krishna, former director of the city's famous archaeological museum, drew my attention to some pages in a mildewed book: *Benares Illustrated, in a Series of Drawings*. Its author, James Prinsep, was an assay master at the city mint during the early nineteenth century, and his records of old Banaras are some of the finest portrayals in existence of the city as it was. 'Prinsep loved this city like no foreigner who had come before him,' said the professor, in his mid-eighties and still a wonderful raconteur. 'He was a polymath, the first to determine the city's latitude and longitude, the designer of the drainage system which is still in existence today. And over ten years he made some extraordinary illustrations of Kashi, including the *Ramlila*. Looking at his book now it seems to describe a vanished city, a city that history has simply swept away. But this one draw-ing of the Lila plays remains very true to how the current performances actually look. It shows us that the Lila is a piece of sacred theatre that is still intact.'

All of which seemed very far from the festivals that are taking place, almost nightly, outside my house on Assi Ghat. Here, the primordial city of white-clad pilgrims is meeting a new world of technology and change, embraced fervently by a predominantly young population for whom ecstasy lies in dance moves and thumping bass, rather than in the gods and goddesses of their parents. As the festival season in Varanasi commences, the waterfront stages nearly nightly events involv-ing rickety bullock carts of speakers pumping out Bollywood hits at volumes that judder through my spine as I try, but fail, to sleep. On some nights, having given up on the possibility of dropping off, I clamber onto the flat roof of my house to watch the proceedings. Banaras was evolving, as it always had – this was how it survived. Although the ghats stretched back into the mists of time, the young people here were connected to a larger global culture that conceived of the world in radically different ways. Everything – quite literally if you considered the impact of subwoofers – was being shaken up.

The *Ramlila* plays, then, seem a perfect antidote, a prism through which to look upon the city as it had once been. Professor Krishna explained to me that, although often translated as 'play', the meaning of 'lila' was subtler than this. 'Think of it as God's creativity,' he said. 'On some level, the world itself is simply a performance, God is amusing himself. Although these performances are telling of epic deeds and great tragedy in some parts, the stories – as with our own lives – are simply a divine unfolding, a play of forms.'

Several months before the performance is due to begin, I start to make plans to watch the rehearsals over at Ramnagar, across the Ganga from my house, about half a mile upstream. Clambering through a maze of frayed electrical cable, I creep past the makeshift stage on Assi Ghat, gearing up later today for a political speech of some kind by a plump local dignitary, no doubt to be followed by several hours of 'Dil Kyun Yeh Mera' and 'Dil To Bachcha Hai Ji', the current season's hits. Waiting for me at the water's edge, boatman Kashi – named after the city herself – waves a friendly greeting, before reaching for the splintered gangplank. In a trice we're afloat, the river reclaiming us into muteness and space. I watch the shoreline receding, a trail of smoke from cook fires painting the sky, beggar children, holy men, packs of mangy dogs. Apart from the city for a moment, I'm reminded how much it baffles me, how much of it I will never understand. It's like a crossword whose clues are continually shifting, so that the word one has tentatively filled in becomes suddenly absurd: a fit of madness. Out here on the water, for a time, the need to decipher slips away a little. I breathe clean air, and enjoy the gurgle of the endless river.

As Kashi rows, a light breeze ruffling the surface of the water, we get into discussion about the *Ramlila*. In his late forties, he belongs to a generation for whom the plays remain vital. During his lifetime television – and now the Internet – has become commonplace, but in his childhood there were none of these things; old forms of entertainment were of paramount importance, and religion remained the guiding principle. The act of rowing tends to make him loquacious: his eyes close momentarily as he recounts the excitement in the community in the weeks leading up to the *Ramlila* performances. I rest my bare foot on the boat's floorboards, transported back thirty years.

'Life was different when I was a boy,' he said. 'It was self-contained. We had our families, our caste, and we were taught to always have one eye open to God. This was enough. The Lila plays were both a holy time for us, and a time of enjoying the old stories. We looked forward to them all through the monsoon. What was always a particular source of pride for my father, as it is for me, is that even we boatmen are a part of the story. When Khevat the boatman carries Lord Rama and Sita across the river, Sita tries to give him her ring in payment, but he refuses. You carry people across samsara towards liberation, he says, while I carry people from one side of this Ganga to the other. When my day comes, I only ask that you carry me across the river, as I have done you today.'

I was struck by this link between Kashi's own profession and the conversation I'd had some time before with the Dom Raja, who tend the burning ghats. This was the second group within the city who seemed to draw a powerful collective succour from their mention in the scriptures. The whole substratum of Hindu collective identity was here: the basis of caste and faith. From the *Ramayana*, Kashi has a sense of his place in the Hindu social order, but it also assigns him a mythical space. Varanasi and the River Ganga are not just material places for him; they exist beyond time. Not for him a humdrum job that breaks his back and ages him prematurely under a baking sun. He is part of a cosmic tapestry, a landscape where the gods themselves once walked, and still do. His two bony shoulders are the meeting place for human and mythic time, and this knowledge seems to help him weather the vicissitudes of life in a wider perspective.

All of which is part of the function of the *Ramlila* plays and what separates them from mere entertainment. After landing on the shore over by Ramnagar, I stroll up a sandy track past a gaggle of reclining boatmen, a fisherman mending his nets, and a motley collection of snack stands. The sun is warm on my neck. A one-eared dog suckles a litter of newborn pups under a broken pot. There are smells of cowshit, frangipani, somewhere some pulses cooking over an open fire. Less than a mile upstream, Ramnagar has a quieter feel than Assi Ghat, free of the burgeoning phone shops and money changers. Neither urban nor fully rural, Ramnagar has the feel of a rustic town a decade after the closure of the factory. It feels peaceful here in its quiet dusty lanes, with one foot in the old India, one in the new.

Under a gnarled peepul tree, not far from two rusting cannons, I rendezvous with Pintu, a young woman of about my age. Though born and bred in Varanasi, Pintu's facility for languages has already taken her far beyond the confines of the city. Fluent in Hindi, Urdu and Bhojpuri, as well as several European languages, she finds work translating for the journalists and Ph.D. students who flock to Varanasi on the path of various esoteric strands of knowledge. Despite her cosmopolitanism, her saris mark her out as traditional by temperament, a combination that makes her invaluable here, where a knowledge of, and adherence to, the old ways is considered so vital by many of the older generation. For the last month she and I have been negotiating the cabalistic webs of bureaucracy that surround the *Ramlila* plays at Ramnagar, so that we can gain access to the rehearsals. Today, eight visits later, and under the strictest instructions not to take so much as a hint of a camera near the performers, the necessary paperwork, endorsed by the Maharaja himself, has filtered through the ranks. It's been a trial of endurance both comical, shattering and illuminating. Pintu is holding the document triumphantly as I draw up, wearing the smile of one who has battled with Indian bureaucracy and prevailed.

Still glowing with this new-found approval, we decide to seize the moment and visit the rehearsals at last, held not far from here in a group of outbuildings owned by the Fort. Away from the river, Ramnagar becomes more village-like still. Passing the Shiv Lassi shop, we head down a tapered path. A round-cheeked cowherd nods a friendly greeting, his hands straining with two wooden pails of fresh milk. Behind him, seven sleek cows bask within a thorn-fenced enclosure; they are cared for reverentially here, symbols of divine plenitude.

In these quarters, since the previous July, the youngest of the *Ramlila* actors have been living and rehearsing, their entire lives given over to prayer and preparation. The *Ramayana* tells the life of Rama, and the first *kanda* or book deals with his childhood, in which Rama and the other gods are reared as princes, educated in scripture and warfare. True to the story itself, the *Ramlila* offers these roles to actual children. We can hear the sound of cymbals as we draw near and, ducking under a heavy wooden lintel, we find a rehearsal in full swing. Leaving his post for a moment, Vyasa (literally 'director') comes over to say hello. His expressive face expands from a central point: a pointed white moustache that would give him a contemplative air were it not for the crimson-checked shirt that he wears over a bright yellow lungi. These primary colours serve to situate him in this garish world of Hindu cosmography, a world that takes form in the young actors depicting the gods who stand about him: Ram, the Supreme Being, Lakshman and his twin brother Shatrughna, Ram's second brother Bharata, and Ram's wife Sita, also known as Janaki. Some distance away, the gods' mothers, here to cook and clean for the young divinities during their confinement, observe us with crossed arms and no small hint of pride, while the gods themselves blink nervously from their huddle, unsure of just what to make of these intruders on their rehearsal. They are, despite this recent incarnation as celestial beings, just eight or nine years old, and carrying the weighty expectations of their community on their slender shoulders.

Vyasa-ji explains a little about the rehearsal process, in its final stages now, with only a week to go until the opening night. Like his father and grandfather before him, his life's work has been to oversee these annual productions. No one knows more on the subject. This is the month of the year around which his other eleven revolve. He crackles with nervous energy and benevolent pride, utterly at one with his work.

'These young fellows have been here since July time,' he explains, 'after selection by Maharaj-ji in the traditional fashion. During monsoon, some forty or fifty local Brahmin boys are brought before him to choose by age, physical attributes or quality of voice. On this day, there is a special puja ceremony and those *svarupa*s [literally 'His image'] are chosen. From that day on, they are no longer referred to by their given name until the conclusion of the festival. Everyone, including their own parents, refers to them by their role in the play. For this community, it is the greatest honour possible to be selected, a sacred duty.'

I ask if all the main roles of the Lila plays are taken up by children. Vyasa-ji says not.

'The *Ramayana* takes place over some twenty-five thousand verses,' he explains. 'For the first part, Rama and the others are just small children. That is what these boys will depict, and it is perhaps the most special of the play's roles because we see children as being anyway close to God. As soon as hair forms on their lip' – he touches his moustache – 'or their voice grows deeper, they must step down and make way for a replacement. The older roles are all played by adults. Many of them become very popular with the crowd over the years.'

An old lady enters the room while we are talking – a village woman, perhaps the grandmother of one of these *svarupas*. She ducks under the low doorway, and as she does so I see her bearing change. She carries some oil, rice and flowers on a small tray, and her lips are silently muttering. She walks over, as if in a temple, to the young gods and bows her head. I notice that they hardly react to this homage: it has become normal for them.

'This Lila is not merely amusement,' Vyasa-ji explains in a low voice. 'That is what separates this from any other play you may see across the world. And these boys cease to be children when they are chosen as *svarupas*. We believe that during these performances these incarnations of the gods become real. As we depict their deeds faithfully, recalling the great lessons of the *Ramayana*, they come to life here for this month of the year. So you see' – he nods at the old woman in prayer – 'she is come here to offer puja. Much of Banaras, in fact, will offer them puja when they come for the performance. And that sense is continued during every aspect of our rehearsals. They must behave correctly at all times. When we eat, Rama must sit first.'

Pintu and I sit quietly in a corner for a time, amongst a group of children from the nearby village come, like us, to spectate. Like many rural buildings in India, this one has a floor of smoothed cow dung, and whitewashed walls. Its smells are of earth and field, devotion and work. The centre of the building opens to form a small courtyard, upon which an old sari lies in the sun, covered with drying grain. Here, as everywhere in this city, the practical and the transcendent find a perfect marriage. The old lady in prayer and the need to process the crops are not two things, but part of a timeless unity, systems of approaching the whole business of living which started five thousand years ago or more and continue to evolve. I think of school plays I was involved in, thirty years before, and remember a time of mischief and giggling, the commonplace high jinks of small children herded into some collective endeavour. Here the atmosphere is quite different. The young gods, with their smooth, androgynous faces, white robes and tonsured hair, hold themselves in a stillness few adults manage. Their faces give little away. It is as if, after all these months of special treatment, they have begun to believe in their own divinity. When not speaking their lines, they stand like sentries, eyes clear and unblinking. It is hard not to see them as different from the rest of us when every detail stresses that they are.

Over the next few days I learn a tremendous amount about the history and functioning of the Lila plays. The hoary Vyasa-ji seems delighted to share what he knows, while numerous village gossips and attendants, appearing and retreating from the rehearsal space with props, makeup, food, or just to pass time at the hub of things, offer their advice, reminiscences and opinions about the plays, past and present, around which this month of the year revolves. Stage designers, costumiers, lighting experts and makeup artists come and go from this tiny rehearsal space, while I watch and listen, struggling to remain both unobtrusive and able to interject a question when the moment allows.

'What make *Ramlila* different are several factors,' Vyasa-ji explains after a long rehearsal of the wedding procession, highlighting – amongst other things – that the wheel of the small wooden cart was by no means properly secured. 'First, there is the notion of incarnation which I have already mentioned, the idea that these actors become avatars during this performance. Second, there is the fact that the play does not have one single location, but many! Unlike conventional theatre, in which a single stage forms the backdrop to the narrative, the *Ramlila* moves around an almost three-kilometre area. Each important event of the *Ramayana* finds its counterpart somewhere in Ramnagar. One day it happens at Durga Mandir [Temple], another at Rambag, then another at Janakpur Mandir. Local temples are used, the lakes and water tanks. Often, several places will be used on the same night, so that the audience follows the actors in silent procession. This makes the audience *part* of the plays, not just spectators. Growing up here, it is part of the way we come to explore and understand our community. If you attend every night of the Lila plays, you know Ramnagar intimately, and you know *Ramayana* intimately. Afterwards, you will never walk through the neighbourhood in the same way, you will feel you are treading on holy ground.'

Towards evening, I meet the harried stage manager for the *Ramlila*, Papu-ji, who works as a carpenter for the Maharaja during the remainder of the year. Papu-ji has green eyes set deep in a craggy visage. So far today he has already walked more than ten kilometres, transporting props and checking details for the first performance. His kindly face has the drawn look one might expect for a stage manager with perhaps one of the most complicated jobs in all of world theatre.

'Regretfully, I can spare you only two minutes, *bhaiya* [big brother],' he says, puffing his bidi cigarette like a steam-train at full speed. 'Because for the correct running of these plays too many burdens fall on my shoulders. We are moving so many items of scenery around, we have lakhs [hundreds of thousands] of props and costumes, and we have an audience of at least twenty thousand waiting very eagerly.' He accepts a swig of water with thanks, tilting back his head in the Indian fashion, so that the stream falls elegantly from the mouth of the bottle without ever touching his lips. 'My predecessor was a very great man,' he says, 'and I struggle to match the legacy he has created. One time when I was a boy he had all the donkeys collected to play Ravana's demons. Now these animals are cantankerous beasts, and keeping them in one place is too difficult. Just before they were due to go on, something got into one of them and the whole lot galloped away into the fields.' He grins. 'A man in my position must be prepared for such things! But at this time of year, I hardly see my family for weeks, preparing. I get up before dawn and retire after they have gone to sleep. Otherwise, how I can I achieve the needful?'

A week later, the day of the first Lila dawns. Pintu and I return to the rehearsal space to witness an important cere-mony. The *Mukut Puja*, as it is known, marks the point at which the five young *svarupa*s are officially crowned, and it customarily marks the beginning of the year's festival. But this is more than simply a cutting of some ceremonial ribbon. Inside the cramped rehearsal space the young gods, now fully made up, with intricately drawn suns and moons painted on their faces, stand in poised expectation. The local priest, carrying burning oil lamps, stands before them intoning sacred mantras, while on the ground before each child lies a gold-painted wooden crown, believed to contain some essence of the deities themselves.

Around this humble building, some fifty people watch with shining eyes, the weight of collective meaning conferring on these children the status of immortals as the crowns are lifted onto their heads. I think of our modern culture, with its *X-Factor* and *Big Brother* mania, and compare these twin forks of human experience, both conferring perceived 'specialness' on ordinary human beings. As if under some spell, the children have disappeared. Only five diminutive mythological beings stand before us now, figures of legend, whose presence casts an otherworldly light on our own. It is hard to look upon them unmoved.

After the gods are led away, Pintu and I make our way through Ramnagar towards Rambag, where the first performance is to occur. It is still swelteringly hot, and we stop for coconut water to hydrate ourselves for the two-kilometre walk. The stallholder selects one from a huge mound rising six feet off the ground, then beheads it with one clean thunk of his machete. The liquid inside is cool, both sweet and salty, and one of the most revitalising drinks on the planet.

Before us, the roads are already thick with pilgrims, and traffic is almost at a standstill owing to the presence of five magnificent elephants plodding their way towards the Maharaja's residence. Jostling and being jostled, we fall into the flow of human traffic, caught up in the flurry of excitement and expectation for what is to come.

'When I come to this Lila,' one man tells us as we walk, 'I forget what I owe the money-lender, I forget my aching back,

I forget even my own name. Only, there is the performance and the feeling of God being very close.' He closes his eyes, visibly moved. 'That is a great gift.'

By the time we reach Rambag – literally Garden of Rama – the crowds are enormous, several thousand and growing. Local vendors are taking the opportunity to combine devotion with a healthy burst of enterprise too, so there are peanut vendors carrying mounds of monkey nuts on their heads, sellers of cheap plastic toys, garish mounds of marigold flowers laid out on white cloth and misted with water. We find a spot to sit down and take in the scene, sitting cross-legged on a patch of grass. The elderly figure on my left wearing the blue turban fans himself languidly, still speaking lines from the forthcoming play beneath his breath.

'Have you noticed how few young people are here?' Pintu points out. 'It is only the old ones who make the effort now. When I was a girl you would see all generations here, but somehow it is changing.'

At around five, a silence falls across the throng. The great elephant bearing the Maharaja is lumbering into view, examining the crowd through watchful, intelligent eyes. Cleverly steered by the mahout, the Maharaja and his retinue position themselves at the front of the crowd, offering one more anchor to tradition. The Maharaja, I notice, is a man of middle age, sporting a toothbrush moustache and a somewhat uncomfortable expression, up on his lofty perch. Beneath him, the elephant is a beautiful female, decorated with green and vermilion paint, and with golden tassels hanging from her tusks, bells around each weighty foot. The mahout, sitting cross-legged on the elephant's neck, sees me watching and offers a toothy grin.

A great roar rises from the crowd. '*Hara Hara Mahadev!*' they shout. '*Hara Hara Mahadev!*' It is a powerful moment, voiced by thousands, for this salutation places the Maharaja, like the actors playing the gods, as something much more than human. Traditionally, the Maharaja of Varanasi is seen as a reincarnation of Shiva himself, an avatar worthy of the deepest reverence. The chant comes again and the Maharaja nods his head, holding his hands together in namaste. With this moment, it is as if the lodestone has been placed. The Maharaj is Shiva, and the actors are Rama, Sita, Hanuman and the others gods, and Hindu cosmography has found human form in this microcosm of Varanasi. From this point on, everything will be simply 'Lila', the creative activity of the divine.

The chants grow silent and at last the play begins. With the Maharaja in prime position at the front on his elephant, the rest of us lean in from the surrounding field towards the small stage, marked out by a series of simple bamboo sticks. Early evening now, the light is gently fading. To a drumroll, the first three actors take the stage: the demon Ravana, wearing pyjamas of a deep scarlet, and his brothers Vibhishana and Kumbhakarna. Ravana's face is concealed by a many-headed papier mâché mask, ornately decorated with gold and silver thread, which fits right over the actor's body like an unwieldy hat and seems very heavy to keep upright. Ravana sways back and forth as he shuffles forward on the stage. Before them, a pit filled with straw is lit in a flash by one of the stage assistants and light flares onto the scene.

Vyasa calls for the audience's attention and, with practised resonance, introduces the events we are about to witness. Ravana is performing a sacrifice, he tells us. By performing certain pujas he hopes to win the favour of the gods. Leaning in, Pintu whispers: 'This is the hook for the whole subsequent plot. The demon Ravana makes such an impressive sacrifice he is granted immortality by the gods, thus throwing the whole of earth out of balance. Everything that happens for the next thirty nights is the story of how it is righted!'

At the centre of the stage, the young actor playing Ravana finds himself the very centre of attention. The Rakshasa king of Lanka, he is a ten-headed demon and as in the great *Ramayana*, all his heads must be thrown into the fire as puja, so the actor tears each head off one by one, tossing them onto the flaming straw.

As the actors recite their lines, projecting the Sanskrit confidently across the field, I gaze across the audience. One old lady smiles with pleasure, while a middle-aged man recites the lines from memory as each actor speaks. Many audience members hold copies of the *Ramayana* open at the appropriate page, while others whisper amongst themselves, pointing out pieces of the set that delight them, or sighing gently while the demons persuade the gods to grant them the powers that will precipitate the tale of good and evil. Having never seen Indian folk theatre before, I'm struck by the simplicity of what I'm seeing here. With only the most modest props, and forgoing amplification or spotlights, this is truly ancient theatre, and as such the very opposite of spectacular. It is quiet and ambling, naïve compared with the high-tech thunder and lightning of a West End stage. And yet there is also something here that can only be understood as one sits in a field, sweating in the late summer heat. For the next two hours, I watch with a range of emotions that seem to encompass the full spectrum: wonder, delight, occasional boredom, amusement, empathy. And slowly, the unfolding magic of this story catches me up: never hurrying, often diverging, but always returning to the central thread of right human conduct, and accordance to the duties we inherit.

'The *Ramayana* teaches us *paropakara*,' Pintu tells me, 'which means "discipline of mind". It's about the consequences of the choices we make, and the basic tensions of the plot are those places where the characters find conflict with the principles of their own dharma. Every Hindu child learns this at school of course. But for those of us who watch these Lila plays, something of this goes into our bones. Whenever I feel some difficulty in my life I remember the story of the *Ramayana* and the difficulties overcome by its heroes. It gives me courage.'

I return often, over the month that follows, to the *Ramlila* as it unfolds. Moving across Ramnagar during this month is like discovering the *Ramayana* on a human scale: I journey to Janakpur and Ayodhya, Rama's mountain home at Chitrakuta, Lanka and Panchavati. Occurring on Dussehra, one of the great festivals of the Hindu world, it is the final night that draws the biggest crowd, ten thousand or more, who line the streets and the verges with candles and cheers as the Maharaja passes. I had been to a Dussehra festival the year before without realising that its very existence belongs to the final scene of the *Ramayana*.

'*Dasha-hara* literally means removal of ten,' Pintu explains, 'which refers to Lord Rama's victory over Ravana in which he cuts off the ten heads.'

Elbow to elbow with a crowd of five thousand, I crane
forward to watch this final battle between good and evil, in
which after some fairly ineffectual shooting of arrows, the
great demon Ravana accepts defeat, bowing down to touch
Lord Rama's feet. Like much in this gentle play, the denoue-
ment is astonishingly low-key, and yet the crowd raises a
heroic cheer nonetheless. After his defeat, Ravana simply
dismounts from his chariot and disappears into the crowd,
lost in the flow of people.

This final exit is deeply touching. For the duration of the
play, Ravana has been a figure from myth, and yet in a single
moment he is part of the crowd again, just a normal human
being. This transition from human to divinity and back again
seems something integral to Varanasi, which celebrates birth
and death continually, in the burning of the bodies, and in the
evening *arti* ceremonies in which earth, fire, movement and
space are depicted by lamps cast adrift on the River Ganga.
The ultimate message seems to me to be that humanity and
divinity are not separate, nor are life and death, form and
emptiness. Everything exists in one seamless tapestry which,
at the play's end, is simply here, and can never be spoken of.

Leaving the crowds behind me, I too merge with the
crowd and am lost.

Sex for Sale

Why do you provoke me and try to wheedle out
of me the facts of my life? What interest can you
possibly have in the life story of a woman like me?
— *Umrao Jaan Ada*

I'm standing, a little sheepishly, on the edge of a long dusty street in Shivdaspur. It is evening and the heat still roiling. A line of decrepit one-storey concrete houses is bisected by the kind of untarmacked road one finds on the edge of Indian towns, designating this as a marginal place, not worthy of municipal attention. Beyond the houses, scrubland undulates towards the city suburbs, a brackish pond providing drinking water for a few bony cattle. Shreds of plastic float over the dry grass in the wind, and there's the distinctive smell of a cook fire fuelled by cow dung, still used here as the cheapest combustible material.

One further detail marks out Shivdaspur as being different. Outside the houses, women sit or stand by the front steps, dressed in cheap, brightly coloured saris and wearing heavy makeup. In their garish clothes they look a little out of place

in this semi-rural setting, but then again no one is likely to
come to this place without knowing the reason for its existence. This is Varanasi's red-light district, where sex can be
bought for an astonishingly low price, and where a small
proportion of what I will later learn is India's estimated 15
million sex workers ply their trade. 'You have no idea the
things that go on here,' Sangeeta, the Ph.D. student who has
brought me here, confides. 'People who call Varanasi the City
of Light should come here to see the darkness.'

The subject of prostitution in India is a thorny one, and
nowhere more so than in Varanasi, where conservative morals
run deep. Though prostitution is officially legal in India,
related activities such as pimping and operating brothels are
not. Historically this has allowed the industry to thrive, while
relegating the sex workers to a murky legal grey area, denied
even access to normal labour laws. What is certain is that
every Indian town and city has an area like this one: there is
Sonagachi in Kolkata and Kamathipura in Mumbai, GB
Road in New Delhi, Reshampura in Gwalior and Budhwar
Peth in Pune. In Varanasi it is Shivdaspur.

I've come here because, as I get to know this city, it's
impossible to ignore this shadow side, evident in a hundred
small details on any given day. Rickshaw wallahs slow at the
lights to pay baksheesh to the traffic cops, drug-dealers
approach me routinely at Assi Ghat offering a veritable shopping list of narcotics: brown, white, opium and charas. There
are purveyors of black magic charms for prosperity or revenge,
and of course offers of girls or boys from gleaming-eyed
characters with worn-out faces. None of this marks out
Varanasi as particularly unusual in the run of modern cities,

save that its public face is one of such piety and its politics accordingly old-school. There are few cities in the world either so closely associated with religion, or so quick to flare up when that impression is questioned.

My first guide into this world is Sangeeta, a student at Banaras Hindu University who has been focusing on this subject for the last several years. Originating from Delhi, she is an outsider here, too. 'I'm Indian,' she tells me, 'so you might think that would make it easier for me to connect with these people, to understand their difficulties. But for them I am from almost as different a place as you. They see that I'm not from here, that I don't speak Bhojpuri. So my first goals are always to try and establish some common ground between us, to try and help them see that I'm on their side.'

With Sangeeta's help, the picture-postcard surface of the city begins to crack. Along the river front, more than a hundred ghats teem with an array of sights and sounds which, as I have been learning, perhaps more than any other place in India has come to symbolise the living traditions of Hinduism. It's a pulsing canvas of primary colour, and a moving exemplar of piety in action. An old woman, wearing widow's white, kneels down with closed eyes before the river. A young man raises his ancient brass water pot to allow an arc of water to stream backwards into the Ganga: this is a tangible contact with the divine.

Close to the Vishwanath temple, the Dashashwamedh Ghat seems to hold too much humanity to countenance. Here Lord Brahma is said to have sacrificed ten fine horses in order to entice Shiva to return after a period of banishment, so it is

especially revered as a place of spiritual power. Many thousands come here daily for bathing, puja offerings, or for the
evening *arti* ceremony in which light from wicks soaked in
ghee or camphor is offered to the gods. The sight of them
floating away downstream, a thousand prayers upon the
Ganga, is deeply stirring.

As we sit one afternoon on the stone steps, pleasantly warm
from the afternoon sun, I watch Italian tourists clicking with
their impressive cameras, and the distant spires of smoke from
the funeral pyres. There are knuckle-cracking masseurs whose
only means of income is their two hands. There are tick-
ridden pye-dogs and bony cows, agile goats and cawing
crows; there are holy men with tridents, one of whom was
thrilling the tourists by wrapping a sword around his penis
and running up and down like a circus performer. This is all
part and parcel of holy India: what the tourists come for, and
without which this would be a church empty of its congre-
gation. But can it be true that even here, in this holy of holies,
there are more temporal ecstasies on offer?

Sangeeta, dressed demurely in the dupatta (a long scarf or
stole draped over head and chest) and Lee jeans of the Indian
middle class, sits beside me behind stylish dark glasses, pointing out the details I've missed. There are touts at work selling
sexual favours to tourists and Indians alike, she explains. There
are children, as young as ten years old, working this ghat
professionally, and there are takers for their services who see
no contradiction between outward displays of sanctimony
and the act of engaging in sexual activity with minors. Under
the bridge there is a place where the sex workers sleep and
occasionally enact furtive snatches of congress with clients,

she whispers. It's also a place where quantities of heroin and glue and pharmaceutical amphetamines are sold or used, just out of plain view. That man there, with his hands in his dirty trouser pockets, is a pimp, feared and respected in equal measure. He'll beat them and burn them if they don't do what he wants. He'll extort the moneys from them and pass them higher up the chain. He's the one, too, who monitors transactions with the local police, whom regular bribes serve to keep silent.

'Are the Indian police really as corrupt as everyone says?' I ask. 'It's one of the great stereotypes, I know ...'

Sangeeta shrugs, a gesture that seems to include acceptance and frustration in the same measure. 'It's just completely ingrained here,' she says. 'One can't blame the individuals. Almost everyone in India is part of this conspiracy.'

I notice the anger in her face, the anger of a generation who want change.

'We bribe the schools to get our kids admitted into nursery. We bribe to pay road tax, municipality tax, get a birth certificate, a death certificate, an electricity connection, a water connection. My dad even jokes that we give or take bribes to get our sons and daughters married – what else is the dowry system but bribery on a grand scale? The fact is India is a great creaking machine that needs rupees to grease the axles or nothing happens.

'I remember one foreigner telling me the biggest shock he had in moving to India was in realising what it was like to live in a society where one can't trust the police,' Sangeeta says. 'That really struck me. I mean, it's equally incredible for us to imagine a society where one *can* trust them.'

'You said you don't blame the individuals who succumb to corruption?' I ask. 'That seems unduly compassionate. *Why* can't you? Surely, every one of them is making a choice at some stage?'

'Look, if the officers want promotion to the next rank they have to bribe their superiors an amount which is several times their annual salary. So they cannot get promotion *without* corruption. The system maintains itself, *yaar* [friend]. This is the subject, I think, that most foreigners simply cannot *understand* about India: the depth of corruption here, the level to which it's embedded in every aspect of our society. *New* India wants to change, it wants to be modern and strong, but *old* India just keeps reaching out and holding us back. I can't tell you how much that pisses me off.'

Our conversation arcs back to the sex trade here: its context against the backdrop of this traditional Indian city. Not so long ago, there were still courtesans here, plying their trade in markedly different circumstances from the slovenly tenements of Shivdaspur, Sangeeta tells me. During the eighteenth and nineteenth centuries, part of what is now Uttar Pradesh was known as Awadh, and was governed by a royal family descended from a Persian adventurer called Saadat Khan. Under these governors or nawabs, courtly manners, exquisite gardens, poetry and refined cuisine were allowed to flourish, giving rise to the image of its capital city Lucknow as a 'Golden City of the East', or 'Constantinople of India'. Within this environment arose a tradition called *tawaif*, a culture of high-class courtesanship with marked similarities to the geisha tradition of medieval Japan. The courtesans were wealthy business people, highly respected, as well as examples of empowered femininity that it would be difficult to match even in today's India.

'The twentieth century saw a massive decline in the status of these women in north India,' Sangeeta tells me, with some sadness in her voice. 'They went from virtual royalty in some cases, to the detritus of society. This hasn't just been a loss for these women, however, it's been a loss for the whole of India. As the repositories of high culture, they were a living library of musical lore, poetry, etiquette and dance. But no one comes to them now for those reasons . . . and so the traditions themselves are dying.

'I should tell you that although I've been studying this subject academically,' she tells me, 'my knowledge is slight compared to that of the man you should really be talking to. You need to meet Ajeet Singh. He runs an NGO called Guria, a local charity focused on improving the rights of prostitutes and trafficked women here. Ajeet has become something of a hero to the thousands of sex-industry workers in the holy city, as well as helping establish the issue of human trafficking as a nationwide problem. He's quite the character.'

Ajeet and I arrange to meet up one afternoon outside the district jail in Chaukaghat, a suburb in the north-west. It takes me an hour in a rickshaw to get there, and I arrive half stunned from the experience: traffic horns ringing in my ears, my eyes stung with diesel fumes.

Expecting a hard-nosed reporter type, I'm greeted instead by a gentle, pot-bellied bear of a man, with round jowls and an unshaven face. He's wearing a kurta by Fabindia in brightly coloured saffron stripes and sweating faintly under the hot sun. He has a thick head of black hair, slightly feminine eyelashes, a gregarious smile.

'So what do you think of Varanasi?' he asks me, as we walk back to his house, through what appears to be an outdoor farmyard running away from the main road. Chickens scuttle across the path in front of us, pursued by some unseen predator.

'It can't be pinned down,' I say. 'Every time I think I've got a hold on it, it moves away. But I love it.'

'That's a good way to begin,' he says, in his sing-song voice. 'Begin with love, but keep your eyes open. The Hindus see it as God's place on earth, but I will tell you that such beliefs make them blind. Most tourists see only the ghats and the Brahmins, and they are also blind. To really *understand* this city will take you some time. And as you say, the city itself is a living thing. One has to see it as such.'

He looks about him, partly with pride, and partly with a great weariness in his face. 'I love this city, too, of course. I would not live elsewhere. But I also hate it very deeply.'

In Ajeet's office, surrounded by a sea of papers, paper plates, paper folders, rolled-up posters, computer leads, cameras and broken HB pencils, he tells me about his life. The city is at one remove suddenly, reduced to a distant hum by thinly painted concrete walls and the overheated fan belt of Ajeet's aging PC. As the conversation grows impassioned, with Ajeet pacing around the room at some velocity, I realise that he is one of those rare human beings incapable of talking about the minutiae of anything. Every subject leads him right back to his central concern, which is the human condition itself.

'My ache is that we are failing to be human beings,' he begins directly. 'Slowly, slowly, we are groomed up to be machines. We are not responsive to the world around us. So I began Guria because I could not turn my eyes away from what I was seeing in my India. Corruption is *everywhere*. The poor have no one to turn to. As a young man I attended a wedding where there was this dancing girl – a prostitute who was singing to make some extra money. And I couldn't *stand* to see the men jeering at her, to see that she was absolutely trapped in this way of life, with no possibility for any alternative. That experience was my initiation, you might say. My eyes were opened that night. Afterwards, I realised that there were thousands, millions like her and that the system itself was self-perpetuating. So, what to do? How to give the women someone to talk to, someone who could address their legal concerns in a society that couldn't give a damn about them. I founded Guria almost on a whim. I had to do something.

'You can't *imagine* how difficult it was for me at the beginning,' he continues. 'These women will trust no one because life has taught them that *no one* is safe. The world they live in is precarious. People are killed or cut over a few rupees and their bodies disposed of in a way that is never discovered. So I couldn't just dance in there and offer my help. First I had to make them trust me. When you're working with these communities this is the crucial thing. Because they don't like outsiders. And to them, the whole *world* is outside.'

'How many such women are there in India?' I ask.

Ajeet shrugs. His face is angry, taut with a thousand unrighted wrongs. 'The government has reported a figure of

several million, I believe. But this number is completely spuri-
ous. There are *far* more than this, I think, and the number is
growing. I would say at least fifteen million. If you drive along
the motorways here there are brothels near many of the roadside dhabas [restaurants] catering to truck drivers. In the
towns the big problem is with organised prostitution, and it
has to be organised because it is such big business. This
involves smuggling people across borders, it involves keeping
them against their will and drugging them if necessary. It is
tied in with mafia money, with international cartels. It is tied
in with so much human nastiness that no book in the world
could contain it. India is very very high up the list, maybe
even top, of countries troubled by human trafficking. Many
of the women I work with here have been taken against their
will, you will see.'

Ajeet's phone rings, a jocular Bollywood ringtone, and he
switches abruptly into guttural Hindi. In a trice he's on his
feet, zooming down the corridor, and through a smeared
window pane I watch him on the flat roof of his house, before
a madcap Varanasi skyline, talking nineteen to the dozen and
waving his free hand about like a traffic cop. These are the
normal rhythms of his life, I soon realise: heated conversation
punctuated by the ringing of the phone. Everyone needs his
help on some urgent matter. He's dealing with getting people
out of jail, and putting others into jail. He's dealing with the
procurement of urgent medical attention, with scores of legal
cases, each one fought down to the last gasp. He's talking to
volunteers and journalists and foreign academics and pretty
much anyone else who'll listen. He's trying to raise money,
raise a family, raise up a whole echelon of Indian society with

his bare hands. His own life, it seems clear, has entirely ceased to exist.

As the morning passes, this pattern repeats itself with small variations. Manju, Ajeet's wife, comes to bring tea: she's a gentle, dark-skinned woman with watchful eyes and a strangely girlish laugh. Her chai is excellent. And there's their daughter, Barsha, whose name means 'rain', with a pixie face and kohl-rimmed eyes, who makes everyone smile no matter how grim the subject matter we're discussing. Barsha puts on my chappals – ten sizes too big for her – and clomps about Ajeet's office like an explorer in snowshoes.

Meanwhile, Ajeet is firing up his DVD player, pushing buttons and connecting leads with a little difficulty, while he struggles to get the machinery up to speed with his own imagination. 'We've been quite succesful in Varanasi,' he tells me. 'I would say this is now one of the only major cities in India where we can with some confidence assert that there are no children working in the red-light area. You go to other places – Kanpur for example, or Allahabad – and you'll see young girls, little children for God's sake, standing outside with the women. I mean we're trying to be a *modern* society. They talk about India joining the world's major economies. *Boasting* about development and democracy and what have you. And this scandal is permitted to be seen in open view in any major city. We are very far from democratic, I tell you. We are very far from developed.'

The screen flares into life and I see, in slightly pixelated technicolour, a street scene taken through what appears to be a concealed camera. Recording from waist level, the camera encompasses a narrow alleyway lit up by fluorescent lights. A group of women huddle together in the doorway flanked by a young man in a red silk shirt, grinning confidently. He's the cliched pimp from 1980s movies: a peacock in flamboyant clothes, with bad teeth and the face of a petulant child. The camera bobs around unsteadily.

'Allahabad has been very bad in this respect,' Ajeet continues. 'Disgraceful. We knew there was a flourishing trade there, and many children involved. But of course the *bhenchod* [sisterfucker] police will do nothing. They are making so much money from payoffs and bribes that the last thing they want is someone like me interfering. I tried and tried but they told me to get lost, *yaar*. So last year I decided to go and find the evidence to force their hand.'

The story he tells is astonishing, even more so because the man narrating it seems like the unlikeliest of heroes. He's a rotund man, staving off the flab like so many middle-class Indians, and it would not be hard to think of him as a shop-keeper: a silk merchant, perhaps, unfolding bolts of fine cloth with a deft flourish of his arms. Instead of such a life, his profession – if that's what it is – has him dressing up as a trader of powders and perfumes, and strolling through the midnight alleys of Allahabad, one of the fastest-growing cities in India.

'I needed to befriend these women first,' he tells me. 'And to do this I needed a reason to be around them. So I used to go and buy discounted makeups and lipsticks from the market, and put them in a basket. Then I would go wandering through the alleyways trying to sell them, and this gave me the excuse I needed to become something of a fixture. For much of last year I slept in the day and worked only at night. I had to get this footage.'

Like an undercover cop – but one working purely of his own volition – Ajeet spent six months infiltrating his way into the red-light districts of Allahabad. Night after night he trawled the backstreets with his wares, learning where the women worked, which pimps ran certain areas, and even some of the women's names, their personalities slipping out while they loitered in their saris under the harsh glare, entreating the passers with salacious words, and even laughing with each other during the quiet times, a testament, mutters Ajeet, to the resilience of the human spirit, and our ultimate necessity to smile.

Some of this is illustrated by the granular footage of the film, which plays on as a background to our conversation. Streets filled with refuse, occasional cows, the harsh static of a radio. Faces emerging through the night gloom. Signs of modernity, signs of a city still tied to its agrarian roots. Groups of men walking through the district of Meerganj on the hunt for sexual experience; a necessity perhaps, in the repressive, male-dominated world of India, where apartheid between the sexes lingers on throughout much of the society. Some of these men's faces are captured by Ajeet's hidden camera and – I don't know why I should feel surprised – there's nothing cruel or unpleasant about them: they don't look like either misogynists or perverts. They're just normal Indian men, doing what has become common in their society – doing it because they need some kind of release, perhaps, in their ridiculously overcrowded world, where there is so little space for liberated sexual conduct, let alone a personal moment of transcendence.

And so I don't blame them, these swaggering fellows looming and receding on the camera lens, many of them drunk or getting that way, some of them puffing cheap bidi cigarettes or spitting livid jets of *paan* from the corners of their mouths. I don't blame them for the things they do, or for the ways they find to survive. But I do look with interest at the faces of the women they're in search of, peering from doorways demurely with the hem of a sari drawn horizontally across their mouths. At first glance they seem coquettish, and their laughs picked up through the microphone concealed beneath Ajeet's shirt sound excitable and fun-loving and just the kind of laugh one would want from a woman who is about to reveal her most intimate secrets in the privacy of a cheap room. It is a laugh that invites disclosure, that suggests an easygoing love of good times. But the eyes, of course, tell a different story. It's hard to see, through the hidden camera lens that bobs up and down under the jacket of this corpulent gumshoe, but the lens does occasionally linger long enough on one of their faces to show guardedness and – if one looks closely – a hint of fear. Fear that one of the men may assault them, says Ajeet when I bring the matter up. Fear that one of the pimps will burn them or starve them for failing to entice a customer. And just a generalised fear, too, born from a life lived in inhuman conditions, a life of vigorous and regular violence.

'And what would have happened to you,' I ask, 'if they had discovered this camera under your clothes?'

'I would undoubtedly have been killed,' says Ajeet without a trace of self-aggrandisement. 'I know that. Killing is a regular part of this industry. It is not a dramatic business, it is simply commonplace.'

Some minutes into the footage comes the most disturbing thing captured on this painful film, which is the presence of not one but several children standing, again in a doorway, in the kind of skimpy clothes that make it clear they're there in a professional capacity. Ajeet's finger quivers before the screen, and I wonder how he kept his nerve at the time, for even a seller of lipsticks is allowed a moral sense.

By children, I mean nine, ten – a pre- rather than a late adolescence. Their black hair is set in bunches, and their thin faces are in need of a solid meal. Seeing them there, observed by passing groups of men in this busy nightspot of Meerganj, it just looks surreal, more so the idea that any man could step forward and request the services of one of them. Is it endemic poverty, I wonder, that has made such things commonplace here, or more complicated factors, deep-seated gender discrimination, the increasing fears about HIV predicted to ravage India in the twenty-first century, and which has increased the demand for younger prostitutes, by some accounts, in the hope that they may be less likely to carry the disease?

Ajeet, however, has no time for such questions just now, because his story has reached the point at which he takes this incontrovertible footage to the DM (district magistrate) of Allahabad. This 'DM', Ajeet says with some disdain, had tried to shrug off his claims before. But this time he literally had no choice. With such footage, and Ajeet's connections to the international NGO community, the DM made his calls to the local police station and a raid was ordered.

'Well, even at this point we knew that the police would make trouble for us,' Ajeet says grimly, clicking off the television to leave us in a sudden silence. 'They had told me repeatedly to stop bothering them. They had made threats even to my face. During my time selling makeup I had found out very accurately how much money they were extorting in that area. The local kingpin was paying them handsomely. The pimps were paying them. The drug-dealers were paying them. So I knew that the police, if it was possibly in their power, would be more of a hindrance than a help. They would do anything to keep this business in place.'

'They must have been livid when the DM forced their hand?'

Ajeet exhales forcefully. 'Not just livid. They were literally mad with anger. They were absolutely *furious*, you see, that I had gone above their head. Once the DM had ordered the raid they immediately began dragging their feet. "Oh there is no fuel in our police vehicles!" they said.' Ajeet wrung his hands together theatrically. '"And we do not have enough personnel for this raid!" Have you ever heard such nonsense! We knew, of course, what they were trying to do, which was to stall things long enough for the pimps to move the children out of Meerganj. So already predicting this, I had scores of our volunteers waiting in all the streets around the brothels, on every side of the buildings. Our volunteers had mobile phones and cameras. We were totally coordinated.'

By six o'clock the raid began at last. The backstreets of Meerganj seethed all at once with angry policemen, swinging their bamboo lathis at anything that moved. Dusk was falling and the punters passed quickly by with their heads down, alarmed by the unpredictable presence of the police. Hundreds of students formed a human chain to protect the children from being snatched away, and were beset by snarling policemen, sirens blaring. As Ajeet describes it, the scene took on the appearance of a fully-fledged riot, what with the screams of the injured and the resolute stand of Ajeet and his volunteers trying desperately not to panic.

And as things calmed at last, twenty children were brought out and escorted to the station.

'Just twenty!' says Ajeet, gravely disappointed even one year later. 'These people are so clever. This was less than one third of the estimated seventy minors counted over the previous months. We felt all our efforts had been wasted.'

'But twenty is something,' I say. 'Twenty is a success.'

He shakes his head. 'You might very well think that. I suppose in your country rescuing someone from captivity and getting them as far as the police station would be a victory. In any civilised society it should be. But here that is very far from the case. Once they get to the police station it becomes even *easier* for them to vanish. Money changes hands and the same prisoner that came in in chains is escorted out of a back entrance five minutes later, avoiding all paperwork. Most of these cases are still pending actually. Things move slowly in India. We are,' he says with a grim smile, 'a small body of determined spirits fired by an unquenchable faith in our mission . . .'

That phrase lingers in my head for the next several weeks, while I pore over an ever-increasing pile of literature: UN reports pushed through my letterbox by Ajeet in brown paper envelopes. He seems determined to make me understand his world, the reach of it, and its sheer human foulness. Knowing my intention to write about the city, it is as if he wished to impress upon me that the side of it he lives in has as much veracity as the other. This is a world where prostitutes are accorded the respect of chattels, where judges are for sale, where policemen beat victims to death with the hard edge of a chair.

Ajeet, it seems, is a man pitting himself against all these things head-on. He prefers to see me in his house because it is less and less safe for him to roam the streets of Varanasi. He goes out from time to time, he acknowledges, as he had on our first meeting, but he does it on a random basis, keeping no routines. Two iron security gates protect the door of his house, bound round with a Kevlar-bound chain. 'It is fairly commonplace for some fellow to ring up and tell me he's going to kill me,' he confides. 'One fellow rang up so many times the other day that Manju finally told him to stop threatening and come and do it, because frankly we were tired of coming to the telephone the whole time.'

I spend a good deal of time with Ajeet and his family over the next months, and grow fond of these obsessive workaholics struggling to make their country a better place through sweat and tears and industrial quantities of chai. I visit the school they've set up, where the sex workers' children find respite from the bewildering world of Shivdaspur, as well as laughter, healthy food and medical attention. I meet Ajeet's lawyer, one of his most frequent visitors, whose 'open case' folder currently includes some 166 cases pending in the Supreme Court of India. 'Even a small woodpecker could chop down the mightiest tree,' he tells me with a smile, 'if it

showed enough persistence! One's beak, however, does grow
a little sore after a time.'

Several times during this period I ask Ajeet if it might be
possible to speak with one of the women themselves. He
seems evasive and, when pressed, tells me there are several
reasons for his caution.

'What you are asking is possible,' he says, 'but it will take
time. You must be patient with me. Even to Manju or myself
most of these women will not tell the truth. Why? Because
they have been beaten and starved and caged for so many
years that they do not even *remember* the truth any more.
There are so many cultural issues at play also. There is shame,
and there is pride, and there is fear, and there is tradition,
and there is honour. These are women who sell themselves
for money but would not dream of entering a temple with
their heads uncovered. For a foreigner here it will be even
more difficult to find the truth. For a male foreigner near-
impossible. I am thinking very hard about the right person,
you see, because unless you are hearing the whole truth you
should hear nothing at all.'

The winter passes before the chance finally comes. I have
been in the city five months, and seen the temperature plum-
met then begin to rise again. Finally, on a Friday evening,
with the call to prayer resounding through the cooling air, I
find myself sitting in Ajeet's front room around a glass table,
with a pitcher of water, some peanuts in a paper bag. I feel
strangely nervous at the encounter, ashamed to be asking this
of someone. But here we are. It is too late now to go back.

Her name is Kamala, and she is Nepali. Ajeet feels that
his presence might hinder things so, after making the

introductions, he leaves us alone, with Manju between us to help with the translation. In her late thirties, Kamala wears a silver hoop through her right nostril, gold bangles on her wrists. She looks undernourished and tired and her smile is a wisp of smoke. It flickers into view, before it disappears into the room's still air.

'I was born in Nepal,' she begins, when the small talk is out of the way. She has a querulous voice, the voice of a child. 'In a small village to the west. When I was a teenager, a young man came through our village in his truck, who promised me a lucrative job in Bombay. My father was dead by this time, my elder brother had left home, so the whole burden was on my back. I thought that if I could earn I might send some money home. So I went with him in his truck, hoping for a better life.

'When I got to Bombay I was immediately locked in a room for three days. By this time I knew that there was no job waiting for me but still I didn't know what to expect. During those days I was with two other girls who'd also been sold. We were crying and begging to be let go, banging on the doors and so on. The brothel keepers used to come and tell us that if we escaped, criminals would brutally kill us, so there was no point even trying. Then they sent the first customer to my room. I was raped for the first time, separated from those two other girls by just a thin scrap of cloth, and that was my introduction to the profession. No one made a sound or came to help me afterwards. Even the other girls were too frightened to move.'

My throat feels suddenly dry. It feels wrong to drag this out of her.

'From this point on they treated us like this,' she continues. 'We had no food and almost no water most days. They kept us in a condition of total weakness so we would not make trouble. At the end of several days I screamed so much I think they began to wonder if I had gone mad. I tore at the walls with my nails so violently that the brothel-keeper came in. "You may go if you so wish," she said. "But you should remember that you are no longer an unmarried girl, a virgin. You are now used goods, and as such your family will not take you back, nor will any man marry you."'

Kamala wipes her face with the back of a hand, her eyes . . .

'It was then I knew this person was correct,' she says, meeting my gaze for the first time. 'Wherever my life took me from here, it would not be back home. That period of my life was over.

'After eight days in that first Mumbai brothel, the brothel-keeper decided my earnings were not enough. She sold me to another brothel – separating me from the girls I had come to know in that first period – and I was moved in the middle of the night across the city, flanked on both sides by her guards. That was the only time in my life I have driven across Bombay. I remember the glowing lights, and more people than I had ever seen in my life. I remember the smell of a dhaba as we passed, and the incredible hunger I was learning back then, and which has been such a constant in the years that followed.' Her hands shake. 'I have been hungry for almost twenty years or more. When I think about my life – worse even than the beatings and the rape has been that hunger. They use it against us like a weapon.

'In Bombay, the second brothel turned out to be even worse than the first. The assistant madam was an exceptionally cruel woman who took a dislike to me. This was one of the bleakest periods of my life – I bore daily beatings with a lathi. Sometimes I would be beaten simply because she was in a bad mood. Sometimes I couldn't work because I was too injured to be able to stand outside and receive the customers. More even than the customers, I grew to fear that woman and what she might do to me. The customers, most of them, were not violent men. But this woman had violence in her blood, everyone feared her. After eight months I reached my limit. Although I had nowhere to go I simply could not take the conditions there and I knew also that, before long, this madam would beat me to my death. I had a friend there, another girl, and we decided that we would try together. By nights I began to make my plan.

'My idea was to arrange a visit to the doctor – that would give me a reason to leave the brothel which it would be very hard for her to argue with. So for several weeks I pretended to have a stomach pain, so that it would appear natural. Finally I said the pain had become so bad that I demanded to see a physician. My friend offered to take me there.

'In the hospital she took her eyes off us for one second. We went out of the back door, through the hospital kitchens, and took a bus to the train station. Not long after we arrived, however, we saw four goondas, thugs, searching everywhere for us, that she had sent to bring us back. The men were combing the station, coming closer, and we were going out of our minds with fear. At the last minute, a female police officer approached and saw us crying. When we told her why we were upset she said OK, I will hide you until your train leaves. So she took us and put us in a room out of plain view, and also helped us get a ticket. We asked to go to Kanpur, which was where my friend was from and which I knew was not far from the Nepali border. As it grew dark and our train was about to leave, the lady constable escorted us to the train. I will never forget that kindness she showed us. In these years since, I have never again met a police officer with such a good heart.

'So that was how I left Bombay and, as we left that city, I felt perhaps the darkness might be over. It seemed certain that, wherever we went from there, it must somehow be a better place. But how wrong I was . . .

'It took three days for us to get to Kanpur. Having spent all our money on the tickets, we had no rupees for food or even water. We grew crazy with hunger on that train. I asked one lady finally after two days for a few even five rupees so we could get some *gram* [chickpea flour]. But she wouldn't help us and turned away. By the time we arrived in Kanpur, we were like crazy women, near collapse. Our only choice was to ask a rickshaw-puller to take us to the nearest brothel and beg for work. So this is what we did. In fact, we found a brothel-keeper very easily who was prepared to give us food in exchange for two new workers. She bought us some plates of dal and rice and we sat there like two madwomen just eating and drinking until our bellies were swollen.

'After we had eaten the food we were senseless. We fell asleep in this small box room. When we woke up there was a lot of noise and we were told there was a police raid. I woke up to find a policeman peering over me with a very angry look on his face. "Who is this new girl?" he was asking. "You haven't paid your entry fee." So he said unless we paid him we would not be allowed to stay there. The madam stepped in at this point and said she would pay for us, but in return we had to pay off our debt to her. The next day this madam said to pay her off I would come to Banaras and work for her here. That is how I came to this city. I did not see my friend again.'

What was your impression,' I say, 'when you arrived here for the first time?'

'Ah, Banaras,' she murmurs. 'Even as a child I had heard of this place as being one of the most holy places in this world. So when I came here I felt happy. I felt that, if this is God's city, perhaps there might be a life for me here.' She winces suddenly, startled perhaps by her own youthful naïvety. 'But none of that is true. Banaras is like any city, all cities. In my case I came here at night and went straight to Shivdaspur. I remembered Banaras was said to be a good place to die. At least that comforted me.

'First, I was put in the charge of the kingpin here called Badruddin, who made us put our names in his ledger. He was a big man, like a bull, and he liked to use his fists on anyone who disturbed him. He was also a very greedy man, and only cared about money. On that first day he made this clear, as he put our names in his book, when he said there was a charge for this, a registration fee, so that from day one every day I worked he took all the money. Not long after, I had my seventeenth birthday here in Banaras. That was more than twenty years ago now . . .'

Kamala's strange and terrible story unfolds. She seems to remember particular details, and wishes to convey them. She speaks of the minutiae of the harsh glare of street lamps, the winter cold that would make her gums ache as she stood outside night after night. But the most touching detail of her story is yet to come. A customer kept returning to Kamala week after week; he claimed to have fallen in love with her.

'At first I laughed at him,' Kamala says, 'because I told him I had no trust for men, and I would not go with him. But he reassured me and he said he wanted to save me. Week after week, year after year, he came back. After two years of this incredible persistence, he began to wear me down. I had never known such determination in a human being. Maybe this person might be good, I thought. And if he's bad then that will no surprise. What could be worse than my life already? So I told him I would go with him and, one night, we fled.

'This man was a Nepali, a Gurkha, which as you may know is a very honoured position for a Nepali, with a good salary. At this time in my life I felt the first twinge of hope I had known since leaving my village. Perhaps everything will be OK, I felt. But this feeling lasted a matter of days. Not much sooner had we arrived at the Cantonment, one of the other soldiers recognised me – he had been a customer at the brothel – and made it known to everyone that their colleague had returned with a prostitute. All the Gurkhas and their wives began to ridicule my husband, telling him I was a bad person, dirty, and taunting us. It was unbearable. Have you just taken her for her money? they said. My husband was so brave, he was prepared to fight anyone, but it was impossible. I told them yes, I had done those things, but I have my dignity. I am starting afresh. But they wouldn't listen. We endured this for months. Finally, my husband was asked to leave the Gurkhas if he didn't get rid of me, they felt I was polluting the camp. He said fine, if saving someone is a crime then I'm guilty. I will not let her go. And so he tendered his resignation from the service and we walked out together. It was one of the saddest days of my life, but inside I was burning with pride for what he had done. We had spent a year in the camp.

'After my husband stopped earning, our money ran low. We had nowhere to stay, and our savings were gone. Finally I told my husband the only option was for me to return to prostitution. He pleaded with me not to but, as we grew closer to starvation, he realised it was our only option. Also I realised I was pregnant. We returned to Banaras and have been living together here in Shivdaspur ever since.'

The saddest part of the story draws into view. Not long before, a persistent illness had beset Kamala, which no treatment seemed to allay. Kamala, it turns out, is HIV positive, as is her husband; the one blessing is that their son remains healthy. Sitting in the waning light of this front room, I listen to Manju describing how, before the diagnosis, she'd had to threaten and cajole the doctors at BHU (Banaras Hindu University) hospital to even treat Kamala. For them she was barely worth the effort. Not worth the time, the expense, not qualifying for even the most basic human compassion.

'The stigma against these women in India is worse than you can imagine,' Manju says quietly to me in English. 'For those with HIV it is even worse. People have a pathological fear of this disease, and believe all kinds of superstitious nonsense about how they might catch it by simply touching a person. To be a prostitute in addition means they are less than the dirt under people's shoes. And yet these people are victims, truly some of life's greatest victims. How can it be that here, in this holy city, we simply let these women fall between the cracks, we're willing to let them die because we are passing judgement upon them as human beings?' She shakes her head. 'Ajeet and I will simply not allow this to happen.'

Later that night I take the long way home, walking in the half-light through the almost silent streets. Simple charcoal fires glow in the streetside tenements, a horse snickers in the darkness. I smell chapattis cooking, see two children curled up under plastic sheeting, pass a businessman walking home with his battered briefcase, all the hopes of the new India gleaming on his patent-leather shoes.

Closer to the ghats there are mendicants, arriving at the river for the first time, their legs caked with dust. Four pigs root through refuse by the side of an open sewer, some students from BHU emerge from a Chinese restaurant, high-fiving each other in a gesture that speaks volumes about the influences the city is absorbing, so far from the solemnity of the young Brahmin boys.

Varanasi houses and gives hope to such a wealth of humanity that at times this city can feel almost overwhelming in its benevolence. But at others, its cruelty is all too evident in the secrets it harbours, some fragments of which I've heard earlier that evening, from a woman who has little to thank the city for, and who will be remembered by few of its inhabitants when she is gone. Rousseau called cities 'the abyss of the human species', and the immensity of them, the cracks through which the unfortunate can vanish, give truth to his words.

The Mice in the Mithai Shop

The Indians have an unparalleled sweet tooth.
– Aroona Reejsinghhani, *Indian Sweets and Desserts*

It's shortly after dawn in Khoya Gali, and most of the shops
haven't yet opened for trade. Metal shutters clank upwards,
cows nose contentedly into their food buckets, and the stall-
holders string up wires to hang their goods from. It's a wintry
December morning, sharp enough for breath to fog the air,
and the Banarasis are wearing khaddar shawls, knitted wool-
len hats, and clustering around the chai stalls for that
all-important first sip of the day. A thin mist lingers over the
streets, obscuring the sun.

Within an hour the scene here will be one of utter chaos,
with enough traffic for ten streets, enough people for a small
city, and the overwhelming din of rickshaw engines and car
horns competing for tarmac space. For now it's almost tran-
quil: a battlefield preparing for the coming assault. Mangy
dogs stretch themselves from sleep; a goat dressed in someone's old shirt nibbles a branch, two sparrows dart to the
ground in search of biscuit crumbs.

For the city-dwellers food is also the first priority. The street vendors are doing a brisk trade and the air is rich with the smell of boiling sugar, samosas bubbling in hot fat, pans of *subzi* or spiced vegetables cooked with fennel, cumin and fenugreek seeds. For the Banarasi, this *subzi* forms one half of a typical breakfast, the other being *kachori* – piquant potato pies that go soft under the *subzi*, enabling easy consumption with a wooden ice-cream spoon.

Known as *chaat*, street food here is an ancient and highly skilled art form, well deserving its place in the culinary hall of fame. The chef is generally a large-bellied man whose paunch stands testimony to his expertise, often under a stained white vest. He sits cross-legged before an enormous *karahi*, the Indian version of a wok, monitoring the heat of the fire, and wielding an enormous iron spatula with great ceremony. As well as samosas, *chaat* includes such delicacies as *pani puri*, which are fried puffs of dough containing tamarind, chilli and potato; *bhel puri*, a tangy puffed rice mix; and *papdi chaat*, a mixture of papadums topped with chickpeas, steamed lentil dumplings, creamy yogurt and coriander chutney. Generally served in surroundings of dubious hygiene, these foods are an extraordinary mixture of sweet, sour, salt and spice, best enjoyed with the roar of street life in the background.

Many other foods, of course, are appreciated and consumed within the Holy City. Aside from *chaat*, there are rich north Indian curries, generally vegetarian, in keeping with the city's orthodox character, and *thandai*, a milk and dried fruit drink that the locals spice up with *bhang*, cannabis resin, so as to join Shiva in a state of divine intoxication. Some people suggested to me that the ultimate Banarasi food is something, in fact, that requires no cooking at all. The local variety of mango, known as *langda aam*, ripens during the blistering heat of June. Its skin is so thin it is described as *aamani* – meaning one can see the sky through it – and its flesh a deep, sunburst orange, almost entirely free of fibre. The poet Bedhab Banarasi eulogised the fruit in a verse that reads:

> *Never leave Kashi, Vishwanath's holy place . . .*
> *When you die, you'll get salvation.*
> *When you're alive, you'll get Langda Mango.*

Even beyond these delights, however, one foodstuff reigns supreme in Varanasi. Known as *mithai*, these extraordinary sweets are the gastronomic hallmark of the city, and it is thought there are more than a thousand separate *halwai*s or sweet makers tucked away in the backstreets. To one who has never seen one, describing *mithai* is not an easy task: their forms are highly diverse, and they bear little or no resemblance to what counts as confectionery in the Western world. Beginning with the raw ingredients of milk and sugar, *mithai* expand outwards from simple fudge-like creations to the most extravagant concoctions of spice, dried fruit and cottage cheese. They can take the shape of cubes or spheres, diamonds, roll-ups, leaf-shaped parcels and a thousand other variations. Their colours include saffron-yellow, pistachio-green, orange, rose-pink, beetroot, chocolate and silver. At their lowliest, they may sell for merely a few rupees – available singly from a grimy plate behind the chai stand. At their most elaborate, they cost two thousand rupees per kilo, and are shipped across India to the great and good, for consumption at feast days and religious occasions.

Afflicted with something of a sweet tooth, as well as a firm belief in the power of food to elucidate the meaning of place, I was taken with *mithai* from the first. Why were the Banarasis so fascinated by them, I wanted to know. What was the history of these edible art forms? How was it that this ancient city, closely associated with spiritual pursuits, should find such fascination in confectionery? Most important of all, where in the city might I discover the finest exponent of the genre, a veritable Mecca for *mithai*? Clearly, it was going to take a good deal of research to find out.

Khoya Gali, the area designated as the wholesale market for dairy products, is an important starting place for understanding *mithai*. Not far from the sacred Vishwanath temple, its marble spire rising some 250 feet into the sky, this market is a thoroughfare of carts and livestock, coal smoke and strident voices, functioning twenty-four hours a day, all year round. Arriving, I'm first struck by the slightly cloying smell in the air, and then by the blackened pans of milk thickening over open fires. Despite the presence of commercial dairy operations like Amul in India, the milk business remains a predominantly local affair here. Each morning farmers trek in to sell the harvest from their one or two cows, the lids of their pails packed with a special type of leaf called dhak, said to prevent souring.

I stop for some time to observe the scene: fistfuls of rupees changing hands, differing grades of milk under assignation, metal trolleys clanking over muddy potholes laden down with kilos of *khoa* – the ricotta-like substance on which most sweets are based. Farmers, traders, sweet makers and housewives throng together in a medley of commerce and boiling lactose steam. The atmosphere is one of energetic good humour. Even in the street life one can notice what is said to be the significant character trait of the Banarasis; that of *masti* or *joie de vivre*. Jokes are ribald and emphasised with a slapping of the hand, food is eaten noisily with much smacking of the lips, tea is slurped noisily. Before long, I strike up conversation with a man named Kunal, a *khoa* maker who learned his craft from his father, he tells me, and has worked at the market for several decades. Kunal has the appalling teeth of the *paan* aficionado, and a narrow, aquiline nose. He speaks a Bhojpuri-English patois from which I glean what information I can.

'For the Hindu cow is number one,' he explains above the clamour. 'It is both a sacred animal and its milk is excellent for health. Just now people are beginning to buy milk in plastic packets, because they think this is the modern thing to do. But traditional Banarasis know that fresh milk is best, because full goodness is there, and zero chemicals. Some rascals, however, have this practice of adulterating milk in some fashion, which is now making people mistrust our fresh milk. Nonetheless we are selling at least two quintals of khoya every day here. [A quintal is 100 kilos.] That is a significant quantity.'

I enquire about the process of converting milk into *khoa* – Kunal is stirring his pan constantly while talking, watching the surface judiciously.

'Basic process is simply to boil off some of the water content from the milk,' he explains. 'Milk then becomes thick, and is classified as *batti, chickna* and *daan-e-daar* depending on how hard it becomes. *Batti* means rock and is quite tough, while *chickna* means slippery and is of medium consistency.

Different flavours are also provided by cow and buffalo milk, depending on what the *halwai* requires.'

Kunal produces a spoon and dips it over the pan to skim off a portion of the white, foamy substance, holding it up to my lips to taste. Never having been that keen on the taste of raw milk, I smile as best as I can, and compliment him. It's a clean, pleasant enough flavour actually – less painful than remembered milk from school break time. This is buffalo milk, he says, from among the more than 100,000 buffalos in Varanasi. The milk is a paler hue than cow milk and, according to Kunal, higher in cream.

'After some time in the pan, milk reduces in volume by approximately seventy per cent,' he continues. 'As you can see here, this has a white colour, but one other benefit of *khoa* is its ability to be stored for some time. Colour then becomes slightly green due to surface moulds and is then known as *hariyali*, or green khoya. This is best for such items as *gulab jamun.*'

I like *gulab jamun* actually – these fried milk balls in sweet syrup are among the most popular of all Indian sweets, slightly reminiscent of suet pudding. The knowledge that they are made with milk that has turned green makes me jot a mental note to self, however, to eat them less frequently in future. I mention as much to Kunal.

'Yes, I am not enjoying them so much these days myself,' he agrees ruefully. 'Not because of flavour but because I heard a story that they have become a favourite method of torture for the police. I cannot enjoy them with this knowledge.'

How is it possible, I ask, for a supposed delicacy to become a torture device?

Kunal draws closer. 'Victim is obliged to eat plate after plate of *gulab jamuns* without a single drop of water,' he whispers. 'Soon, his mouth is like the Thar desert, and he will sign whatever confession is required! These policemen are ruthless fellows I tell you.'

Witnessing the milk market in such spate made me reflect on the ancient veneration accorded to all things bovine in India. With this in mind it was plain and simple why Indian sweets should be primarily milk-based. It was Brahmanism, the direct historical predecessor of Hinduism, that exhorted people to venerate the cow. Cows are referred to no fewer than 700 times in the *Rig-Veda*, the great collection of Indo-Aryan hymns. They're described as celestial beings, brought about by the churning of the cosmic ocean. The god Krishna is perhaps the greatest cow lover in any world scripture. Often known by the sobriquet 'Gopala', meaning Finder of Cows, he is said to have once lifted the entire Govardhana hill into the sky in order to prevent the devastation of its pasture land by the god Indra.

While the second main ingredient of *mithai*, sugar cane, is not quite as sacrosanct as the first, it is no less indigenous. One of the tall perennial grasses of the genus *Saccharum*, sugar cane is mentioned in the *Atharva Veda* (*c.* 1500–800 BC), where it is called *ikshu*. By about 1000 BC Indians had discovered the process for boiling the sugar-cane juice until it reached a crystalline state. Sanskrit literature refers to *phanita* (a thick juice), solid *guda* (jaggery), *sharkara* (brown sugar, unrefined *guda* crystals)), *matsyandika* ('fish eggs', maybe some sort of crystallised sugar) and finally *khand* (crystalline lumps).

With these two foodstuffs at the heart of Indian life, *mithai*, in their most basic form, seem the most logical evolution. One of the most charming stories in Indian culinary history recounts one of the first experiments to combine the two. In the late fourteenth century, cows belonging to the sultan of Mandu were fed sugar cane for weeks to make their milk sweet for use in puddings.

Sweets, however, already existed in some form long before this stage. By the time of the Buddha, pastries called *samaya*, made from wheat flour, milk and ghee, and often flavoured with cardamom, pepper or ginger, were being eaten. Rice-flour preparations shaped like figs were another creation, as were *shastika*, cone-shaped pastries made from barley flour. By late Buddhist times, some sophisticated sweets are mentioned. The *mandaka* was a large paratha stuffed with a sweetened pulse paste, which was then (as now) baked on an inverted pot; *madhusarika* was a sweet cake; *morendaka*, made from *khoa*, was shaped like the eggs of a *mora* (peacock).

Finding a Banarasi *mithai* shop that somehow encapsulated all these venerable traditions proved to be more difficult than I'd supposed. Many of the *halwai*s I spoke to seemed baffled by my interest in the history that lay behind their work, while others baulked at the idea of allowing a foreigner into their kitchens. One quite famous *mithai* shop did allow me access, only for me to find myself absolutely gobsmacked by the sheer squalor within. There was, in fact, no kitchen to speak of, but only a series of decrepit concrete cells in which mice scuttled in harrowing numbers. I counted ten in one room alone, swaying in a kind of diabetic stupor as they gobbled up stray morsels.

'We don't mind these mice,' said the owner, echoing my landlord. 'They don't bother us if we don't bother them.'

I wasn't so sure, however, and left shortly after, my memory imprinted with the image of a trio of mice tightrope-walking along the edge of a *karahi* full of cooling sugar syrup. I wasn't sure I could bite down on a *ladoo* in that place with the full confidence required . . .

Several weeks pass before I strike gold at last. Interviewing a musician from Ramnagar, I am offered a *mithai* from a box of delicious-looking sweets. They are from Ksheer Sagar, in Sonapura, he says – 'Best in the city by far.' It seemed I had been walking past the shop almost every day without realising how close I had been to confectionery nirvana.

The following evening I stroll down to meet the owner. From Assi Ghat, I pass by Lolark Kund – the ancient water tank famous for its ability to confer progeny on those having difficulty conceiving – then past the Ma Anandamayee Ashram, where one of the great recent saints of the city lived until 1982. On the main road, I pass the government *bhang* shop, where Shiva's favourite intoxicant is sold in the form of potent sugar balls and biscuits. Finally, I arrive at the glass-fronted Ksheer Sagar, one of the most modern-looking sweet shops I've seen in the city.

Inside I know at once that my hunch is confirmed. By far the largest and most impressive selection of sweets I've seen yet is displayed before me. Refrigerated glass cabinets reveal every conceivable size and shape, every shade and ornament of *mithai*. At least fifteen customers are already browsing the display, and the place rings with the animated chatter of sugar junkies expecting an imminent fix. Behind the counter, four

workers dart from end to end packing orders into brightly
coloured boxes. I estimate at least a hundred different types of
sweet here, and with each one priced by weight, electronic
weighing scales are constantly beeping in use.

For the first time, I can examine the full array of this culinary tradition. There are *ladoos*, *motichurs* and *gujiyars*, *barfis*,
cham chams and *sohan papdri*. There are *narkel naru*, *malpoa* and
shrikhand, *jalebi*, *rasgolla* and *pilar pedha*. Many of the names I
haven't even heard of, and I marvel at the sonorous sound of
words like *balushahi*, *abar-khabo* and *shankarpali*.

The owner, Anoop Kumar Yadav, comes out to welcome
me – pausing en route to inspect the quality of a tray of fresh
kajoo rolls on their way to the display case. In his early fifties,
he has a vaguely harried air about him, his well-trimmed
moustache twitching anxiously in the middle of a kindly face.

'I was nine years old when I started working in this shop,' he
explains, as we begin our walk through the immense series of
rooms that lie behind his shopfront. 'My father had founded this
place in 1966, but for a long time it was a small enterprise, with
just a handful of workers. As a child I knew at once that I could
build on what my father started, and I would dream – even
during my classes at school – of changing my father's small
mithai shop into something like this. But' – his face fell mourn-
fully – 'for a long time my father was very resistant to these
ideas. It wasn't until I was in my late thirties that he would give
up the reins, by which time I was extremely frustrated. He was
a traditional man, quite threatened by the possibility of change.'

'What was the shop like in the old days?' I ask.

'It was one room only!' he says. 'And we did a mere handful of basic sweet recipes. A very cramped place. Like many of

the shops in Banaras even now, we had no refrigeration what-
soever. We had our own cows back then too, and the milk
would come over from Ramnagar Fort by boat every morning. I used to go with them sometimes and collect the milk
pails in this small rowing boat, which we would row along
the Ganga. Ah, that was a happy time.

'After my father retired, however, I wasted no time before
major expansions. There are many sweet shops in Banaras, as
you must know, but it was my intention to create the finest
shop in the city, keeping some of our native traditions of
course, but also bringing in some of the Bengali sweets. My
father was a good businessman actually, but I knew that what
I could bring to the table was my taste buds. They are' – he
blinks proudly – 'my finest asset.'

'How many sweets are you selling a day here?' I ask, raising
my voice as some gigantic machine roars into life beyond our
line of sight.

Anoop considers for a moment. 'At least three hundred
kilos, I would say. We have one hundred and twenty-five
different sweets here, which require a total of about seven
hundred litres of buffalo milk per day, and five hundred litres
of cow's milk. That is why our shop is called "Ksheer Sagar",
which means "Ocean of Milk". This is a spiritual reference as
much as a culinary one.'

I ask him why he thinks it is that the Banarasis have such a
fascination with confectionery.

'It is true. Nowhere in the world has such a fascination for
mithai as Banaras! Yes, they love sweets in Calcutta – but what
makes *this* city different is the religious festivals. Only twelve
months in a year, and yet there are fourteen major festivals

here. For each of those, people may come here to buy sweets. Not only for themselves, you understand, but also for the gods. So this gives them great opportunity to celebrate.'

I mention Ganesha's supposed fondness for *ladoos*.

'He is liking any type of sweet actually! When you see him in pictures, his trunk is often turning sharply to the left so that he can taste one. At the time of Ganesh Chathurthi, his birthday, people come to buy *modak*, which are dumplings filled with coconut and palm sugar. Ganesh is giving many blessings to those who remember his sweet tooth. I myself never forget him in my offerings.'

After passing through a series of storerooms, we come into the first of the Ksheer Sagar kitchens. At least ten women clad in brightly coloured saris are sitting cross-legged on the floor around a small mountain of what appears to be white dough spread out on muslin sheets. This is *chenna*, explains Anoop, which is the chief ingredient of the Bengali-infuenced *mithai*. It's cold in here, and a little gloomy, but the women are chattering animatedly while they work, occasionally breaking into peals of laughter.

'In Banaras, *mithai* are generally using *khoa*, which is basically thickened milk,' he says. 'These Bengalis learned how to add a souring agent, like lemon juice, to the milk, which forces it to separate into curds and whey. The curds are then strained through cloth, and hung up for some time so that you get a soft cheese, or pressed between blocks of wood. We add a little flour to this to make what we call *chenna*. To this you just add some sugar, and perhaps some rose water, and you have something delicious. But it can also be used in much more intricate ways.'

We move into the next room, where piles of raw ingredients lie stacked up in hessian sacks. There are cashews from Goa, hulled almonds from Himachal Pradesh. There are dried apricots from Ladakh, green cardamom and cinnamon bark from Tamil Nadu. All the smells of the Orient seem to meet in this room: saffron from Kashmir, orange zest from Madhya Pradesh, fragrant black vanilla pods from Kerala. In one corner, several men are preparing spice mixes relevant to particular *mithai*, then twisting the weighed portions up in sections of the *Hindustan Times* ready for the chefs. In the background, a radio emits Bollywood film songs.

'Certain ingredients are used specifically for flavour,' continues Anoop, as we savour the intoxicating smells of the spice room. 'Others are used more for colour. Almost every other shop in Banaras is using chemical colourings these days, which is why you will notice how bright their sweets are. But I have watched these fellows at work and, though Health and Safety permits only three milligrams of allowed colour, they are pouring it in like nobody's business! This is not good for either health or flavour. So here we use entirely natural colourings, like turmeric for yellow, beetroot for pink colours, rose and orange, and even spinach for green. This was my invention actually, and it works perfectly. We cook up the spinach and then use only the water that is left to colour the *khoa*. These are my secrets.'

By this stage my stomach is rumbling keenly. Towering trays of sweets are passing by me at eye level, gleaming with ghee and sugar crystals.

'And now,' declares Anoop theatrically, 'we come to the main kitchen. Please be careful in here because there are many potential hazards. There are sharp things and hot things, so keep your hands in your pockets. Our first aid kit is in too much regular use.'

Coming round the corner, I enter a room the size of a small aircraft hangar. A blast of heat hits me like a flash fire, and for a moment I simply stop in my tracks, absolutely flabbergasted. At least thirty people are at work here, all of them in bare feet, and a good many of them before enormous fire-pits interconnected by metal pipes. Giant woks the size of bathtubs are balanced over the open flames, roiling with milk or sugar syrup, while the backround rumble of some titanic generator gives the whole scene the air of heavy industry. It's like the engine room of a battleship, roaring with steam and clamour.

'This is quite something,' I bellow to Anoop, still shaking my head. In summer it must be literally unbearable.

He grins proudly. 'You have no idea! We are using diesel-fired furnaces here. They are most effective!'

Never was a truer word spoken, I think to myself. Surely no one who has ever consumed the dainty creations that are Indian sweets could ever imagine a kitchen of such biblical proportions. At one end, colossal quantities of milk are being churned by powerful mechanical whisks, at another sausage-shaped pastries are sizzling in cauldrons of oil. There are men crushing nuts into powder, and breaking coffee-coloured palm sugar into manageable rocks. There are machetes glinting, pestles pounding, and a great shimmering heat haze over the whole kitchen. Over this rhythm come the regular calls of Anoop's staff, hollering for a sack of sugar, a lowering of heat, or for someone to step back as a glowing pan is eased off the flames.

'Bare feet seems a little unwise,' I point out, wincing as two men carry a cauldron of boiling sugar just inches over their uncovered feet.

'They can't be persuaded otherwise,' he says, with a look of meek acquiescence. 'Even though we have had some quite serious accidents over the years. They find it inhibiting, you know.'

'What's your favourite sweet?' I ask. 'If, in fact, you still eat them after all these years.'

'Certainly I eat them,' Anoop assures me. 'How can I run this shop and not do so! It is true our India has something of a problem with diabetes, but I am something of a keep-fit fanatic. That is how I can keep a stern eye on quality control without putting on too many pounds. My favourite are *rasgolla*. Follow me,' he says, 'and I will show you the cooking of one.'

In one corner of a room we come to the *rasgolla* workstation. It is here that the kneaded balls of *chenna* that I'd seen in the other room are being turned into *rasgolla* via a large pressure cooker. A sharp-nosed man wearing a white rumal (cloth) around his head stiffens to attention as he sees the boss approaching.

'This fellow has a particularly light touch with the *rasgolla*,' expains Anoop. 'He came here as a cleaner, but we gave him promotion when we saw him always watching our techniques. Wait till you try one! It's a unique sweet because it combines the richness of cheese with the sweetness of sugar syrup. Our speciality here is to add orange zest, and we sell literally hundreds per day. Inside this pressure cooker the *rasgolla* are boiled for about seven or eight minutes then left

to cool. They are best eaten cold. This is not a traditional
north Indian *mithai*, actually, but even the Banarasis have
come to regard this as a favourite now.'

With our tour of the kitchens over, we retire to Anoop's
office for a tasting at last. It feels strangely quiet after the
cacophony of the factory floor. First there are the celebrated
rasgolla, delicately flavoured with orange, and with a spongy
texture that is undeniably unique. Then the Monkey God
Hanuman's favourite *besan ladoo*s, made with chickpea flour,
and just a hint of cardamom. We eat *kalakand* crunchy with
pistachios, *lal peda,* a soft, milky fudge, and *rabri* – condensed
milk infused with sugar, spices and nuts.

'*Mithai* are an important part of life in the city,' says Anoop.
'They are the truest Banarasi food. During the battle for Indian
independence, one of the city's oldest *mithai* makers even used
them to increase nationalist sympathies. He made a *barfi* from
saffron, pistachio and *khoa* so that it resembled the tricolour
Indian flag. Later, he invented a sweet called the Jawaharlal to
present to our prime minister when he came here.'

'What are your feelings for this city?' I ask. 'Are you positive about the future of Varanasi?'

'Who could claim as much?' says Anoop, consoling himself
with a final *barfi.* 'It was once the greatest city in the world,
but now it is getting too crowded. Population is out of
control. The government of this state is not paying any attention to us. Moneys are spent in Lucknow first, then even
Kanpur, before Varanasi. Electricity is constantly failing, so
that without generators no business can operate efficiently.'
He sighs gently.

'Will your son take over this *mithai* shop when you retire?'
I ask.

'He is looking forward to it,' says Anoop proudly. 'I shall not
be so resistant as my own father was. He has many big ideas
for the shop. Like me his life is only sweets. When we take our
family vacations, we go all over India finding *mithai* shops to
see if anyone can match our own. I'm not boasting,' he says
with a gleam in his eye, 'but no one has surprised us yet.'

The Ganga

I am the shark among the fishes, and
the Ganga among the rivers.
— *Bhagavad-gita*

I come a fallen man to you, uplifter of all.
I come undone by disease to you,
the perfect physician.
I come, my heart dry with thirst, to
you, ocean of sweet wine.
Do with me whatever you will.
— Panditaraja Jagannatha, *Ganga Lahari*

They have always worshipped rivers in India. Originally
revered as a source of life's most sustaining force, over the
millennia, rivers have become actual gods in their own right,
replete with personalities, preferences and whims. The great
Mela gatherings were originally river festivals, commemorat-
ing a creation myth of Hinduism in which drops of sacred
amrit, ambrosia, fell from heaven. In India, river water is sprin-
kled upon heads, consumed; the ashes of the dead are

consigned to it. And of Varanasi it is said that an *arti*, or devotional ceremony, has been offered to the Ganga both morning
and night for five thousand years. Before even the earliest
recorded history, it may be that the location of the city
provided annual respite from floods that covered the
surrounding plains entirely.

I will never forget my first sight of the river in Varanasi,
from the narrowness and constriction of the alleys, thronged
with activity, to the sudden release of the waterfront, the
labyrinth's end. It was not the river in isolation, perhaps,
that stunned me so much as the river and the ghats as one
entity, and the open plain beyond it, and the spires of dark
smoke before it, and the silence, and the white sky, and the
sense of being utterly at the centre of a profoundly ancient
world. Beside my feet, the great river glittered. At the burning ghats, where bodies are consumed by Agni, the Vedic
god of fire, and where I would later meet the Dom Raja, I
was struck by the logic of making fire by water; the significance placed on elements here, not merely as metaphors,
but as central participants in the grand process of life. 'Life
is like a river, always flowing,' said the Buddha, whose first
sermon was delivered not far from here. 'Do not hold on to
things.'

If a city could be condensed into a single phrase, the one
that might well stand for Varanasi is 'the Great Cremation
Ground', a place provided by the gods for humankind to end
their days in. Within this microcosm, the river itself as it meets
the holy city may be the most powerful symbol of them all.
Ganga is the feminine essence, a celestial river so powerful
that, save for Shiva's bending to withstand the impact – thus

tempering the flow with his matted hair – the entire universe would have been destroyed.

During my first months in the city, in need as much of open space as anything else, I formed the habit of taking protracted boat rides down the river. From my front door bordering Assi Ghat, it was merely a short hop to the edge of the river where any number of boatmen loiter in the hope of passing trade. In this way I met Kashi, the boatman who would later ferry me back and forth to Ramnagar to see the *Ramlila* plays. He became my friend and regular ferryman along the slow-flowing river. I gravitated towards him because his prices were fair, and because he was named himself after the city itself. 'I am Kashi from Kashi,' was a phrase I heard him practising regularly on newly arrived tourists. For me he refrained from the patter, for which I was grateful, and once the price was discussed on that first meeting he never touched the subject again. That alone made him unique.

Kashi's boat was a small wooden skiff about 12 feet long, functional though not exactly elegant. It had uneven floor-boards, innumerable splinters on its poorly sanded woodwork, and rowlocks made from loops of pink nylon string, since the originals had fallen overboard during some briefly alluded-to altercation. Kashi was proud of this vessel, nevertheless, and kept a close eye on it even while relaxing at the nearby bidi stand, lest any child be seen to tamper with it, or fellow boat-man dock his craft too close. Such provocation would unleash a torrent of abuse, punctuated with a cascade of sparks from the cigarette the fist was clutching, and occasional frantic head-waggling. Kashi's temper was quick to rise, but even quicker to subside. His wrinkled face, sun-baked from a life on the river, shone with a natural ease and good humour. His voice had a sing-song lilt to it, ever poised on the cusp of laughter.

From this humble craft – as well as from its grizzled owner – my knowledge of the river grew exponentially. For the boatmen, stories of the river are their patois, part and parcel of their role as surrogate tour guides, but also born from genuine reverence. The mighty Ganga forms at Gaumakh in the southern Himalayas on the Indian side of the Tibetan border, I discovered, beneath a glacier known as 'the Cow's Mouth'. Over 1,500 miles long, it passes through twenty-nine cities with a population greater than 100,000, and twenty-three more with a population greater than 50,000, before it meets the sea. The silt it deposits covers an area of 230,000 square miles, enriching some of the most fertile soil in the world. Perhaps as a result of this fertility, a magnet for those who cultivate the land, the Ganga river basin is now the most densely populated region of our planet.

From the Himalayas, the ice-cold river debouches into the Gangetic Plain at the pilgrimage town of Haridwar, another of the great holy river cities. There, a dam diverts some of its waters into the Ganga Canal, which irrigates the Doab region of Uttar Pradesh, while the rest begins its journey south-east through the plains of northern India. After eight hundred kilometres it reaches the city of Kanpur before being joined from the south-west by the Yamuna at Allahabad. Swollen by further tributaries such as the Kosi, Son, Gandaki and Ghaghra, the Ganga swells as it heads east towards Bengal. It is during this leg of its journey that it meets Varanasi, where for a stretch of about 7 kilometres it passes temples, ghats and shrines, many built in homage to it.

'Were you aware, *bhaiya*,' said Kashi to me one morning, as we sculled upstream towards the bridge at Ramnagar, 'that here is the only place on the whole course of the Ganga where she turns north again towards her source? This is merely one example of the great relationship there is between Mother Ganga and Banaras.'

'Why is this?' I asked, feeling sure Kashi had some theory he was angling to share. Letting the oars trail in the water, his face assumed a pensive cast. 'Well, Lord Shiva comes from the Himalayas, it is said. So it may be that when *Gangamaiyya* reaches his city, she turns back north to the mountains out of respect to him. This is actually my feeling on the matter.'

'Tell me, Kashi,' I asked, 'do you see the Ganga as a river or a goddess?'

'She is absolutely both,' he said. 'She takes on all the sins of the world for us. But as a river, she is carrying away bodies and dirt, and providing us food. As a goddess, my father told me that even one glance at her waters is enough to clear thousands of negative karmic actions. Both these things are true here. They need not be separated.'

The natural symbiosis of these worldly and celestial forms of the river needs no explanation for the citizens of Varanasi. As children they're nourished on her mythology, fed on her fish, spiritually and physically cleansed by her. During monsoon her sheer power is capable of intimidation as she rises above the banks, bubbling with millions of litres of snowmelt. For Kashi, as well as a good portion of the 18 per cent of this planet's inhabitants who call themselves Indian, this river is a celestial being before it is a natural watercourse. For a non-Hindu visitor like me, however, her form is less clear. She's tired, overburdened; her pollution is a terrible sight. Now the most contaminated river in the world, the faecal coliform bacteria levels at Banaras are 60,000 parts per 100 ml, or 120 times the official safe bathing limit. DDT factories, tanneries, paper and pulp mills, petrochemical, fertiliser and rubber factories use the river as a free dumping ground. Some stretches are now devoid of all aquatic creatures as a result, while the health implications for humans may only unfold over many years.

Boatmen like Kashi generally bear the situation with the great enduring acceptance that outsiders, rightly or not, have always seen as a quintessentially Indian quality. Economic poverty and the ancient discriminations of caste tell them they have no power to change things. Hinduism views acceptance as a logical attitude towards the vicissitudes life presents. Just occasionally, however, I saw a scowl cross Kashi's face at the state of the river water. Once, beside Raj Ghat, near the site of Krishnamurti's former residence, we crossed a spew of white bubbles several inches deep. Looking up the tributary from which it emanated, we saw it lathered with industrial foam from one bank to the other. It stank with an acidic tang, not just polluted but palpably venomous.

'When I was a boy we used to swim in her without any thought she could be dirty,' Kashi said quietly, shaking his head in wonder. 'Her water was so sweet. Her current was strong also. Now look what has become of her. Mahadev, we have forgotten who she is.'

*   *   *

The state of the Ganga began to occupy a lot of my thoughts. How had things become so bad? Was anything being done to change them? Were the Hindu leaders, whose faith sanctifies its every drop, involved in cleaning the river? Or is spiritual purity seen as entirely disconnected from such worldly matters as bacterial counts and faecal coliform levels? Everywhere in India now, there's an overwhelming sense of movement: first the never-ending struggle to survive, and then the need to turn a profit. Were these pressures now so overwhelming that maintaining the health of the river simply fell off the radar? At what point would it grow so bad that the government would have no choice but to act? Surely, with so many millions depending on the river for their lives and livelihoods, the health of the Ganga should be a national priority?

One name quickly emerged in conjunction with these matters. There *was* a man sounding the call to action, and his story sounded intriguing. Sometimes referred to as Mahant-ji, the honorific accorded him as the head priest of Sankat Mochan temple at Tulsi Ghat, his real name is Veer Bhadra Mishra. A former professor of hydraulic engineering at Banaras Hindu University, his role as high priest at Tulsi Ghat made him one of the city's most revered spiritual figures. Since the early 1980s he has almost single-handedly championed the issue of pollution on the Ganga, even making the United Nations Global Roll of Honour in 1987, in recognition of his environmental achievements. More than twenty years later, I wanted to meet him, both to see what he felt had been achieved during the last decades, and to understand a little more about the great fight for the health of India's holy river.

Such a seemingly simple task, however, proved to be akin
to scaling Everest. Veer Bhadra Mishra, now in his late seventies, is a busy man, and his health is failing. First, I spent many
mornings at his office, fended off by the thorn hedge of
bureaucracy that is India's primary hurdle to an outsider.
Endeavouring to wear down his retainers through sheer
persistence, I dutifully filled in forms, returned with a typed
letter, returned again when the letter yielded nothing. I
brought recommendations, notes of character reference,
copies of published work. The attendants seemed almost
maliciously inured to my plight, greeting me each morning
as if for the first time, scoffingly wagging their heads at the
very notion of finding time in the Mahant's schedule. I found
the situation, by turns, frustrating, farcical, perhaps even some
sort of divine test. Some mornings I could even see the back
of the Mahant's head beyond a doorway, apparently drinking
chai by himself, but the notion that I should be allowed to
speak with him seemed close to impertinent.

Finally, one morning, after noticing Professor Mishra once
more ensconced on his chair in the room adjoining the office,
I simply go in and sit down. None of the four people in the
room make pause in their conversation, so I settle in as if I
belong there, waiting for a chance to speak.

Up close, Veer Bhadra Mishra is a slender, dignified-
looking man with a shock of snowy hair and a bristling white
moustache. He is handsome, even into his seventies, and his
voice is an educated one, that cultured Anglo-Indian diction
which echoes a forgotten world. All of this is at one remove,
however, behind the deep weariness that seems to pervade
him. More than tired, he seems broken, perhaps beyond repair.

I sit perched on a sofa for an hour or more while visitor after visitor comes in seeking a blessing, touching his feet in the traditional Indian manner. Retainers hold papers under the Mahant's nose which he signs indifferently like some ancient king. All the while his eyes constantly scan the room as if in search of something, barely noticing these devotees who come to him on their hands and knees, let alone the would-be interviewer perched expectantly upon his sofa.

At last he turns to me with the air of someone waking and asks me what I am waiting for. I say I am waiting to speak to him, and explain my desire to write about the city, and especially its relationship with the river. I wax lyrical about the river, and try to get across how disturbed I am by its condition. But even as I plead my case I see that he isn't listening, his eyes searching, searching for something beyond my line of sight.

'Do you know, young man,' he says at last, looking down at the lines upon his hands, 'how many journalists come here to see me?' He leaves a long pause. 'And how many have been coming for year after year for twenty, thirty years? They tell me their newspaper, their television channel, will promote our cause. They tell me people will be moved by what's happened to this river. I'm afraid I don't really believe that any more. I'm afraid I have lost faith in your trade.

'Anyway we are busy today,' he continues, before I have time to reply. 'We have an important case reaching the high court imminently. After that, you may come. I hope I will have more time. And please have some tea before you go. Come in a month, no, six weeks. And a biscuit, look there are biscuits. Please, take one before you go.'

*   *   *

Despondently, and clutching a crumbling Good Day biscuit, I find myself ejected into the bright sunlight of Tulsi Ghat. It's one of my favourites of the ghats because of its tranquillity, and the impish rhesus monkeys who play around the ancient ficus tree, its roots intertwining with the stonework. One of them dutifully accepts the biscuit and runs chattering up onto a nearby parapet clutching its prize, while I sit and watch the river. Sweat beads faintly at my temples; within an hour or less, it will be necessary to find shade.

After some time a man comes and sits beside me. It is one of the Mahant's assistants, a retiring, thick-spectacled fellow who has nodded at me from time to time from the corner of the office. He is carrying two glasses of tea and he offers me one.

'You are looking disconsolate, sir, if I may say,' he begins. 'So many mornings you have been coming here. And now he is telling you to come back again. I am sorry for your trouble. Please, would you accept this tea?'

'Another six weeks to wait!' I lament. 'But it's not your fault.' This sudden gesture of entente seemed to absolve him from any part in my previous difficulties. For Indians, chai resolves most things, consoles for the things it can't.

We sip our tea with an eye to the river. An overloaded boat carries pilgrims – a group of women in vivid saris – across towards Ramnagar Fort. They are laughing elatedly, snapping each other's photographs with their mobile phones. They have the levity of holidaymakers, the children and husbands long since forgotten.

'You see, Mahant-ji has been speaking about the problems of this river since the 1970s,' says the man, who introduces himself as Shiva. 'He started the Sankat Mochan Foundation, for which I have been working these last seventeen years. This is a non-governmental organisation which aims to alleviate the problems of the river, but also to campaign at a national level for something to be done. But this country has some corruption problems, as well as some bureaucratic problems. So progress has been severely limited. It's most tiring.'

At this I almost spit my tea out of the corners of my mouth, given that his own office is upholding the bureaucratic side of things at the highest level. However, since it is clear he is empathetic, I restrain myself.

'I will tell you one joke, in fact, regarding the corruption in Banaras,' Shiva continues. 'Of all the cities in India, they say this is the worst! A man dies and goes to God. He sees hundreds of clocks moving at different speeds on the shelf. God says: "Each hand shows the speed of corruption in different places." The man says: "But God, I can't find the clock of Banaras. Have you forgotten us?"' Shiva snorts pre-emptively. '"It is not here," says God, "because I am using that one as my room fan." So this anecdote may tell you how things work here. When we started, we had such high hopes. But many years have passed now.'

I ask Shiva why their hopes *had* been high at the beginning. He is in his mid-forties, I imagine: one of Kafka's nameless bureaucrats, yet overlaid with the deep religious sensibility common to so many who live in Varanasi.

He removes his spectacles, and begins to clean them with an impressively white handkerchief. It seems a distinctly Indian gesture.

'Well, the government was different, back then. Rajiv
Gandhi was in power. In 1986 we launched the Ganga
Action Plan with the mandate to clean the river of pollution. There was a huge ceremony of course. Prime Minister
came here to Varanasi, and launched the project. TV cameras
were whirring, so Mr Gandhi was getting a lot of political
mileage out of his promises to clean the river. He made it
clear that GAP was to be a hundred per cent centrally spon-
sored scheme. And the idea was, by 1990, to have completed
the initial task of cleaning more than eight hundred million
litres a day of waste water along the river in Uttar Pradesh,
Bihar and West Bengal. This would have made a great difference, because that is really the largest source of pollution in
the river.'

'And how were things looking when 1990 arrived?'

Shiva tilts his head unhappily 'So many Ganga meetings, so
little Ganga action. In 1990, the deadline was suddenly post-
poned again till 2000. We felt disgusted. 1989, you see, had
brought a major defeat for the Congress Party in India. Did
you hear about the Bofors scandal?'

I say I have not.

'Rajiv Gandhi himself was accused of taking kickbacks
from a Swedish weapons company who wished to secure a
bid to supply India with some weapons. Before this, everyone
was thinking Rajiv Gandhi was a thoroughly honest fellow.
After this, everyone saw that he was the same as the others. So
perhaps, in 1990, his focus was not on Ganga, but on being
re-elected. We felt very let down. Beside her banks here' – he
gestures to the murky waters – 'we see her condition daily.'

'And then Rajiv Gandhi was assassinated?'

'Indeed. A great tragedy for our country. In 1991 Rajiv was killed in south India by a Tamil militant. After this, the whole of India was in disarray. We were concerned about this, of course, but our main focus was still the Ganga. She is more important than all of us. So we continued to pile on pressure even as the government changed. But by 1993, when we tested the quality of the river water ourselves, it was seen that the quality was scarcely improved.' Shiva lets out a deep sigh. 'So many millions wasted. And still she was full of poison. The Ganga Action Plan proved to be a total fiasco.'

'But you haven't given up?'

Shiva looks appalled at the notion. 'This is not merely a river we are saving,' he said. 'Every molecule of her is sacred to us.'

While I wait for my next chance of the meeting, I return to the river in my spare time, commandeering Kashi and his aged craft for some longer journeys that require him to recruit a friend, Mukul, to assist with the rowing. Mukul is another boatman of the city, with laughing coal-black eyes and a ready turn of wit; his hands bear the deepest calluses I have ever seen. Inspired, perhaps, by the presence of a comrade, as well as by the sheer time some of these journeys give us on the water, Kashi and Mukul begin to offer up their stories of the river. They have the banter of all good double acts.

'Being a boatman is a constant game of luck,' Mukul declaims one morning. 'If the Ganga offers us a customer, we can be blessed. But sometimes there is no custom. We return home to our families without even one rupee! Our wives become very angry.'

'Tell him about the fat man!' says Kashi.

Mukul assents. 'There was one day, however, back some two or three years, when a Swiss gentleman gave me fifty American dollars for a journey. He was a very fat man actually, and my arms were getting too tired while I rowed him. Afterwards, when he gave me this money I told him he had overpaid and tried to hand it back. He said that actually he had *underpaid* for such an experience as seeing Ganga *arti* by boat. I went straight home to my wife and bought a chicken! The rest I used to repair my boat.'

Occasional generous tourists aside, their lives, it seems, are a constant battle for survival. Like most trades in India, too many boatmen – some 2,000, Kashi surmised – now compete for business here, giving rise to a fierce competitiveness, and the ubiquitous hassling that confronts any visitor daring to walk the Varanasi waterfront. Most boatmen come from the Mallah caste, I learn, a large group that encompasses boating and fishing people, and which has occasionally earned a criminal reputation. Traditionally seen as a ritually inferior caste, many Mallahs partake in alcohol and eat meat. Poverty, worsened by marginalisation and dispossession under colonial rule, remains endemic amongst them.

'That was a very fine day,' continues Mukul, still wistful over his legendary tip. 'Other times we get so little work we do many other things, but always around the river. Some fellows become divers who collect the bodies from the bottom.'

'*Gotakhors*,' adds Kashi, providing their official name. 'Mainly, *gotakhors* are from the Raj Ghat area. They become good swimmers by collecting coins from the river bed. So many pilgrims are throwing rupees in for the good luck, so the *gotakhors* make a good living by retrieving them. Then, when the police want to find a body they get asked to swim down because only they understand the currents here.'

'And not just bodies,' says Mukul. 'All manner of items find their way into Ganga. There are guns down there, stolen goods, animal bodies also. Many people cannot afford even the wood to burn their cow when it dies, so they simply bring her to the banks and throw the corpse in.'

'Is the current that strong?' I ask. 'It looks placid.'

'Oh Ganga can be very fierce,' said Mukul. 'During monsoon so much water can flow through here that it is necessary, by law, to have two boatmen in each vessel. And many people are getting washed away. Last year three students from BHU made the foolish choice to be drinking a great deal of whisky and then going swimming. Not even the *gotakhors* could find these fellows – military frogmen were coming and searching for several days. Finally, they were found swollen like buffaloes. Even I had to hold my nose when they pulled them out.'

It is still early out on the river, not yet 9 a.m. This morning Kashi and Mukul have suggested we dock on the river's far bank to see what they grow on the seasonal vegetable patches that utilise the highly fertile river bed exposed when the monsoon rains recede. As the boat slides aground on the damp sand, we jump out into the shallows. The water sloshes around my ankles, still carrying the chill of its Himalayan origin. I turn back to scan the famous waterfront vista, with its temples and spires, from this new angle. From this distance, minus the crowds and the dirt and the hawkers, it has the glory of an open-air cathedral, or the silence of a mosque's inner sanctum.

'Some time before, we would take sand from this bank for construction companies,' explains Mukul, drawing my attention back to more temporal matters. 'It was hard work for us, but we could make money that way when times were hard. Now even this is forbidden. New laws are making life very hard for us. Fishing is even forbidden in some places.'

'The pandas [priests] do not like us, actually,' says Kashi. 'They pretend the fish are eating the dirt in the river and so they should not be fished. But the real reason is pandas say all fish who swim within the area of the holy city are sacred.' He chuckles. 'We say they are sacred also. Everything which Ganga provides is sacred. But we say she provides them for us to eat. Mothers provide food for their children.'

We begin a discussion of Veer Bhadra Mishra's Ganga Action Plan, about which all the boatmen seem well informed. As we sit on the dry sand away from the water's edge, where Kashi smokes one of his bidi cigarettes, it grows clear that while Kashi and Mukul feel a deep concern for the state of the river, and indeed a reverence for Professor Mishra, they are embittered towards the river-cleaning campaign, which, they say, has damaged their livelihood.

'Last year they tried even to make us pay fifty rupees per day to use the river!' Mukul says angrily. 'Can you believe this! Forest department said there were river turtles that were eating the dirty water and so, in order to protect them, we must pay fifty rupees per day. How can we pay this? And why should we, who are born on this river, and who see her as our mother, have to pay? So we went on strike immediately. No boatman in all Varanasi would work. We made a big protest along the ghats. Even the tourists could not see the burning ghats from the water because there was no one to take them. And of course they had to change their decision.'

'Problem is,' adds Kashi, 'that we boatmen always suffer. It has always been like this. Government does nothing to curb the factories which are poisoning the Ganga, and yet they tell us we cannot fish, or we must pay fifty rupees. They are very stupid fellows, I think. And they do not take responsibility for the problems they are creating.'

'How did you eat,' I ask them, 'during the ban on fishing?'

'It was not easy,' says Kashi, scratching his stubble. 'We became very thin during this time. Actually we had to make some baksheesh to the police and then fish at night. This way we could feed our families.'

'What about these gardens over here?' I ask, turning to the neat rows of musk melons, cucumbers and water melons which are already emerging from the rich soil. 'These vegetables look very good.'

'The Ganga is so powerful she even provides us fruits and vegetables!' says Mukul delightedly. 'Mainly our wives are looking after these crops over here. We bring them over here in the morning time and they make sure things are watered. Water level comes down last month, and we have to be fast because crops must be harvested before she rises again in May time. Again, the Nagar Nigam [municipal authority] has been making trouble for us over this because all these turtles they say must come here for sleeping and mating practices. They say we boatmen are disturbing these creatures and also eating them.'

Kashi tilts his head thoughtfully. 'Actually it is true that some boatmen are doing this. These are very tasty creatures,

you see, and there are too many of them over here. My wife
is cooking one in a particularly tasty ...'

'Yes, but that is not the point,' interrupts Mukul hurriedly.
'This is the land we have always cultivated. So we should be
allowed to use it.'

He eases himself off his haunches suddenly and strides to
the river's edge. Mukul is one of the more politicised of the
boatmen, and he often speaks like this, but today he seems
especially fired up. Perhaps it is being on this side of the river,
so that the city itself is at a distance, which allows him to put
his thoughts into perspective. Or perhaps it is because I am
asking questions that strike to the heart of his identity. He
bends down and, with hands forming a makeshift cup, scoops
some Ganga water into the air. He takes a long drink, letting
the remainder trickle back into the stream.

'When Lord Rama and his wife Sita were married they
departed from Varanasi,' he says. 'They were going to perform
yatra – a pilgrimage. And because they needed a way to cross
the river, a boatman offered his services. In return Lord Rama
gave him a blessing, and a *dan* [donation]. For our people this
story has great significance, for we believe that God himself
has blessed our lives here. But whether there will be a way of
life like this for our children, we do not know. Times are very
hard for the Mallahs of Varanasi.'

The weeks passed. Winter weather descended over the river,
bringing with it flocks of brown-headed gulls, escaping the
snows of the central Asian mountains: Turkestan, Gansu and
Tibet. A South Indian visitor called them by their Malayalam
name one day, *vichikaka*, which translates poetically as 'wave

crow'. My boatmen friends added a new string to their bow by mimicking the gulls' sounds for the pleasure of tourists, attracting wheeling colonies low over the river surface with their curious cawing. Morning pilgrims still flocked to the water's edge for their dawn prayers, though many confined themselves to a brisk splashing, I noticed, rather than the full immersion of the warmer months. In the mornings, an icy wind whistled across the water, fanning the coals, as well as the sales of the nearby chai stalls, to a fever pitch.

Still I tried to understand the river, with all its meanings, its problems and delights. Like most houses in Varanasi, the place I lived in had a flat rooftop upon which one could dry washing or chillies, practise yoga or fly a kite. From mine I gained an extraordinary view over the river itself. There was the bustle of Assi Ghat, with its frequent festive occasions, snake-charmers and buffalo. There were the widows holding out their hands for alms, the one-armed beggars, the ascetic sadhus bearing magnificent beards and robes the colour of tangerines. There were goats dressed in old cardigans during the cold weather, and peanut sellers with monkeys on their shoulders, vendors of sliced guava and chilli powder snacks. For several days I noticed a horrifically wounded dog, its ear torn off in a fight to expose a suppurating wound. Though I tried to pour anti-septic over it, it died two days later, its head merely inches from the great river. A holy man passed me while I took stock of its fly-ridden corpse. 'This creature knew where to die,' he said with a warm smile. 'It was drawn to Ganga.'

It was the first time in my life I'd lived this close to a river, and I began to see how much a river's personality could affect the day-to-day life of those who lived nearby. If a rough wind ruffled its surface, people seemed a little surlier; if a spitting rain moved in, people hunkered under wide-canopied trees, their spirits simultaneously dampened. When the waters shrank during the dry winter months, people fretted over Ganga's health, cursing the government for her upstream dams, for the poor monsoon that hadn't bought the replenishment she needed. And in the first days of the following year's rains, as the river thirstily drank the contents of the immense Himalayan clouds, the river-dwellers sang and danced, and held up their hands in thanks for the reassurance that all would be well for another year.

Towards Lanka, an open-air fish market sold a selection of river fish caught daily from Varanasi's waters. They were primeval, bony-looking fish, and I wasn't tempted by their greasy complexion, yet the locals – those, at least, who put their stomachs before the pure vegetarianism espoused by most Banarasis – haggled furiously over weight and price, while the pye-dogs hovered eagerly for any offcuts. This was the Ganga as mother, providing for those who lived along her banks. This same source washes clothes, allows easy transport, carries away one's deceased, and even offers spiritual solace in a hostile world. I could think of no single thing – except perhaps money – that carries as much significance for us in the developed world, where nature is, more often than not, a resource for our pleasure and profit, and rivers merely something to picnic beside on a sunny day.

At long last the Mahant's retainers manage to solicit his attention for long enough to tentatively pencil me into his diary. Almost five months have gone by since my first attempt, and

this interview has taken on a somewhat exaggerated significance. It is now February, and the temperature climbs daily.
Nevertheless, having passed through the stages of frustration
and despair into a sort of gleeful nonchalance, I have been
growing to enjoy my trips to the Mahant's crumbling residence, with its cool pockets of shade, powdery blue paintwork,
and temple to Lord Rama. One early morning, I even discover
a wrestling *akhara*, where men practise *kushti*, an ancient form
of unarmed combat said to have come from Persia with the
Mughals. Caked in red mud and wearing only loincloths, the
wrestlers' primordial form of discipline seems a fitting thing
to discover beside the river banks. One wizened old man,
claiming to be one hundred and three, tells me he has never
missed a morning's training, nor his dip in Ganga afterwards.
'Too few young boys are coming to *kushti* these days,' he
laments, after demonstrating to me that he could still manage
a press-up. 'They go to the gym instead. But gyms have no
discipline, no honour, no sacred aspect. *Kushti* maintains the
old ways, it maintains respect.'

The soil of the wrestling ring, he explains, is considered
sacred to them. Mixed with mustard oil, turmeric, ghee and
milk, it is worshipped every day before the wrestlers fight, and
then used liberally to adorn their bodies, for it is said to bring
strength and health. Hearing this, I realise I have found a spiritual
significance accorded to yet another of the natural elements in
Varanasi: fire, water, and now earth. Everything is interlinked
here, it seems, and everything is considered sacred. And yet the
wrestling, just as the old man said, is dying out in modern India,
superseded by more modern pursuits. I shared his sadness for
the state of things, felt even that I understood the hint of

desperation in his rheumy eyes. India's tryst with modernity is destroying far more than simply the respect accorded to the elements that sustain us. The river herself is a symptom of a whole civilisation hindered on its journey by a surplus of people, waste and corruption. And yet still she survives, occasionally sparkling in the light to remind us of who she is.

The Mahant, when I arrive, does not appear pleased to see me. He looks like a man who, after continual pressure, bows to an outcome he resents, and resolves to drag his feet through the entire process. 'How long will this take?' he mutters. 'I have a very important meeting in twenty minutes.'

'It will take twenty minutes, then,' I say. 'Twenty minutes to discuss your life.'

'Very well,' he begins with a sigh. 'I suppose I can tell you the basics. In my family the role of priest at this Sankat Mochan temple has passed from father to son since the sixteenth century. So I always knew this would be my dharma. I expected, however, to assume the role once I had reached manhood. What happened was that in 1952, when I was just fourteen, my father died. So I had to assume the role somewhat earlier than expected.'

'I understand you're a professor of hydraulic engineering also,' I say. 'How did this come about?'

He shrugs. 'Indeed. I had an aptitude for learning at quite a young age. My father acknowledged that this might be worth pursuing. So I learned to cultivate two roles in life: that of a religious leader and that of hydraulic engineer – which became my vocation.'

'Tell me about the river. What do you remember of it from when you were a child?' I ask.

'I bathed in it every morning,' he says, increasing frustration creeping into his voice. 'Each day at dawn I would descend to Ganga to do my prayers. As I grew older the river grew more poisonous. My expertise as an engineer, combined with my hereditary role and religious beliefs, gave me a special perspective on what was happening, and what should be done. I have spent my life talking about the problems of the river. A wasted life, I sometimes think.' He shouts suddenly into the next room, so that one of his retainers comes scurrying in. Has any post arrived, the Mahant wants to know. And has there been any news on their pending court case?

I feel suddenly very tired. It seems wrong of me to have corralled this weary old priest into an interview when it is so palpably against his wishes. Two minutes into our discussion and he is already involved in another conversation.

'Look, I apologise,' I say. 'I don't want to force you into an interview if it's upsetting you. Let's call it a day then.'

He blinks at me, caught off balance.

'I think that would be best,' he says. 'You see I have spoken about these things too many times. And while I have been speaking about them, again and again and again, I have grown old and tired and sick. And time is running out.'

'For you, or the river?' I ask.

He holds out both palms facing up. 'For us both.'

I get up to go. Slumped in his chair I pity him a little, and admire him too, and know it is time for me to be on my way.

'Just write about the river,' he says, as I reach the door. 'My voice has been heard too many times. Perhaps the Ganga herself will speak to you. Let us pray her plight is heard by someone before it is too late.'

The Warp and the Weft

The loom and the shuttle
lie forgotten:
His Heart is full of Ram's name
day and night.
— Kabir

If a competition were to be held for the sound most typical of
Banaras, the slide and click of a shuttle moving across a traditional loom would probably be a strong contender, even today.
Towards a century that has already brought us cloned sheep
and space tourism, the ancient river city shows only hesitant
signs of curiosity. Yes, since 2006 there has been a McDonald's
here, where the city's aspirational class munch flash-fried Aloo
Tikki Burgers and McPuffs. Yes, there are multiplex cinemas, a
water park, a trendy art gallery showcasing photographers
from New York and Paris. These are the signs of a globalising
India, the outer layer of a beast that is slowly fitting itself to a
new world order. In the background, however, the traditional
city follows patterns of work and worship that have scarcely
changed for millennia. Water is carried by hand, fragrant spices

are ground on heavy blocks of stone, distinctions of caste remain supremely important. There is a poetry to this world, and sometimes a galling cruelty.

At the centre of this ancient city are the weavers, known as *paat* in Eastern India, *pattu* in the south, and *resham* in Hindi and Urdu. The silk which is their raw material may first have arrived in India along the eponymous trading route. Recent archaeological discoveries in Harappa and Chanhu-daro, however, suggest that sericulture, using wild silk threads from native silkworm species, could have existed in South Asia during the time of the Indus Valley Civilisation, roughly contemporaneous with the earliest known silk use in China.

Varanasi, in any case – probably for climatic reasons – has never been a centre of sericulture. It is the art of weaving that has thrived here, for much of the lifetime of the city. As a young prince, before setting out on his path of self-realisation, the Buddha himself wore the city's garments.

I was delicate, most delicate, supremely delicate. Lotus pools were made for me at my father's house solely for my use; in one blue lotuses flowered, in another white, and in another red. I used no sandalwood that was not from Benares. My turban, tunic, lower garments and cloak were all of Benares cloth.

The thought that the young Siddhartha may have been clothed in Banaras cloth is a pleasing one. True or not, Varanasi has long produced some of the world's finest fabric, initially from cotton, later from silk. Perhaps it was Gujarati weavers, fleeing famine, who brought such skills to the city. Other theories point to the influx from royal workshops in Delhi at the close of the Tughlaq Empire at the end of the fourteenth century, or a migration from Jaunpur with the collapse of the sultanate a century later.

Much of this information was imparted to me by a young Muslim, Bahadur, who'd come recommended not merely as someone well informed about the city's weaving trade but as one of its most enthusiastic spokespeople. I meet him in early December, on a morning chilled by the first cold snap of the winter. Wrapped in a crimson-checked shawl, he sports the lustrous beard and white topi of many Banarasi Muslims, with eyes set wide apart, and wearing a slightly quizzical expression. He is leaning proprietorily against a yellow rickshaw and smoking a Gold Flake cigarette when I arrive. The slightly battered vehicle belongs to his cousin, he tells me, and we will need it if we are to see some of the differing sides of the city's weaving industry.

'When I was younger I used to love driving with my cousin,' he hollers merrily back over his left shoulder as we get under way. 'Every corner of the city he is knowing. Muslim, Hindu, Sikh, Jain, he has friends from every community. He knows the shortcuts. He knows where to get the best prices for all manner of goods. And as a boy I used to be very impressed with the variety and delivery of his cursing.' Bahadur waggles his head with amusement. 'If someone cuts him off he will unleash such a torrent of abuse that fellow will be running home to his mother. He wields these phrases like a blade I tell you!'

Bahadur, it seems, has something of his cousin's skill at driving. We are heading for the southern part of the city, a mohalla known as Madanpura. The narrow *galis* of the city

hum with commerce as we fly by. All business is a form of
theatre here: food is flipped with comical panache; chai is
poured from an absurd height into glasses for it to cool.
Wherever possible, basic procedures are complicated by elaborate movements of the hands, exaggerated shaking of the head
or a downturned mouth. *Masti*, love of life, trills into every
second of time, so that food is savoured more loudly, complaints
are more vociferous, spiritual practice is more intense. In a blur,
I watch a mother and daughter descend from their shiny
Ambassador car, snapping up a parasol to protect their skin
from the winter glare. On a corner, a haze of fat from a mutton
cutlet stall shimmers in the air, then comes a Kali temple, a
guest house, an ancient tree that has become a shrine.

We leave the rickshaw on the edge of the weaving quarter,
then continue on foot, past the Katuni Fancy Store, the Big
Cinema-C-In-Nai-Ki, a small pottery centre producing
grandiose life-size figurines of local political figures. It's
mid-morning and the workday is in full swing. Already we
can hear the clatter of looms in the distance: an old-fashioned,
metrical noise, like a steam train rattling over rails. Fingers of
sunlight reach down into the alleys, picking out potholes, a
window half ajar through which an old woman watches the
street, the brown hindquarters of a mongoose disappearing
through a crack in the wall. It turns to look at me briefly
through the same crack before disappearing, allowing a
glimpse of intelligent eyes, with their distinctive oval pupils.

'Most people think Banaras is purely a Hindu city,' says
Bahadur, as we duck into a tapered alley leading off the main
drag, a smell of sewage assailing our nostrils, 'but this is not

true. There are more Muslim shrines here than almost any
other city in India. And a large population of Muslims,
perhaps thirty per cent of the total. Most of the Muslims here
earn their living, in one way or another, from the loom.'

'But not you?'

He grins. 'Well, I never wanted to be a weaver, this is true.
My father says it's because I can't stop talking but I say I'm
interested by too much to be tied down to one job, especially
if it requires me to keep still. But actually the industry does
support me, because people like yourself ask to be shown
around, and I work with charities to improve the conditions
here for our people. So even though I am not spinning silk, I
am spinning stories about it.'

We flatten ourselves to the wall while a Honda Dream
Yuga motorcycle holding four people roars its way down the
constricted alley, making no reduction in its speed for the
sake of us pedestrians. The sound of the looms grows audible
again as the motorbike recedes, and I dream, as how often
before, of a city before the advent of motorised vehicles.

'It is said there are more than a thousand shops selling saris
here in Banaras,' Bahadur explains. 'And there are crores of
Julahas doing this work. North of the city there are places like
Jaitpura and Adampura, but in the city centre the main places
are Reori Talaab and Madanpura. It is a world within a world
here, you will see.'

I ask Bahadur to explain the world Julaha to me. It is often
used as a synonym for weavers, I know, and yet its meaning is
more complex. He explains that while Islamic theology is
opposed to caste in principle, Muslims in India have long
since taken on board some of the caste distinctions recognised

by their Hindu counterparts. Julahas, weavers, are among these, he goes on, as washer-people are Dhobis, sweepers Lal Bhagi and butchers Qureshi. Julaha comes from a Persian word meaning 'ball of thread'.

But those who actually own weaving firms, are not Julaha, Bahadur points out; they call themselves Ansari. 'Ansari is a term of respect for us,' he clarifies, 'whereas over the years Julaha has come to take on some negative connotations of poverty, or low caste. Many people are not liking this term for this reason. They wish it to be banned as insulting.'

At the end of an alley we turn past a *paan* shop no bigger than a cupboard, then arrive at our destination, the house and workplace of a Muslim weaving clan. Behind a substantial gate lies a courtyard with metal hand-pump, crumbling walls of earth and brick, a broken charpoy, missing several of its strings. There is a feeling of simplicity rather than poverty here, and a stillness that persists despite the clacking of the looms. Order and routine pervade this inner world, while religion provides a foundation. I feel intensely the distance between here and the city I have come to know.

An elderly man and his two sons come out to greet us. They wear identical pristine white kurta pyjamas, the patriarch distinguishing himself with a coal-black waistcoat unbuttoned to display its fine silk lining. All three wear Muslim skullcaps, as well as spectacles – a legacy, I suppose, of a lifetime examining thread count and stitches. They look affluent and conservative.

'*Asalaam alaikum*,' comes the greeting, accompanied by the traditional Indian gesture of the right hand raised to the forehead.

'*Wa alaikum salaam* – Peace be upon you too.'

I'm speaking with Haaji Mohamed, a placid, glassy-eyed man of kindly disposition, who also happens to be one of the great living Ansaris of the city. While his sons both sport dapper beards, Haaji is clean-shaven, further reinforcing my impression that he is a rigorous, ordered fellow, concerned with the fine details of things. We move inside and sit down in his showroom carpeted with mattresses covered in white sheets, thick bolsters of the same fabric running the length of the walls. It is spotlessly clean and we sit, without shoes, at our ease, while tea is called for, and the serious business of discussing the weaving trade commences. I find myself slightly startled by the brightness of this interior space: it has an almost medical cleanliness compared with the world just beyond the walls. It's so meticulously clean, my own slightly scruffy clothing and odd socks seem to draw embarrassing attention to themselves.

Tea arrives and special cumin biscuits. I hold my glass gingerly, and try to avoid spraying the showroom with crumbs. These are fastidious men, I feel at once. They live their lives in showrooms and mosques, unravelling bolts of fine cloth with careful hands. There is a particular aura about them: mercantile but retaining a strong connection to the craft; wealthy enough, by local standards, but it is a new wealth, perhaps one generation old, so that the bleeding fingers of their forefathers throb beneath their own. They spend their money wisely, are traditionalist, do not yet foresee a life beyond weaving for their own children. Unlike Bahadur, these are men of an older world: they are pious, insular; they speak in level voices.

Haaji, as the family head is known, has done the Haj to
Mecca twice. This is a measure not just of his piety but his
wealth, for such a trip is costly. It gives him enormous respect
in the eyes of his family, and the subject comes up at once, a
matter of honour.

'Government is paying some donation to Air India,' he tells
me, with a raised forefinger. 'However, I chose not to accept
this, because the stipend should be for those Muslims who
really need the assistance. In any case, this issue of Haj subsi-
disation has been causing some ruckus between the
fundamentalist factions of our society. Some Hindus say only
India should be *pitribhuumi* – fatherland – and they resent the
fact that we Muslims wish to do the Haj, which lies in Arabia.
However, from our perspective, we love our India as much as
the next man, but religion is something different. For the
purposes of Islam, we must go to Mecca. It is one of life's
most important acts for us. The Prophet himself, peace be
upon him, said that "One who offers Haj and doesn't speak
obscene language, and doesn't commit sins, will come back as
pure as he was at the time of his birth." So you see' – he tilts
his head and offers an open hand – 'one cannot refuse.'

He gazes fondly at the large framed picture on the wall of
the place in question: the Kaaba adjacent to the Grand
Mosque in Mecca, circled by a crowd of astonishing magni-
tude. I imagine he looks at this image often, recalling the
spiritual and temporal zenith of his life. In this minimalist
room, it hangs as a bold statement of purpose.

'But making the Haj is the end of my story really,' he says,
smoothing away an invisible crease in his kurta. 'My story
began in this complex of buildings. As a child I learned to

weave almost as soon as I could move about. Many children now spend their time with toys or bicycles, but for me there was only the loom. This was during the 1940s. Already, India was moving towards her Independence.'

'Your father was a weaver?'

'Not just *any* weaver. A master weaver,' says Haaji, with a twinkle of pride in his eye. 'My great-grandfather, I should tell you, sent textiles to the Great Exhibition in Hyde Park during 1851. His work was among those chosen to represent all India. We like to think Queen Victoria may have stood before him. You see, weaving is in our blood.'

I ask about his childhood.

'As soon as I could walk I was working,' he remembers. 'These days people talk of child labour and all these things. All kind of restrictions are there about what children may or may not do. But we didn't *know* of such things. My family are weavers. In fact, I *wanted* to learn – I used to race home from school with excitement. Learning this craft was so vital to my understanding of the world. Now they are saying children should not work until fourteen or something, but the skills required by a master weaver *cannot* be kept until this age. In some cases there are thousands of steps involved in a singular piece, perhaps tens of thousands. It takes literally years to gain the dexterity, the endurance, the finesse required to work at the highest level. If one starts so late to spare the feelings of a child, the craft will be lost!' Haaji smiles. 'In my case I was quite proficient by about seven years of age. But to learn the extent of the business, how to manage other *karigars* [artisans], how to articulate a design properly, these things take years longer; I am learning them still.'

We talk of quality. This is the moment I have been waiting for, when the Ansaris, with the ease of long practice, reveal their silks from hidden cabinets, startlingly vivid against the white mattress. The saris arrive as if from nowhere in their hands, so fine one can see the light through them, with an iridescence that is all the more striking for the plainness of the room itself. Such colours! Azure, crimson, peacock green ... It is as if a bird of paradise has appeared suddenly in this whiteness. I sense a tiny glimpse of the wonder a bride must feel to be greeted by such finery in the build-up to her big day. And the Ansaris, I realise, cultivate great skills of showmanship along with their weaving skills. They are like magicians pulling things from hats, colour exploding suddenly into empty space.

'We Banarasis do not claim to have invented the sari,' explains Haaji, 'because this garment has been around for longer, even, than this ancient city. But it can be said that Banaras is the place where this garment has achieved its highest expression. From all over India, brides will make the pilgrimage here with their mothers to choose their bridal trousseau. It is one of the most exciting moments of their lives, so we have a responsibility, you see, to ensure they are not disappointed.' He gazes lovingly at an example in his hands, still fascinated with his craft after all these years.

From having known nothing of saris, I'm soon sated with facts. Saris range from four to nine metres in length, I learn, and are as varied in style and design as the women who wear them. One end is richly decorated, known as the *pallu*, while the blouse that bares the midriff, traditionally worn underneath, is a *choli*. The garment finds different incarnations in every state, explains the Ansari. There is the Kanchipuram from south

India, the bright tie-dyed Bandhani from Rajasthan or Gujarat. In Andhra Pradesh one finds cotton Gadwal saris with silk borders, and in Maharashtra there are intricate designs of silk and gold woven saris with peacock designs known as Paithani.

'It was in Banaras, however, that something special occurred,' Haaji tells me. He speaks in Urdu to one of his sons, who selects a particular example and passes it over. It has elaborate swirls and patterns, a particular green colour somewhere between jade and emerald.

'The Moghuls brought with them a highly complex iconography of symbols and patterns which the weavers of this city were able to incorporate into the brocades. If you see some of the greatest buildings left behind by the Mughals you will find such patterns: flowers and birds, delicate leaves and paisleys.' He points to the matching designs in his cloth. 'Now no one is making such buildings any more, but these saris remain a living tradition. You have probably read about all the problems our community has been facing since the advent of mechanical looms, and especially cheap imported silk from China.' Haaji looks to his sons with pride. 'Insha'Allah, we have escaped facing too many problems in this family because we have never tried to be mass producers. We only do the very finest work on the handlooms, and this work can *never* be replicated by machine.' He nods his head emphatically. 'It takes a lifetime of dedication to become a true master weaver. But once that has been achieved, you have done something no one can take away from you. Our silks have been on catwalks in Milan and New York City. Even some designers like Kenzo are now commissioning things from us.'

My legs are getting cramped beneath me; it is time for a

change of scene. On Bahadur's prompt, Haaji asks his eldest son, Aziz, to show me the weaving process itself. Adjacent to the showroom, we enter the simplest of workshops, the source of the noise peculiar to this district. The handlooms are astonishing devices, a seeming chaos of strings and threads, pulleys and beams, cleverly positioned over a well in the floor into which the weaver's lower torso can fit. Six men work in here for at least ten hours a day, manipulating these machines as though they are extensions of their own bodies. If Haaji's house is itself a world within a world, entering the weaving room takes me a stage further into a microcosm of Banarasi society. This room is absolutely outside history, without a single sign of its location in the twentieth century. It smells of sweat and new yarn, and thrums with clicks and whooshing sounds.

The weavers greet us warmly, clearly pleased to have their work appreciated. Handloom weavers are almost always men, Aziz explains, while many of the subsidiary processes such as carding, preparing the yarn for weaving, rolling it onto bobbins and shuttles, and cutting and polishing the embroidery threads are done by women. In all my time amongst the Muslim weavers of Varanasi I very rarely, in fact, even *see* a woman, let alone have the chance to speak with any of them. While their role is clearly integral to the silk industry, their position is an insular one and their dealings with the outside world few.

'The first step is to dye the yarn,' Aziz tells me. He has a high, querulous voice, not yet embodying his father's authority. 'We do this by dipping it in coloured water that has been boiled. The higher the temperature of this process, the more strong the yarn becomes. Attention must be directed to make sure the colour is applied uniformly. When this is done, it is put to dry in the shade only – never the sun, because this can damage the finished product.

'The next step is to load the coloured yarn onto a frame so that it is held in tension. This becomes what we call the warp. The yarn that is inserted over and under the warp threads is called the weft. These are just some of the stages before the weaving itself.'

I notice a strange series of cards hung above one of the looms, made of cardboard and filled with intricate holes.

'After the design has first been drawn onto grid paper, it is then perforated onto cards,' Aziz continued. 'It is a kind of binary system that is an ancient precursor of a computer. These tiny holes guide threads through the handloom according to the motif, each card corresponding to a single line of weaving. All of this must be set up before the weavers sit down to work, and if there are mistakes at any stage it can ruin the sari. So we are totally vigilant. Each sari must be prepared with patience, or we can lose time and money.'

The weavers return to work, and we stand quietly and watch them for a while, their brows furrowed in concentration, the most exquisite silks forming in slow increments between their hands. There is something profoundly satisfying about observing this work in its natural setting here, far removed from the anarchic traffic, or the sharp light. One of the weavers is older than his colleagues, perhaps sixty, and I wonder how many years he has spent in this very room, measured out by the rhythmic clacking of these machines. After a while we leave them to their craft, the rhythm of the looms following us even as we walk away through the narrow streets of Madanpura.

*   *   *

Several weeks later I meet up with Bahadur again, this time
to visit a different side of the Varanasi weaving community
entirely. Whilst last time we had been to a Muslim Ansari
family, working with only the finest materials and with lucrative connections to Western fashion brands, now we are to
visit the opposite end of the spectrum, some Hindu weavers
struggling for survival. As we drive, Bahadur explains that
although the weaving industry in Varanasi is largely split
between Hindus and Muslims, with the Hindus mainly traders and the Muslims weavers, there is a small coterie of
lower-caste Hindus who also work with the handlooms. The
enormous surge in mechanised Chinese silk production over
the last years has hit these lower-level weavers particularly
hard. While Haaji and his family concentrate on a quality so
high that not even machines can match it, the poor handloom weavers are producing simple cloth in a way that is
effectively in direct competition with industrial production.

Starvation, suicide and extreme poverty now afflict this
ancient world, with the result that the plight of the Varanasi
weavers has become a national issue. Many of the major
Western newspapers have carried articles in the last few years
citing this horrendous state of affairs, the story making for
highly saleable journalism owing to its picturesque setting,
and to the fact that it points to the larger issues of globalisa-
tion. Man simply cannot outpace the machines, and in any
historical situation where people have been forced to try, the
outcome has been dire.

Zooming through the outskirts of Varanasi, with the irre-
pressible Bahadur chattering at a rate that matches the velocity
of his driving, I find myself leaving the blare of the modernity

that has colonised the city in recent years, for an India of mustard fields and bullock carts. This is a world I'm drawn to, and from which many Indians are anxious to escape. It is insular, restricted and constrained by poverty, but also by the codes of conduct that govern a society evolved on religious lines. We foreigners rarely see the whole picture in such places; I know this too. As outsiders we are free to cross the lines of caste and religion that rule the choices that Indians are able to make. Occasionally this can allow for a clear perspective – in that an outsider may be a less threatening person to tell the whole truth to – but it can also entail the opposite: we may see only the façade rather than the finer details, and cannot decipher the inner meaning of things. This is partly inevitable, I suppose, in such a complex world as the weavers of Varanasi. A Hindu journalist from Delhi told me that he'd felt uncomfortable during his visit to a Muslim weaving quarter of Banaras. 'The Muslim boys did not feel happy speaking to me,' he said. 'I'm from a different class, a big city, and Hindu of course. In Delhi we think India's changing so fast, but after that visit, I saw that some things haven't changed at all.'

With this in mind, I'm interested too by the fact that the Muslim Bahadur feels free to take me to a Hindu village. Especially in a city that has come to symbolise the whole underlying structure of the Hindu faith, I'd wondered how relations would be between the two communities, especially in the weaving industries that have always been historically connected. In response to this question, Bahadur tells me that relations in general are cordial. 'Some people call this relationship like the warp and the weft,' he said. 'Because one cannot have a cloth without both parts. Yes, sometimes there has been some trouble – especially around the subject of Ayodhya – but for the most part we work alongside one another. Many of these fine saris that Muslim weavers make are for the weddings of Hindus. Haaji has made crowns for temple deities in the past, too. We live together, and we respect one another. It is only a few troublemakers who try to stir things up.'

I press him on the issue. His response seems like the kind of thing he is used to telling foreigners, but I know from several sources that there have been serious flare-ups over the previous decade. Few issues of recent years, in fact, have caused so much Hindu–Muslim friction in India as that of Ayodhya. Located in the district of Faizabad, not far from Varanasi, this ancient sacred site is believed to be the birthplace of the Hindu god Rama, as well as that of the first Tirthankar of the Jain religion, Shri Rishabh Dev. Since 1527, however, there has also been an important mosque there, the Babri Masjid, constructed by the first Mogul emperor of India. Hindus have always claimed that the Emperor Babur built this mosque over an existing Hindu temple and, especially during the second half of the twentieth century, Ayodhya became an increasing focus of inter-community dissent. It was in 1992, however, that the friction flared to a serious flashpoint during a political rally, in which 150,000 rioters tore down the mosque. 'They used hammers to knock down the three domes of the mosque,' reported the BBC the following day, 'and then tore at the bricks with their bare hands until the building was totally destroyed.'

At a level crossing Bahadur and I pull over at a convenient chai stand while a long cargo train – Rameswaram–Varanasi Express 14259 – rattles past. We stretch the cramps from our

legs and accept a tea from the gap-toothed chai wallah, while
Bahadur rustles around in his pocket for a crooked cigarette.
The nicotine makes him loquacious and, warily, he begins to
speak.

'I was quite young in 'ninety-two,' he tells me, exhaling
thoughtfully. 'Maybe only ten or something. But I still
remember the terror we felt. Tensions had already started to
build in Banaras for a few years before the destruction. The
BJP had realised that the more they spoke about this issue of
Ayodhya, the more seats they seemed to win. Then they came
up with this plan for a Kar Seva, which is a kind of cleaning
of a historical place, and was of course directed at cleansing
Muslim influences from Ayodhya. In 'ninety-one we actually
had a huge riot here in Beniabagh [an area of Banaras near
Chowk] which resulted in a curfew for several months. There
was a frightening atmosphere here during that time. We felt
any spark could start a war.'

Had he witnessed this riot, I ask, noticing the chai wallah's
son, about the same age Bahadur would have been, grinning
at us from his position behind the stand.

'Not that riot.' He shakes his head. 'But then later that year,
in November, there was a bigger one that I did see. My God.
It was at Kali Puja, when some Hindus let off firecrackers not
far from where I live in Madanpura. They were on their way
to Dashashwamedh Ghat to immerse their idol in the Ganga,
when a firecracker was thrown into the house of a Muslim
person. Somehow after this rumours started spreading, and in
Godowlia the made-up story filtered through that we
Muslims had broken the Kali idol. Three Muslim boys were
dragged from the Sushil cinema and stabbed to death.

Violence immediately spiralled between the communities. Many families lost their sons.'

I spoke to many people during the following months, about what it was like to live in Banaras after the destruction of Ayodhya. All of them remembered fear, and a tinderbox atmosphere hovering over the city. But it is this particular conversation, at the chai stall with Bahadur, that lingers on in my mind. His memory had a keenness to it which perhaps can only come from someone whose mind was youthful – open to everything – when the event unfolded. Usually so jovial and full of banter, his voice took on a haunted tone in the retelling, so that I could see he thought of those dark days still, replayed them in his mind as he went about his business in the holy city.

'After the destruction of the Masjid, the area we call Lohta was the worst hit,' he tells me. 'Huge crowds tore through there leaving twenty or thirty people killed, houses were burnt to the ground; you could see the black smoke for miles. The army was sent into the city, especially around the area of Kashi Vishwanath Mandir, because it was supposed that Muslims would try to retaliate in some way for what had happened. In some parts of the city, despite the efforts of the police, the two communities advanced on one another throwing stones and glass. All the Hindus were shouting "Hara Hara Mahadev", and the Muslims "Allahu Akbar". My father said it was the most frightened he had been since Partition.'

Bahadur drains the last of his tea and stares into the bottom of the glass. 'Recently, I have studied these events actually to try and understand what happened. Back then I was just a boy, and the fear overwhelmed everything. But now I feel it's important to really see things clearly.'

'Can one ever really understand that kind of violence?' I wonder aloud.

Bahadur stares at me. 'I feel that I do understand this. Both communities were so wounded by Ayodhya. It was a terrible thing for India. Both sides felt personally attacked, personally insulted. When a man feels like this he may pick up a knife first, and think second.'

We drive on in silence for a while, both of us mulling over what has been said. On the edge of the Hindu village, the road ends entirely and, leaving the rickshaw, we continue on foot down a rutted track. The immense silence of the Indian countryside surrounds us. Everywhere there are bright primary colours: marigolds, poppies, blue sky; in a tree, a green barbet, red-beaked, with a streaked brown head, its plumage a luminescent flash.

After a small field of chillies comes a cluster of dwellings: uncomplicated structures made from mud bricks. A gangly dog with a black ring around one eye lopes forward to meet us, and behind him I notice chickens, two goat kids, a buffalo tethered by a coir rope. Nothing is extraneous here: the ground swept clean, the chilli field carefully fenced by thorn branches. And the villagers, when they emerge, seem to share this impression of being pared back to the essentials. They are lean, neatly kept, there is a solemnity in their eyes and a little sadness. Passing an open door, I glance inside one of their houses. Utterly plain, there is a bed, a cow-dung floor, a stool. A technicolour poster of Ganesha provides the only decoration. Classic Indian kitsch, the image shows the Elephant God wearing pink kurta pyjamas and holding a vast bowl of sweets.

We spend some time getting acquainted. Bahadur, it seems, is a well known figure, but the arrival of a *gora*, a white person, in this village is something of a first. Faces of all ages appear from doorways, and soon there is a small crowd gathered round us, blinking with interest under the midday sun. I'm offered a ladle of well water from a chrome bucket. A cow is ceremoniously milked for me and I struggle over a cup of the warm liquid, a privilege, I know, which any of them would have relished. The weavers are fascinated, full of smiles, and I feel the slightly embarrassed honour of a foreigner feted merely because of his difference.

The natural spokesman is a man named Hari, of about forty, who – in accordance with the Indian belief in moustaches as a sign of virility – sports a fine example. It gives his face a slightly authoritarian look, tempered by squinting eyes. The villagers lean in when he speaks, nodding from time to time as he describes the tribulations of their lives.

'We are about three hundred people in this village,' he tells me, when I find some respite from my dairy consumption. 'All of us are related in some way or another. Ten years ago there were many more here, and all would have been employed in some way by weaving. That is our traditional occupation. But in these last years, a crisis has come to this business in India. Now we struggle to find enough work.'

It is a story I have read many times. Beginning in the 1980s with Rajiv Gandhi's 'New Textile Policy', the whole economic thrust of weaving in India had shifted towards productivity rather than employment. Technology-intensive mills rapidly overtook the traditional handloom sector, a move that hit Varanasi harder than anywhere else in the country. Trade liberalisation and the devaluation of the rupee made matters worse still, with the final blow coming from China's boom in silk production during the same decade. By the early 1990s, a catastrophic decline was hitting the ancient weaving sector of the city.

'In my father's day there was too much work here,' says Hari, sweeping his hand across the village landscape. 'We worked hard but it was a fair return on our efforts, we had enough food, and we had a good life. But since the last fifteen years or so, we are barely getting by. Our family has a good relationship with the *gaddidar* [literally cushion or pillow, but meaning middleman], so that, when times are tough, we can be lent money to tide us through, set against future employment. Without this, we would surely starve.'

Hari's wife interjects angrily, adding – from what I can gather – that although the *gaddidar* offers this service, he charges a hefty rate of interest for doing so, more than 10 per cent.

Hari acknowledges the point. 'He may take his interest,' he says, 'but without this option the crows would pick our bones clean. In other parts of the city – Sareyan, Bazardiha, Lohta – many people have died. Some people have not even been able to feed their children. Others' – and here his face looks ashen – 'have killed themselves because they could see no hope any more.

'Some men here – myself included – have taken jobs on construction sites, working with lumber, or carrying soil. This work is very hard for us, and it ruins our hands for weaving, but we make more money this way, and we can look our families in the eyes. Some of the women do sari cutting also, or take jobs as domestic workers for some of the Brahmin families. By these methods we are putting food on our plates.'

I ask about the economics of weaving as it is continued in the city. There are looms clacking in several of the houses, I notice, so there is obviously some work going on.

'One sari may take ten to fifteen days,' Hari says, 'and there are four people involved in this work. At the end of this we may expect around eight hundred rupees.'

I do a quick calculation. Assuming it takes ten days, that is eighty rupees, or approximately £1, per day, split between four people. This is far below the poverty line and, with the increased food prices in India of recent years, not enough for even the most basic of needs. I feel a sudden hollowness in my stomach at the plight of these people, and the rhythm of the loom – previously such a romantic sound to my ears – takes on a haranguing quality. The global economics are largely beyond my grasp, but the basic fact of mechanisation replacing artisanal labour is one I can understand. These weavers are working in a fashion little changed since the time of the Buddha. I think of the American folk hero, John Henry, who raced against a steam-powered hammer and won, only to die in victory with his hammer in his hand. These weavers can never outpace a machine loom, and perhaps they lack the skills or the contacts to follow Haaji's family's lead in competing on quality instead.

'Do you feel sad,' I ask Hari, 'when you have to do building work instead of working at your loom? After all, weaving is your family heritage, and important for the city of Banaras.'

He shakes his head and traces a forefinger, absent-mindedly, over a jagged scar on the back of his hand. 'Mahadev, I feel no sorrow about this,' he says. 'Why should I feel loyalty to something that has not provided for my family? Why should I feel pride for something that has made our lives so difficult? No,' – his mouth sets into a hard, flat line – 'I just want to survive, and I want my family and village to survive, and I want my children to have some opportunity other than this. If the tradition is important for Banaras, they should make some provision for our survival. If not, both we and the tradition will simply disappear.'

The City of Ten Thousand Widows

> In childhood a female must be subject to her father,
> in youth to her husband, when her lord is dead to
> her sons: a woman must never be independent . . .
>   – G. Bühler, *The Laws of Manu*

'When the world becomes too much there is always Banaras,'
said a stranger to me one day. I was sitting on a corner of the
main ghat, Dashashwamedh, observing an old lady whose
extreme frailty made me wonder whether she would even
survive the night. Thronged with pilgrims and noisy as a foot-
ball stadium, the ghat was its usual kaleidoscope of colour and
form, but for now I was seeing none of it: my eyes were locked
on the widow, whose situation seemed grave. Whether through
extreme old age or infirmity – it was hard to tell – she had the
mesmeric stillness of someone very close to death. Before her,
a dented begging bowl had accrued seven rupees in alms, as
well as two Britannia biscuits which I suspected she would
lose to monkeys or goats unless she ate them fairly rapidly.

    I turned to nod assent to the stranger. His was the kind of
observation one grows used to here, a place where metaphysics

and mundanity find easy company, a city of armchair philoso-
phers and tea-stand saints. He was explaining the city to me.
But for once I was tongue-tied. With her watery cataracted
eyes, set deeply in a raven-like face, the old woman crouched
in a bundle of rags, scarcely aware of my presence. Perplexed
by those quandaries that India provokes like nowhere else,
I wondered yet again about the line between help and inter-
ference, and what the responsibilities of a visitor in a strange
land should be. When I turned to ask the stranger his opinion
on these matters he had gone, vanished into the teeming
crowd.

Returning next day, I looked for the old lady in the same
spot, but there was no sign of her. Finally I asked one of the
other beggars if he knew what had befallen her. The man
looked up at me with penetratingly blue eyes, then simply
pointed his finger up to the skies. She was gone.

Upon arriving in Varanasi, I had noticed at once the numbers
of these women who populate the verges. Usually found
outside the temples and Muslim dargahs (a Sufi shrine), most
of them wearing widow's white, they appear part of the fabric
of the city. Unlike most of the beggars, whose entreaties range
from plaintive to outright badgering, they rarely speak, lost in
grief perhaps, or surrendering to the will of God. It was
impossible not to see in their numbers some manifestation of
the city's mythology, for they had come here to die, thrown
into Varanasi's arms by a cruel world that offered no other
place for them. I found them, in turn, distressing and fascinating. There was a way they held themselves. There was a
remoteness to their gaze, an emptiness of purpose, that seemed

particularly remarkable when almost everyone else in this city was moving, racing in one direction or another with purposes too many to count. But the widows were still, for they had nowhere to go and nothing to accomplish. They stood, or sat, at the road's end, waiting only for the eternal to strike them.

At BHU, I meet Atma, a Ph.D. student constructing a thesis on the plight of widows in North India. He is three years into the project and lost in a sea of statistics. Like a cross-Channel swimmer beginning to doubt the existence of the further shore, his work is threatening to drown him. Discussion with me, therefore, offers him a welcome break from the daily grind, as well as a chance to reconnect with the actual situation which has prompted his study in the first place. 'Are you writing a guidebook?' he asks. 'Trust me, no one wants to read about this . . .'

I'm trying to understand the city, I explain, via certain broad themes. At the heart of it all, a city that promises salvation. Running from that, certain threads exploring how the city's heart beats, what is its dream life, the fuel it runs on.

'Well, money!' says Atma flatly, and with a cynicism I will come to see as intrinsic to his character. 'That's the first thing. The main thing also.' He takes a swig of his Thums Up Cola, reaching in his pockets for a crumpled cigarette. 'People come here to see religion and yes, down by the ghats, this is what you see. But that's just a small part of the city. Away from the river things get a lot simpler and a lot uglier. People want money and they'll do anything to get it. Everyone is trading, bartering, angling and haggling. It's damn tough here. There's too much corruption, too little work. The city lacks the opportunities of Delhi or Mumbai, it's not really set up for international tourism, it's not got much to offer all these young people. Except the university of course.' He waves a hand to take in the bucolic greenery of the university campus, which offers a stark contrast to the anarchy beyond. 'BHU is one of the country's best schools, but people study here with the expectation of leaving.'

'You're cynical,' I say. 'But you don't believe this city is quite as generic as all that.'

He shrugs. 'There are things about it that are unique, yes. But I can't believe in the crap they teach us at school any more. I mean, what's the point in religion unless it makes you behave like a decent human being? What's the point in any kind of belief unless it makes you look after your fellow man and stop trying to *cheat* everyone you meet? When you live here, and especially doing the kind of work I do, one comes to see the worst in people more often than not. Throw away your bloody Vedas, I want to say. Get real!'

I like Atma. I had expected someone cerebral, but he is grounded and at home in the world. With his two wings of black hair, neatly parted in the middle, he is the clean-cut eldest son of a middle-class family, yet his appearance belies a street-savvy swagger he's picked up from several years of fairly tough field research in Banaras and Vrindavan. He has his eyes open to the worst in life, I feel at once, and yet the cynicism conceals a soft heart.

'Actually anthropologists love to paint Banaras with all these grand themes,' he continues. 'People love stories. But it's also just a town that happens to have this long-standing religious tradition. Most people are just trying to pay their bills,

send their kids to a good school, or whatever. Most of it is
absolutely humdrum. It's a dirty machine on its last legs. But
one thing I will say is that human nature is on *full* display
here.' He nods emphatically, cupping a hand to strike his
match. 'You will not find any place where you can see
everything so clearly, so openly. You can see people *dying* in
the streets, you can see people burning their bodies, you can
see people reaching for Ganga like she will cure them of all
the problems of the world.' He exhales forcefully, a long
stream pushing out into the hot sunlight. 'They'll be waiting
a long time for that, *yaar!*'

I keep my ear to the ground over the weeks to come for
information about the widows here. What are their numbers?
Their condition? And who can they turn to once they arrive
in the city for support? I watch the affecting film *Water*, by
Deepa Mehta, which depicts the plight of widows in Varanasi
shortly before the Second World War, while India was still
under British rule. Mehta had originally tried to film in
Varanasi itself, Atma tells me, but was forced to relocate to Sri
Lanka after several thousand angry protesters stormed the
ghats: one particular strand of the plot involves a young
widow forced into prostitution.

'Nowhere on earth will you find people so ready to defend
any slur as the Indians,' he says, with a chuckle. 'Indians will
take to the streets over *anything*, their egos are tender as the
eggshells of a newborn chick! And *Water* provoked one of the
biggest shit storms in recent years in daring to depict the situation of widows as it *might* have occurred half a century ago!
One fellow, a member of Shiva Sena, I think, offered to commit

ritual suicide owing to the slur Mehta was offering on the
Hindu faith! He said he would drown himself in the river like
a holy man. Ha ha, what a joke! The BJP sent people here, and
the VHU [Vishva Hindu Parishad, the World Hindu Council],
it was total chaos I tell you. And why? Were these vigilantes
claiming Hinduism does *not* classify widows as unclean? Were
they claiming theirs is a virtuous faith when it comes to the
well-being of widows? On these fronts they were totally quiet.
Of *course* they were, because they don't have a leg to stand on.
They just wanted to parade through the streets burning effigies
of Deepa Mehta, because they felt affronted, they felt that some
core set of their values was being held up to negative scrutiny.
And perhaps they were a little bored that day.'

Reading a draft of Atma's thesis, I learn more about the
sociological context of Indian widows, of whom there are an
estimated 40 million today, or 10 per cent of the female population. Traditionally, widows have three choices: to marry
their husband's younger brother, to commit sati, or to commit
to a life of sexual renunciation on the margins of society.
Forbidden to wear colours, use henna or turmeric on their
skin, and certainly to remarry, they are expected to sleep on
the ground, to shave the hair from their heads, to fast regularly and pray for their departed husbands. Although sati is
extremely rare these days, many of the practices remain, especially in traditional settings such as Banaras. How have such
rigid codes evolved, I ask Atma. How has the status of widows
descended to such lows?

'Well this has been a core part of my research actually,' he says.
'Trying to look back to the origins of Brahmanical Hinduism
and really understand this. Why do Indians treat their widows so

poorly? It's almost as if they are afraid of them, to treat them like this. There is a Turkish social anthropologist, Nur Yalman, who has done some fascinating work on this subject. He talks about this Brahmanical obsession with the notion of maintaining the purity of their caste. Now go back five thousand years or so and imagine a small tribal group who are living in a somewhat hostile environment. The more they can close the structure of their society, the safer they feel. So they try to preserve their land, their women, and mainly this sense of special purity which they feel they possess. We are talking about caste here, the very origins of caste. And what lies at the very core of caste purity but *women*? Women are the life-givers, the ones who continue the line for the next generation. So it is through *them* that the men try to exert control, it is upon *them* that the men place stricture after stricture to prevent them from polluting their bloodline. So all of this comes from men who put it onto their women, purely out of fear.'

'But how do widows play in to this?' I ask.

'Well a widow is most likely no longer a virgin! Can you imagine the risk! She is a sexually mature woman who, when the husband has died, is now in a position to have another relationship, perhaps bear children again. Look at the way they used to force very young girls, children even, into arranged marriages. Why was this? Because they would try to take the females *completely* out of the loop of having any opportunity to pollute caste. Their marriages would be arranged for them, and then if they became widows they were expected to be sexually abstinent. This is all to prevent the ultimate taboo in Hindu society which is *varna sankara*, or caste miscegenation. Let me quote to you from the *Gita*:

Dosair etaih kula-ghnaanam
Varna-sankara-karakaih
Utsaadyante jaati-dharmaah
Kula-dharmaash ca shashvataah

This means, basically: "By the inappropriate actions of those
who destroy the family tradition and thus give rise to inter-
mixed children, all kinds of community projects and family
activities are destroyed."'

'Sounds like they wouldn't have liked the hippies!' I say
facetiously.

Atma cackles. 'That is great! Because the hippie movement
basically was a generation who were sick of the old structures.
They wanted to be free of it all! And what were the Brahmins
terrified of more than anything, but just that: people who might
step outside these boundaries! They were trying desperately to
keep themselves safe by living within rules and regulations. So
their idea of a society that transgressed from that was basically
hell! Arjuna even says something like this in the *Gita*.'

'So how does that leave widows today?'

'These women exemplify the paradox of modern India,'
says Atma. 'That is why I chose this subject for my thesis,
because all other subjects about our India are contained within
it. Widows are trapped between tradition and modernity,
between a way of life stretching back probably to the Vedas
and an increasingly Westernised, cosmopolitan existence. How
can these two modes of living possibly meet? They are oil and
water. What we have here is a clash of civilisations, because
those who believe in so-called morality feel that they may as
well not go on living if they give that up. But those coming up

in the new India look at the older people who've lived that way all their lives and we say, "Well, you don't look so happy. Why should I follow your path if it's made you so bitter?"'

Several weeks later, I make my way to Asha Bhavan, a widows' home in Banaras funded by a Dutch charity, where a fraction of the estimated five to ten thousand widows of the city are finding shelter. As it's located on the road to Sarnath, the journey takes me through the heart of the city: onto Sanskrit University Road, then Premchand Road, named after one of Varanasi's most esteemed literary sons, then Gautam Buddha Rajpath Road. As usual I baulk at the incessant honking of horns, the burning dust, the stench of exhaust that stings the eyes, and as usual I smile, because somehow all this anarchy functions, indeed there's a kind of poetry to it. As the rickshaw spins by, I see a melon vendor slicing open a ripe fruit and carving a flower into the surface of one yellow half. Further on there are monkeys tightrope-walking electrical cable, a Muslim butcher's filled with hundreds of caged chickens, several of which are being beheaded with a long curved blade as we pass, so that long ribbons of blood trickle down onto the street.

The traffic slows to a crawl and, while the rickshaw-wallah jumps out to see what's causing the delay I examine a hotchpotch of roadside tents made from cheap canvas, from which a cook fire burning the cheapest coal exudes a toxic smoke. Here the families and dust-covered infants of local construction workers live in a kind of medieval squalor, caught between the country and the city, belonging now to neither. A small child with wild-man hair watches me with open curiosity, holding up a hand to wave as the lights change to green.

Asha Bhavan, or 'House of Hope', is an unobtrusive modern building of limewashed concrete, set down a nondescript street. Away from the main drag, and now outside of the city's heart, it's possible to hear the birds once again, and to breathe the hot, clear air of early summer. Two goats on long coir leashes nibble leaves from the roadside. Run by a Christian organisation, Asha Bhavan was set up in response to God's call to care for widows in James 1:27. Whilst their endeavour is laudable, and the building that greets me clean and welcoming, I'm struck by the irony of a situation in which one religion persecutes widows on the basis of scripture, and another saves them. Nevertheless I'm touched by the calm, restful environment I find myself entering, where some twenty-five women of various ages have found refuge. They are just beginning, they tell me, and plan to house several times these numbers when they have the infrastructure in place.

Elsa, a Dutch volunteer, leads me around the home. Everywhere there are women in simple white cotton saris, mostly occupied in cleaning, preparing food or baking bread, which the organisation sells to hotels around the city. The women look at me with mixed reactions: curiosity, a touch of unease, sometimes total indifference. Some of them are in relative good health, quite active and talking animatedly. Others lie as if half dead, supine on their metal beds, staring at the ceiling with vacant eyes. It's a much more uplifting scene than the widows' home depicted in *Water*, yet the women bear the same air of being exiles, outsiders in a society that has all kinds of ideas about who they are and what they represent.

'Many of these women are so close to death when we find them,' Elsa tells me, 'that it may take a long period before they are prepared to re-enter the world. And some of them simply will not engage with reality. They are completely broken. They ask for poison, or that we throw them into the Ganga.'

We come to an old lady with the traditional shaven scalp expected of widows here. Pure white, it crowns a face so deeply wrinkled I can scarcely see her eyes, which are half-closed, as if she is afraid to fully confront the world. I can hear the short, uneven rasp of her breath.

'When we found her she was filthy, without even proper clothes. She had a petticoat, that was all. We took her to a hospital but they wouldn't take her.'

I ask why not.

'Well, they said we don't have a bed. Which was palpably not true. There is something inauspicious about widows here, you see. People don't want to touch them. We think she is Bihari, but we haven't been able to find out yet. The last few days she just hasn't been able to speak. You can see her bones, you know. And she's not the only one. This is common. So we don't know yet. We don't know if she will make it.'

'Who are the youngest widows you have here?'

'Well, Savithri must now be late twenties. Her son is eleven, and she had him when she was fifteen, I believe. Her husband was shot. Now she works here in the widows' home. You know life is not worth much here. Our own landlord is a widow because her husband was shot. There is one little boy you may see about these parts, he is living with his grand-mother only because his parents were shot. And there are no social services here to step in when these things happen. There are the streets. They claim everyone and, if you can stay alive, they become your home.'

I ask if, over the years, Elsa feels she's come any closer to some cultural understanding of the reasons for this kind of behaviour.

She shrugs. 'It starts from birth. If you're a girl you're worth nothing. Even before birth. If you're a girl, they abort you. In the whole culture the girls just mean nothing. They just say to these children: "You should have been a boy." One of our staff members, she has two teenage girls and she was pregnant again. Well there was some kind of medical issue and as soon as the baby girl was born they just threw her on the floor and said you don't have a child. They were letting it die. So another one of our girls here, who was assisting at the birth, she said: "Look, for God's sake just give her some oxygen!" Under pressure they did, and actually now she is OK, she has some medical issues but she is surviving and she can have a life. But the way they behaved was just disgusting. If it had been the longed-for boy they would simply have moved heaven and earth to give it a chance. The women here are very strong, they can be great leaders, but they're just not getting the chance.'

I ask what's so preferable about having a boy.

'Well at the risk of sounding very cynical I would say it comes down a lot to money. The whole thing boils down to dowry. We don't want a girl because we will have to pay a dowry. So she represents a burden to them. On the other hand, a boy will *bring* us a dowry! So, in purely financial terms the odds are very much stacked against girls.'

I mention a case I've just seen in the Banaras edition of the *Times of India* about a dowry burning, a fate that a wife may suffer when her husband or his family feel they have had a bad deal with her dowry, or could obtain a better one.

Elsa nods. 'Yes, I saw that. Well, that is another manifestation of what's going on. Dowries bring so much money
people want a second chance to get one. Shortly after we
moved here, our neighbours opposite us killed their daughter-
in-law. They wanted to make their house bigger, so they were
demanding more and more and more money to do this from
the wife's parents. But when they didn't have any more to
give they hanged her. The mother-in-law went to the
women's jail here in Chaukhaghat. But she was out in three
months. For premeditated murder! And this was not on bail,
mind you, this was full release. Rupees passed behind the
scenes and the case was simply quashed. That is what happens
here. If you are poor, you won't get justice.'

Tea is brought, and we sit, cradling the scalding metal cups.
Wisps of steam rise in the still air. Wondering aloud, I ask Elsa
if some of the women don't start to believe in this prejudice
after a time, if centuries of oppression make them feel that
perhaps they really are worthless.

'You know,' she tells me, 'when we first started Asha Bhavan,
our intention was to train up the women and have them run
this place. Because we can't be here all the time, so we wanted
it to be self-sustaining. But when we started asking some of
them about taking some responsibility, they all of them –
without exception – said: "Oh no, I can't do anything." So,
knowing they are all fantastic cooks, we started the bakery,
because that was something they were comfortable with, that
was a domain in which they did have a sense of their own
accomplishment. Outside of that, their confidence is non-
existent. I remember the first lady we taught how to ride a
bicycle. We spent a whole summer teaching her. Finally, when

she was proficient, we suggested she leave the precinct and ride the bike somewhere. But she refused. She said what will people say when *I* ride the bicycle? What will they *think* of me? You see they're afraid. A woman shouldn't leave the house, a woman shouldn't be independent. But now she has begun to set an example, so some of the other women are interested to learn.'

A klaxon screams some distance away on the main road. I hear echoes of women chanting in the yard. In the stillness, I sit beside the bed of a Bengali lady. She is in her eighties, and her body has shrunk now to almost nothing. Her name is Bhagwanti Mazumda. She was found outside the train station, Elsa tells me, with a fractured arm. When they weighed her, she was only 27 kilos, the average weight of a nine-year-old. She has a broken tooth, thin birdlike arms. Despite this, her eyes gleam with life. Bhagwanti's is the face I will most remember from this day, with its transparent blue eyes of one who has left everything behind.

'I came to this city alone,' Bhagwanti says, tilting her head. 'And I will be going alone. Everyone I know is dead now, my parents, brothers and sisters. I am waiting to join Him. I lived in a very quiet place a long way from here in West Bengal. We had no electricity, no cars, none of those things. One day some Naxalites (a communist guerrilla movement) came from the fields and attacked us. Those men took everything from me, they burned the village to the ground and many people lost their lives. After that I had nothing left, so I said I will go Banaras.'

What can she tell me about this city, I ask.

'For all the things that have happened I am glad at least to be ending my life here in Varanasi,' she says, jabbing her childlike finger emphatically. 'If this body can be burned on the ghats by Ma Ganga, I am sure to attain Shivalok [the realm of Shiva] here. At this point I even feel forgiveness for those men who burned my village. Perhaps this city has made me feel like that.'

Harmony, Rhythm and Order

> In the East, music has been always accepted as a spiritual
> phenomenon. If your music cannot create silence
> in the people who are listening, it is not music.
> – Osho, *The Great Pilgrimage from Here to Here*

A folk saying from these parts warns: 'Beware the four perils
of Kashi: widows, bulls, steps and holy men.' On this particular morning, I'd encountered all four and it was barely 6 a.m.
First, our neighbourhood bull had accosted me as I tried to
step past him through a particularly narrow intersection,
resulting in my lurching suddenly backwards into a cowpat to
avoid being gored. Soon after, outside a crumbling temple, a
line of widows held up their alms bowls and a succession of
careworn faces entreated me to sponsor them breakfast. Next
there'd been a regiment of Naga sadhus, the most fearsome of
the holy men, en route for their morning ablutions in the
Ganga, chanting *Har Har Mahadev*, Glory to Shiva, lustily as
they approached the water. Finally I had tackled been faced
with a vertiginous flight of several hundred steps leading
from the river ghats upwards into the alleys beyond. Out of

breath, but fully immersed in the current of the city, I looked
for a resting place and spotted a tea stand beneath a vast
banyan tree. The tree looked as old as the city itself; the aerial
roots, characteristic of the species, had grown through brick-
work and concrete, reminding me that this city emerged out
of forest and would, perhaps, return to it one day.

Exploring in the early mornings like this made sense on so
many levels. It was like creeping round the belly of a dragon
during its final hours of sleep, treading gently for fear of
waking the beast. The great river, serene and windless, was an
empty mirror that offered the Banarasis a chance to see themselves reflected in a non-human space. These were the hours
for contemplation and sacrament, before the necessary business of the day. Shopkeepers swept the grime from their
forecourts, barbers scraped away the encroaching stubble, the
river washed away the sins of the previous day. At this hour,
too, it was possible to hear one of the most hallowed sounds
of the ancient world: the Vedic recitation that is one of India's
greatest cultural legacies. On this particular day, I was no
more than two sips into my tea before I heard a sudden wave
of chanting from the building beside us, announcing that
here were young Brahmin boys reciting the most sacred syllables of the Hindu canon. I sat there hypnotised – forgotten
tea expelling wisps of steam – while the sheer power of this
chanting washed over me. It was as if I'd stumbled on a choir
practice inside the Vatican, an art form performed at the heart
of its own cultural setting. This chanting can be heard all over
Varanasi; it is the beating heart of the Hindu faith.

If one has never heard traditional Vedic chanting, it is difficult to convey either what it sounds like, or the power of it.

It is said that the rishis – forest sages – were the original tran-
scribers of a series of sacred or cosmic sounds or, as one *pujari*
explained to me, 'the breath of God himself'. In essence these
primordial earth hymns represent some of our earliest contact
with the ancient world and its conceptions of the divine. They
contain accounts of the origin of the world, hymns to various
gods and fragments of narrative depicting a mobile, semi-
nomadic culture, with horse-drawn chariots, oxen-drawn
wagons and metal weapons. Pre-dating the advent of alphabetic
writing in India by several centuries, these chants were considered the ultimate in sacred knowledge, and a tremendous energy
went into transferring this knowledge to the next generation.

Sitting there on an old slat of wood by the tea stand, I was
hearing a tradition that went back to the time of Homer. That
in itself was remarkable, but more than that, the sounds themselves had a profound effect on me: the rhythmic slightly
atonal chants, perfectly in unison, pouring out in the dawn. I
let them wash over me, sensing the power in them, and it was
as if muscles long accustomed to clenching were coaxed open.
I didn't know what they meant but, on some level, that was
the point. The vibrations themselves were the message. Even
today, priests are called upon to chant these mantras for the
sick and dying, and in former times the chants were employed
to bring rain, or to cleanse an environment of negativity.

A few weeks later, I return to discuss the art of chanting the
Vedic scriptures with the priest, Prakash, who has agreed to
explain the fundamentals to me. Vedic chanting seems somehow
elemental to the city: I want to know more about its purpose.
Prakash is, in some senses, the epitome of one aspect of the city:

his saintly white robes, worn *mala* – bead necklace – and serene countenance bestow an otherworldly air. Everything about him is measured and precise and, as he ushers me to a small room adjoining the temple, I find myself drawn immediately into the stillness and order of his world. As the resident guru (literally teacher) of some twenty students, his is a life based on ancient principles of hierarchy, ceremony and discipline.

'Should I call you Pandit?' I ask, aware of the importance placed in these parts on correct recognition of rank.

'I am a Pandit,' he says, a swift smile exposing even white teeth. 'Though most of the students call me "Acharya", which has the connotation of teacher. But actually, perhaps we can begin our discussion there. If you are asking about our tradition of the Vedas, then you should also know that the word Pandit is given to one who has memorised a significant proportion of the Vedic scriptures. For us this is the most important aspect of our training.'

'I heard some of your students the other day,' I tell him. 'Already they were producing an extraordinary sound. I understand they spend a large proportion of their youth learning these chants by heart.'

'Powerful discipline is required,' he acknowledges, 'to really learn the needful. It takes around six years' initial work to learn the twenty thousand verses of the Vedic Samhitas. But their task is far more complex than merely memorising words. These mantras are the purest sacred vibrations, mystic sounds. There is a meaning, yes, but we believe just to experience that sound has a healing power. They can heal sickness, cause rains to come during a time of drought. So it is paramount that these boys learn the correct way, without one error. Every syllable must be precise! We Brahmins see ourselves as the custodians of this knowledge – it is our dharma to preserve it for the next generations. Full training takes twenty-five years actually. And this has been going on, we believe, for between five and ten thousand years.'

With my mind still boggling at the notion of 20,000 verses, I ask Prakash how such a feat is possible. Brahmins, I know, have evolved some of the most complex methods of rote learning in the world.

'This is an incredibly complex subject,' he says, adjusting his pristine robes carefully around his shoulder. 'Scientists have often studied our methods to see how such a feat is possible. We use mudras: sacred positioning of the hands to assist the memory. That is one way. But the main thing is dedication, surrender to God. One must give one's life to this study, without hope of reward. Some students find it harder than others, but eventually, with true persistence, the sheer power of repetition starts to pay off.

'Also we use *patha*s, which are recitation styles. The students memorise the same chants in multiple ways, first by continuous recitation, then word by word, then broken up into pieces, and next in what we call *karma patha*, in which words are arranged in an AB, BC, CD fashion. There are others too, but you see the genius of this very comprehensive method is that it allows for continual comparison. We are continually checking the pronunciation of each syllable, the notes, the points of emphasis, the continuity, the pauses or punctuation. Since the goal of the tradition is to preserve this knowledge, these *patha*s allow us to see the same thing from different angles, thereby keeping it perfectly intact.'

'What do you feel is the future of this ancient tradition?' I
ask Prakash. 'Surely, as Banaras keeps getting more modern,
there may be fewer students willing to commit to such a
rigorous training?'

Prakash looks thoughtful. 'It is true that fewer families now
send their boys for this instruction than in my father's time.
In the old days, it was truly the greatest honour for one's boy
to become a priest. Now they are dreaming of America in the
same manner: we priests are not immune to the changes India
is undergoing. But when you think how long this tradition
has lasted, so many thousands of years, you can also see that
we humans can never fix our view at a point in time and
understand God's will. We must simply continue preserving
this sacred knowledge as best we can, with an open heart.
Everything else is none of our business.'

As well as being the home of Vedic chanting, which uses tone
in its most primal form, Varanasi has long been one of the
centres of north Indian classical music, with students from all
over India coming here to learn their craft. Just as the young
Brahmins seek out gurus like Prakash from whom to ask
guidance and the transmission of sacred knowledge, musicians in India must also apprentice themselves for sometimes
many years to a master. Known as the *guru shishya* tradition,
this thread of Indian culture dates back into Vedic times, in
which a guru was regarded as the metaphysical father of his
disciple, esteemed higher even than biological parents. Such
profound reverence for one's teacher persists today, as does
the notion that musical skill represents far more than a pleasing artistic accomplishment. Like everything in India, and

especially Varanasi, music is understood as holy, a divine gift to mankind. *Raag*, in the Sanskrit dictionary, is defined as 'the act of colouring or dyeing', meaning that the ragas, the melodies of north Indian classical music, are recognised as having a direct influence on human emotions: it is our minds which are coloured by a particular mood. Musicians are therefore far more than mere performers; they are conjurors of heavenly energy, able to influence both our frame of mind and our attunement to the sacred. At their highest evolution, musicians are seen as figures of literally priestly reverence.

Banaras produced two musicians during the twentieth century who came to exemplify these qualities. The first, Ravi Shankar, was born in the city, though he came to fame abroad and returned little in subsequent years. The second, the late Bismillah Khan, a virtuoso of the shehnai, not only spent most of his life within the city precincts: he loved it to a degree that his name has become for ever linked with Banaras, spoken of with the greatest affection by Hindus and Muslims alike.

His story was recounted to me often during my time in the city, but most memorably one sultry morning in February, while I sat on the flat roof of a local musician's house, reclining in a hammock. Sameer was from Allahabad, but had moved to Varanasi in his early twenties to learn sitar. A decade later, and supported by his family's moderate wealth, he inhabited a strange middle ground that allowed him to move between the tight-knit world of the old Banarasi families and the tie-dye and restless spirituality of the Western backpacker crowd, many of whom lent authenticity to their presence in the city through adherence to various artistic or yogic disciplines. Sameer was something of a novelty to me, in terms of the Indians of my acquaintance. Money had freed him from the relentless pursuit of material security towards which so many of his countrymen were helplessly compelled. His parents, for whom such freedom had come hard-earned, were appalled by this fact, though marginally placated considering that he was putting his energies into classical music and had chosen to live in India's holy city. After I overheard Sameer speaking with some eloquence at Kashi chai stand, a popular Assi Ghat hangout, we'd become friends. He was my way in, I realised, to the musical life of the city. His knowledge and contacts could give me access to an inner world generally denied to outsiders. Added to which he was excellent company, a font of anecdotes, and with a near-encyclopaedic knowledge of the city's music scene.

On this particular morning his rooftop – little more than a concrete space adorned with a few mats, an overflowing ashtray and a wilted Naga chilli plant – has already seen a steady string of visitors in the half-hour since my arrival. Sameer sits cradling his antique sitar, elaborating his sentences with the occasional flurry of notes. His landlady brings *tulasi* tea, and a rug that she hangs in the sun to dry, then beats with a rod of bamboo so that dense clouds of saffron-coloured dust cover the sun. Next comes a young Belgian couple who, like Sameer, are in Varanasi to study music. They bring with them a clay chillum pipe and a sizeable quantity of Kasol charas which they proceed to smoke hungrily, before vanishing to a local cafe in search of banana pancakes. I suspect little musical study will occur today.

Finally comes the household's youngest son, a six-year-old bearing a five-rupee kite of pink and purple crêpe. It's the school holidays and he finds himself with time to kill. He is portly, with the round jowls of a child regularly placated with sweets. After trying to fly it in the muggy air for a few minutes, he retreats downstairs with a mournful expression on his chubby face. 'Come back evening time,' calls Sameer consolingly after him. 'Maybe there will be some breeze!'

When the visitors have dispersed we turn to the real purpose of my visit, which is a discussion of the music scene in the city, none of which, in Sameer's view, can be touched upon without referring to the great Bismillah Khan. Khan is his hero and his inspiration: it was *The Call of the Shehnai*, a film to which he had provided the soundtrack, that first inspired Sameer to the musician's life.

'Not only can you not discuss music in the city without mentioning Bismillah,' says Sameer animatedly, 'you can hardly discuss the city at all. Banaras is not just a Hindu city, but a city where Hindus and Muslims have lived together harmoniously for hundreds of years. In the twentieth century Bismillah came to really symbolise that relationship, in the way he lived, not just the music he played. He was that great man who retains a total simplicity. He accrued no possessions, hoarded no money.'

Briefly, he recounts the story of Khan's life. As the story goes it was Khan's grandfather, Rasool Baksh Khan, who gave the boy his name. When the old man saw the newborn child he was so delighted he let forth a vociferous exclamation of 'Bismillah!', which means, for Muslims, 'In the name of God, the most Gracious, the Most merciful'. And the legend was born.

By the time he was six, Bismillah was already showing an interest in music. His uncle Ali Bux was the official shehnai player of the Vishwanath temple, and as such was required to play there each morning, noon, evening and night. Bismillah would follow him like a shadow, soaking up every aspect of the ragas. He lived in Benia Bagh, and as his uncle's student, would accompany him each day to the great Hindu temple, pestering his uncle to buy him some *mallaiiyya*, a delicious street snack of whipped cream, saffron and pistachios, en route.

Was it really true, I ask, that devout Muslims worked as professional musicians in Hindu temples? In all the media coverage of conflicts between the two communities, such a fact had fallen between the cracks.

'In Banaras this can happen,' Sameer nods. 'Although they were Muslims, Bismillah's family saw no difference in paying homage to God at the Vishwanath. There is something very illustrative of the city about this. People talk a lot about the fighting, they emphasise division. But they don't mention the many things that work just fine.'

I confess to Sameer I'm still not entirely sure of what the shehnai is, or how it sounds. He rifles through his iPod collection for an appropriate recording and sets it playing. The sound issues forth over the rooftops of the city, immediately familiar to me. It is like an oboe – horn-like, with a nasal, snake-charming overtone. Sameer's elderly neighbour, busy with her washing on a nearby rooftop, turns and looks in our direction at the sound, her face poised in the act of listening.

'You may have heard this at Indian weddings,' Sameer says, 'because its sound is considered auspicious. Like the conch shell, it has a mystical quality. For that reason it is also played at temples. For me it is one of the quintessential sounds of this city.'

The story of Bismillah unfolds. The young boy absorbed the devotional repertoire with ease, but he didn't stop there. He listened to *thumri*, a lyrical Banaras-influenced school of north Indian classical as well as vocal music, and the folk traditions of the surrounding regions of India. In his hands, Sameer explains, the shehnai could no longer be confined to its previous role as merely a festive instrument. Bismillah bought something new to it: an immense subtlety, a tenderness that had the power to convey the deepest pathos. He revolutionised the way the instrument was understood.

'This is not an easy instrument to play, I should tell you,' Sameer informs me. 'I know because I could not play it *at all*, so I turned to the sitar. Mahadev, it is *too* difficult! It has four reeds to begin with! One's breath control has to be incredibly strong just to play a basic tune. To get the melodic variation that Bismillah employed is just so extraordinary that one must conclude, as perhaps he did, that he was an instrument of God. You know, not long ago I was at this *thandai* stand not far from where he used to live, and I got talking to the older *thandai*-wallah, who used to know Bismillah very well. This old guy just started to sob when we got talking about him. "There will never be another like Bismillah," he said. "Some orthodox Muslims, you know, believe music to be a sin, and they say it should not be played. But Bismillah used to say '*Aur haraam karo, aur haraam karo*' – If music be a thing of sin, sin on."'

I heard a lot of music as the months flew by, from impromptu *bhajans*, devotional songs chanted by holy men, to *Qawwali*, Sufi devotional music praising Kabir, and *bol*, the mnemonic syllables used by tabla players to define the rhythmic pattern, and which are themselves a form of music. Not far from my house, a tabla guru offered lessons in the distinctive Banaras style of percussion, and his vociferous teaching style, each tabla note sung aloud, offered a pleasing soundtrack to my passing. Everywhere, the echoes of the traditions perpetuating themselves told me that, despite a rapidly changing India, the heart of Varanasi remained alive and well.

As a centre of performance, however, it seemed that Varanasi's heyday was past. Professor Ananda Krishna, the man who introduced me to the Varanasi cityscapes of James Prinsep, painted evocative descriptions for me of the city as it had once been, ruled by a maharaja in the not too distant past, from whose court a large number of the region's greatest musicians received patronage. One afternoon Professor Krishna described the extraordinary flowering of musical culture that had occurred in India under the Mughals, and its continuation in the royal courts of north India, even after they were supplanted by the British Raj.

'Mughals like Akbar supported vast retinues of musicians, as well as scientists, astrologers and poets,' he told me, sitting in his garden one afternoon to the sound of bulbuls. He had a hoary voice, tiring easily. Nevertheless, it was a privilege to hear him speak. 'As well as these figures, some of the main custodians of this intellectual and artistic culture were the courtesans, who were important figures in the courts of medieval India. Far more than prostitutes, they were schooled in sixty-four different art forms ranging from singing and dancing right through to mineralogy and metallurgy. Courtesans from different cities became famous through the whole kingdom.' He paused to clean his glasses with a crumpled blue handkerchief. 'It was the British in India, however, particularly in the late nineteenth century, who began to frown on these women. An obsession with social purity came in with British missionaries to India and spread throughout the East India Company. Suddenly, this ancient tradition which had encompassed so much more than mere sexual activity was relegated to a sort of moral black hole. Women who had been revered by kings became social pariahs. Unable to pursue their arts due to these social pressures, there became little incentive to maintain artistic standards. In such desperate circumstances, the *tawaifs* had no recourse for survival other than the common prostitution of which they had been accused.'

The mounting heat drove us inside. With its thick walls and stone floors the house was cooler within, but nevertheless I was sweating still, and grateful for a glass of lemon water. We sat on a mattress in the Professor's study. Around the room I noticed copies of his many published books, an ancient statue of Saraswati, goddess of knowledge and the arts, a red plastic analogue telephone. There were spiders' webs, a dated air-conditioning unit, a get well card for the Professor's wife, currently in hospital with a broken leg. This was a house of no great wealth, and where possessions were few, and yet the passions of those who lived here, the sense of a high culture that contained so much of what made life valuable, was palpable in every mote of dust. I felt a sudden sadness for what would pass with this man; it was as if he was a living connection to the city I had been searching for. And yet, even as I sat with him, he grew frailer.

The Professor began to talk of *thumri*, the particular form of Indian classical music for which the city was famous. I saw him, years before, with his eyes gently closed at some evening performance, debonair in a white kurta. His favourite performer, he said, had been a woman named Girija Devi, the daughter of a zamindar (hereditary landowner), who'd shocked her social class by announcing that she wished to pursue a career in music. It was the *thumri* that shocked them most of all, he said. The music had evolved during the eighteenth and nineteenth centuries as a sort of rebellion from *dhrupad*, a formal and austere mode of singing long favoured by the courts of India. *Thumri* was a devotional music generally sung by the *tawaif*, the courtesans, evoking a girl's love for Lord Krishna. Unlike much of traditional Indian classical music, *thumri* allows for playfulness, explained the Professor, and the parallels of divine love found an easy mirror in the human realm. When the courtesans sang of Krishna dancing with the gopis, women cowherds, in the Vrindavan forest, the twinkle in their eye conveyed many meanings for the members of the audience.

'Steeped in tradition, *thumri* finds room for manoeuvre even within such strictures,' the Professor explained. 'This was the music for which Girija displayed a precociousness. Somehow it has become known as "light classical", but this couldn't be further from the truth. It demands prodigious skills in *raagdari* and *layakari* – these are technical aspects, playful modifications of rhythm within the overall structure of the piece. These may sound like fine points, but these things were understood by all of us in those days. Girija was one of the last to learn music in the traditional way here in India. As she and I have grown old, *thumri* has all but vanished, and the city we lived in has become unrecognisable. We are, perhaps, the last who will remember it as it was.' He cleared his throat.

'But to hear Girija in her day was something very special. All those years of training, all that knowledge, all the formality of the tradition, somehow softened in the *thumri*, and in her performances. She made us feel so human, you see, and yet we felt the presence of God.' He shook his head sadly. 'She had a great student you know, called Manju, who became famous in her own right, and who lives in the city still. If you like, I could arrange something?'

And so it is that one Wednesday evening, a month later, I find myself arriving at the gate of the Theosophical Society head-quarters, off the seething Guru Nanak Road. In terms of my own love affair with India, it seems a pleasantly synchronistic moment, for the Theosophical Society, a *fin-de-siècle* spiritual group founded by Helena Blavatsky, had been one of my earliest inspirations to turn East, many years before.

As one would expect from an organisation that had boasted nearly 50,000 members during the 1920s, the headquarters has a faded grandeur about it, and vast well-tended grounds. After negotiating my way past the security guard, I begin to realise just how vast, as the bustle of the polluted city outside recedes to a distant memory. I find myself removed to a more placid realm, in which tall trees and perfectly clipped bushes curve gracefully around sandy paths.

To reach Manju's house, the aged guard gestures, follow this path. How is it possible, I wonder, just a few metres from the anarchic traffic of the main road, to find such pastoral silence? It somehow deepens the expectation the Professor had instilled that Manju Sunduram, considered one of the greatest living exponents of *thumri*, has opted for a spiritual seclusion. She lives, I understand, in the same house that was once occupied by Annie Besant, a close friend of George Bernard Shaw, and who had been instrumental in establishing Jiddu Krishnamurti as one of the leading spiritual figures of the twentieth century. I thought of those revered people walking here, under these same tall trees, in the years before India's independence. Annie Besant had also founded the Home Rule Movement, the first political party in India to have regime-change as its main goal. She was a complicated, remarkable woman, and her protégé, Krishnamurti, one of my greatest influences.

Manju Sunduram meets me at the door. In her sixties, she offers a cerebral though sympathetic demeanour, the face of a librarian or a mother superior. As I sit down inside, I take in the details of her house: refined, full of history, a bookish house, the house of a musician. Her instrument, a sarod, sits gleaming upon a stand. I observe it coolly while a maid brings us tea and puffed rice with spices. We sit quietly for a few moments, sizing one another up. I have that subtle sense of having broken through to the inner circle of the city once more. Incredible tranquillity fills the room, there are dust motes circling in a slender beam of light.

Noticing my gaze Manju smiles, and clasps her fine hands together in her lap. She has an extraordinary presence, a deep inner calm.

'I very rarely perform now,' she says. 'Music has been my path but, at a certain point, one leaves the path behind. Music in the West has a variety of purposes, a variety of functions. Here it has always been used as both a means of touching the divine, and an expression of that essence itself.' She sings a sudden note that sets my spine tingling. 'Sound, you see, is an exact miniature of the cosmic laws. It contains harmony, rhythm and order. So when we study music we are not just learning how to make beautiful music, we are studying these laws. We are moving towards the inner truth of things. That is why Varanasi remains a special place to study music, because here the total picture is understood. One is studying life only.

'Some years back,' she continues, 'some famous musicologists came to India with all kinds of questions. They couldn't understand why we Indians have particular songs for particular times of day, for example. So one of my own teachers said to them: "I would like you to just experience the music and find out for yourselves what it evokes, what imagery." He was a sarod player, and first he played one raga to them for ten minutes, and then a second. The musicologist was quiet for a few moments and then he requested it to be repeated. After this he said: "It's extraordinary, the first raga made me feel that the world was waking up from slumber, from deep sleep. The second piece was when the cattle, after grazing all day, were going back to their pastures when the day ends."'

Manju smiles, her blue eyes twinkling. 'You see, nobody had told that musicologist which raga was which, nor what time they are supposed to be played, but he himself could feel it. He was attuned. This is a window into the nature of our classical music. We are trying to align the vibrations of the notes at that particular moment with the cosmos. And then the beauty of the raga unfolds completely. So harmony is the essence. It is to be in tune with the universal harmony.'

We turn to the nature of the relationship between a pupil and a guru, which seems to be one of the marked differences between Eastern and Western traditions of education. Her own teacher, Girija Devi, is now very aged and confined to a retirement home in Delhi. Manju's memories of her, however, sparkle with fondness and respect.

'Of course it is different!' Manju says. 'Because in the West a teacher is imparting knowledge of a particular skill. Here, that teacher is imparting knowledge of the universe itself, the way to approach life. That's why, for example, the disciples used to live in their guru's house. I'll tell you one thing. When I went to Girija Devi first I was the only child of my parents, and in my family there was no tradition of touching the elders' feet, as is the old custom in India. So it was not that I was very proud or I didn't want to do it, I simply didn't have this custom. But anyway, at fifteen I used to just do namaskar to Girija Devi and then, after some days, she told me: "Look, it's good to touch your guru's feet, it makes you aware that you are in the stage of learning, and when you're learning you have to bend."' Manju pauses to see that I have understood. 'You cannot climb when you are straight, you see. You can climb a steep hill only when you bend a little. So, it doesn't boost the ego of the guru, but it keeps the disciple aware that they are *learning*. So, this was imparted to me and I saw the beauty of it. By stooping down, you see so many things you can't see from a distance. This is learning the truth of life. Not just music. There are so many stages in life when you learn by bending a little. She was teaching me not to resist. Learning life, through music. Girija gave me the truth of life like this, the ultimate knowledge. So the *guru shishya* tradition is not just confined to the subject, be it music, sculpture or whatever. Along with that, the disciple has to be receptive. Girija used to say you have to be very sensitive to nature. Hear the birds singing. Hear the waves when you are on the sea shore. Hear the water rising, the leaves murmuring. Watch how a leaf trembles in the wind then falls. All the phenomena of nature. This will then be reflected in your music. Absorb it, then you can express it. It's not music in particular, but it has everything to do with music. To bring out the wholeness of music. Don't just sing the grammar, the technique of music, this is about something else.'

Leaning over to her sarod, an intricate lute-like instrument with some twenty-five strings, Manju touches one of the strings very gently. It hums very slightly in the still air: just a single note, but enough so that I can sense the whole room shifting. She leans in with her eyes closed.

'Music affects us,' said Manju. 'Who can tell what goes on within a person? Your state of mind might change. Your patterns of behaviour might change. Your outlook, the things which you used to react to, you might not respond to them any more. So you respond to music, and then the analytical side of the brain is not there. The intellectual speculations are not there. It finds its own way. That is the beauty of music. You know when I went to Salzburg for the first time, the director of music there, in the Academy, was kind enough to play the organ in that church for me. For forty minutes he played that, and the tears rolled down my cheeks. What reason could I give for this? When I'm telling you this I feel a lump here. But I don't care to know what it did. It was something good, very positive, full of bliss. I was in ecstasy, with no need of indulging in why. It comes on its own. One has to be sensitive, and receptive to this. Let it come.'

What of *thumri*, I ask, and how Varanasi itself became a centre for the style.

'Have you been here in summer?' she asks. 'May and June? Have you experienced the hot wind we get here? So, the scorching sun, you can't stir out of your house after nine, nine-thirty. The heat can be fatal if you go out if you don't cover yourself properly. After that, the day you hear the clouds gathering in the sky, when you see the thunder, when you see the lightning. Just imagine the state of mind of the farmer who has been waiting for the rain, for the first showers after such scorching heat. Then, the ecstasy, the experience he goes through. When there is the intensity of any emotion you burst out in singing. Where there is no argument for that, when you feel very happy for no reason, you just feel like singing. And when the farmer, his wife and children are a part of the soil, when they see the clouds gathering, they can't help but start to sing. This is the origin of folk music. It's not stylised, but very beautiful. Sensitive compositions, portraying nature. Swings on the branches of mango trees, the young girls singing. And what the showers do, the lady who has a beloved by her side, what her feelings are. And the lady who is waiting for her lover. What she is undergoing. All that is depicted in those songs. And when those songs are sung in the classic mode, stylised, they take the form of a *thumri*. *Thumri* basically has to do with the instinct of love. It is delicate. As somebody rightly said, the melody of a *thumri* enters the heart with felicity and leaves with reluctance. And *thumri* doesn't follow very strict rules of classical ragas, the taboos, the do's and don'ts of classic singing. It starts in a particular raga and it can just follow the flight of imagination, it can change its strength, it can go into another raga. So it's a world of fantasy, with no taboos. All is fair in love and war, no! So, in *thumri*, wherever your emotions take you, you go.'

I'm deeply touched by Manju Sunduram, she has a quietude and charisma that tell me she must have been a mesmerising performer in her day. Looking down I notice, with some embarrassment, that I've dropped several pieces of puffed rice on her immaculate floor. Hers is the kind of house to make one acutely conscious of any imperfection. She smiles as I lean to pick them up – all is forgiven.

'When the urge to perform fades away, then what remains?' I ask her. 'Do you not miss the musician's life?'

Manju interlaces her fine fingers together in her lap, nodding slightly.

'There is a time, yes, when you strongly desire to see people applauding, see enjoyment, see standing ovations, hear the praises. Then you sing *to* them, you sing *for* them, and that is, in itself, a beautiful thing. But the time comes when your music is for the sake of music. Of course the listener is there, but the stage comes when you yourself are the listener of your music. So you sing for them, but that is no longer the primary aim. And the deeper you delve, you see the beauty of its being unfathomable. To be an artist of any kind, and to live in this city especially, one comes to look upon the world like this. Girija Devi used to tell me: Ganga is not just a river, water flowing, but life itself in flux. That's the message! Every morning, people go to Ganga for their dip. But they're not taking a dip in the same river, it's always a different one, in every moment.' She tilts her head. 'That river has no end, it has no beginning. It's ever fresh. If you understand that, then you have left music behind, you might say. You have left even the world behind. And this city, with all its colour and devotion, has evolved for one reason only, which is to pay homage to that.'

Afterword

Are there not thousands of cities full of treasures
at every step? But Shiva, I swear to you, I have
nowhere laid eyes on a city such as Kashi.
— Kashi Khanda

Between the eleventh and the seventeenth centuries, virtually
all of Banaras was demolished by successive invaders. In the
late twelfth century Qutb-ud-din Aibak, a former slave who
became a sultan, almost levelled the city to the ground,
destroying more than a thousand temples in the process. The
sixth Mughal emperor Aurangzeb razed many more, including, in 1669, the Kashi Vishwanath temple, Hinduism's holiest
site. This litany of destruction confirms the sense that the city
itself is not bricks and mortar, but something more resilient.
No matter what history throws at it, it seems to survive. And
yet part of me wonders whether, at long last, the city might
have met its match. The much-feted modernisation of India
is affecting changes in the social landscape here that might
prove as destructive to Varanasi's makeup as any army. India's
growing economy and the explosion in connectivity to the

Internet are changing the aspirations of its young people in radical ways. Caste and faith — the ties that have held Indian society together for so long — are fraying, as the Western model, based on individualism, enters the picture. This is all going to affect Varanasi in ways no one can predict.

In the newest districts of the city — little more than clusters of new concrete buildings, really — the old structures are noticeably absent. It is as if a painter, schooled for several thousand years in a certain mode of creation, has suddenly discarded all that has gone before. These districts have no wells, wrestling arenas, shrines or headmen. They are simply groupings of featureless architecture in which human beings find refuge and try to make a life for themselves. In the days when my explorations took me to the fringes of the city, I found myself grateful for return to the familiarity and lyricism of the river bank. From this I concluded certain things: that we humans are comforted by order and ritual, are threatened by change and are nourished by modes of living that appear to lead us to a kind of fruition. Whether we can live without these things represents the great uncertain experiment of the future, but not one entirely without hope.

My year in Varanasi was an opportunity to witness the continuing evolution of an ancient city in real time. Just as in Hindu scriptures Vishnu takes the form of a fish, a turtle, then a boar, so India's holiest place is reincarnating herself moment by moment. Yet what is most striking about this apparent battle here is that the city's personality seems almost entirely allied with the older mode of being. This is a conservative city, a city that draws its identity from the past, unlike, say, Bombay, whose lure for many Indians is its newness — a place, like America, where one can reinvent oneself. Varanasi is a place where reinvention is something of a dirty word. If people flock to Bombay to embrace modernity and find material wealth, they flock here to seek salvation and to leave the material behind.

I had an encounter, on one of my pre-dawn walks around the city, a conversation that seemed to encapsulate so many of my feelings about this shifting kaleidoscope I was trying to freeze-frame. At Chauki Ghat, I fell into conversation with an old man drawing sketches of the river: free-form, quite avant-garde approximations of the Ganga, using biro on old torn scraps of notebook. The pictures had a power and authority about them that far exceeded the artist's technical skill. He wore the black robes of a mendicant, and spoke precise, eloquent English in a soft voice. We sat taking amiably as the first rays of sun broke through the clouds, talking of art and philosophy and the city we were both attempting to sketch. Before us, the surface of the river was utterly still, except where bisected by the prow of a solitary fishing craft.

'You will never know this city,' he said, while his bony fingers scratched the crescent sweep of the river. 'You will never know it because it only exists in here' – he tapped his skull. 'It is merely an idea. So there is my city, your city, his city' – he pointed to a passing boatman – 'and all the millions of cities that coexist. That is the true meaning of Varanasi, it is a city of the heart actually, that place we're all trying to get to.'

I nodded back at the old man. This was the kind of conversation Varanasi seemed to engender like no other place on earth. And he made a lot of sense. The city was an idea, a totemic symbol as much as it was bricks and stone.

'I'm echoing Kabir really,' he continued. 'He was this city's greatest son: a poet, iconoclast, but ultimately a unifying figure. Kabir would go to the yogis and tell them: "If levitation is so impressive, how come the kites and crows can already do it?"' He chuckled. 'He would go to priests and say: "If shaving your head brings salvation, why aren't all the sheep saved!"'

I found myself laughing too. 'Sounds like he knew how to stir things up.'

'Oh yes,' the old man dabbed at his eyes. 'But he did it for a reason. He was pointing to a place beyond division, beyond categories of any kind. In this city so many things meet. Everything pools together: the present and the past, all the ways humans have tried to comprehend God, and so many of the great cultural traditions of north India, too. But the message of this place, and the reason for the city's long association with death, is that everything that is static dissolves in the end. It dissolves into the place Kabir was pointing to: the Great Mystery itself.'

The old man turned back to his drawing, tore it from the pad and presented it to me.

'Like the mighty Ganga herself,' he said, pointing to the silently flowing water in front of us. 'Everything just keeps on flowing.'

Select Glossary

abar-khabo – a type of Indian sweet

Aghori – ascetic shivaite sadhus

Agni – Hindu God of Fire

akhara – originally referring to training halls for professional fighters, the word can also mean regiment

amrit – nectar

Assi Ghat – the southernmost ghat in Varanasi

avatar – usually translated from Sanskrit as incarnation

Ayodhya – one of seven holy places for Hindus in India, believed to be the birthplace of **Rama**

– the founding father of **Baba Kinaram** the ancient Aghora, considered an incarnation of Shiva

balushahi – a type of Indian sweet

Banarasi – local term for a citizen of Varanasi

Bazardiha – district of Varanasi

Bandhani – a type of tie-dye practised mainly in the states of Rajasthan and Gujarat

barfi – condensed milk and sugar sweet

batti – rock

besan ladoo – a ball-shaped sweet made with chickpea flour

Bhairav – a Shiva temple in Varanasi

bhakti – devotion

bhang – a preparation from the leaves and flowers of the cannabis plant

Bharata – Rama's second brother in the Ramayana

bhel puri – a snack made of puffed rice, vegetables and a tamarind sauce

bidi – thin, hand-rolled Indian cigarette

chaat – a term describing savoury snacks

chai – spiced tea

cham cham – a type of Bengali sweet

chappals – sandals

chenna – fresh curd cheese

chillum – a straight conical pipe, traditionally made of clay

Chitrakuta or **Chitrakoot** – the 'hill of many wonders' is a town and district of Madhya Pradesh, said to be where Rama, Sita and his brother Lakshmana spent eleven and half years of their fourteen years of exile

choli – a midriff-baring blouse or upper garment in the Indian sari costume worn in India

crore – a crore is a unit in the South Asian numbering system equal to ten million, or the equivalent of a hundred lakhs

dargah – a Sufi Islamic shrine built over the grave of a revered religious figure

Dashashwamedh Ghat – the main ghat in Varanasi on the Ganges River. It is located close to 'Vishwanath Temple'

dhaba – roadside restaurant

dhak – a leaf used to prevent milk from souring

dharma – can mean duties, rights, laws, conduct, virtues and 'right way of living'

dhuni – sadhus' sacred fire place

Dom Raja – caste whose traditional role is to tend the funeral pyre in Varanasi

dupatta – a long scarf worn by women in South Asia

Dussehra – one of the most important Hindu festivals, celebrating Lord Rama's victory over the ten-headed demon king Ravana

Faizabad – city in Uttar Pradesh, India, situated on the banks of the river Ghaghra

gaddidar – middleman

gali – alley

Ganesha – also known as Ganapati and Vinayaka, Ganesha is the Elephant Headed God of the Hindu pantheon, also called 'the remover of obstacles'

Ganga – the goddess of the river Ganges is known as Ganga, and she and the river are worshipped as one

GB Road – GB Road (full name Garstin Bastion Road) runs from Ajmeri Gate to Lahori Gate in Delhi and is the city's biggest red light area

gend balla – cricket

ghat – a series of steps leading down to a body of water

goonda – thug

gora – white person

gotakhor – diver

Govardhana hill – a hill located near the town of Vrindavana, said to have been lifted by the God Krishna with his left hand, thus providing shelter for the townspeople and their cows from a devastating storm

gram – chickpea flour

guda – Sanskrit word for jaggery, a concentrated product of date, cane juice or palm sap

gujiyar – a sweet dumpling, resembling a samosa filled with dry fruits, khoya, coconut and wheat flour

gulab jamun – one of the most popular Indian desserts. Dumplings traditionally made of thickened or reduced milk, soaked in rose-flavoured sugar syrup

gulmohar – *Delonix regia*, a flamboyant tree

haldi – Hindi word for the spice turmeric

halwai – sweet maker

Hanuman – Hanuman is the Monkey God, central character in the Indian epic *Ramayana*, renowned for his courage, power and faithful, selfless service

hariyali – a ricotta-like cheese made by simmering milk in an iron cauldron for several hours

ikshu – Sanskrit word for sugar cane

jalebi – a popular sweet made by deep-frying a flour batter in circular shapes, which are then soaked in sugar syrup

Janaki – another word for Sita, consort of the Hindu God Sri Rama

jati – caste/characteristic

Julaha – a term referring to weavers, may derive from the Persian *julah* (ball of thread)

kachori – this spicy snack is usually a round flattened ball made of flour filled with a stuffing of yellow dal or *Urad Dal*, chickpea flour, and spices

kalakand – a popular sweet made out of solidified, sweetened milk and cottage cheese

Kar Seva – Seva refers to 'selfless service', work or service performed without any thought of personal benefit. Kar Seva refers to the construction or cleaning of a religious place such as a temple, originating from the Sanskrit words *kar* (hand) and *sevak* (servant)

karma patha – a pattern used in the traditional learning of Vedic chants

Kashi – Sanskrit name for Banaras

Khevat – the boatman who ferries Rama across the Ganga in the Hindu epic *Ramayana*

khoa– dairy product made by milk thickened by heating in an open iron pan

kushti – wrestling

ladoo – a round Indian sweet, said to be the favourite of the Elephant God Ganesh

lal peda – traditional Indian sweet made from milk and sugar

layakari – a term used in Indian classical music to describe the fluid relationship between basic timekeeping and the changeable tempos of a performance

madhusarika – a sweet cake

Mahabharata – one of the two major Sanskrit epics of ancient India, the other being the *Ramayana*

Mahant – a religious superior, in particular the chief priest of a temple or the head of a monastery

Maharaja – a Sanskrit title for a 'great king' or 'high king'

Mallah – the traditional boatmen caste and ethnic group of North India

mallaiiyya – a sweet made of whipped cream, saffron and pistachios

malpoa – sweet pancake often from flour, semolina, milk and yoghurt

mandaka – paratha stuffed with sweetened pulses

Manikarnika – One of the two traditional burning ghats in Varanasi

mardana – traditional name for a weaving room

masti – love of life, said to be a defining characteristic of those who live in Varanasi

mithai – sweets

modak – dumplings filled with coconut and palm sugar

mohallas – Islamic equivalent to 'parish'

moksha – enlightenment or liberation

morendaka – ancient Indian sweet shaped like the eggs of a peacock

motichur – smaller variation of the traditional ladoo sweet

mudra – a symbolic or ritual gesture in Hinduism and Buddhism

narkel naru – spherical sweets made from milk and coconut

paan – is the Hindi word for betel nut, a mouth sweetener, freshener and digestive widely appreciated in various forms in India

pani puri – sometimes known as gol gappa this is a popular street snack in India, consisting of a round, hollow pur filled with a mixture of flavoured water (*pani*), tamarind, chilli, potato, onion and chickpeas

papadum – a thin, disc-shaped Indian food made from black gram (chickpea) flour, fried or cooked with dry heat

patha – a musical recitation style

pattu – weavers

phanita – thickened juice of sugar cane

pilar pedha – semi-soft sweet from the Indian subcontinent made with milk, sugar and spices

puja – a prayer ritual performed by Hindus to host, honour and worship one or more deities, or to spiritually celebrate an event

raag – a melodic mode in Indian classic music

raagdari – a term for the combined effect of multiple sounds, melodious in nature, which are pleasing to the ear

rabri – condensed milk infused with sugar, spices and nuts

Rama – the seventh avatar of the Hindu God Vishnu, and a king of Ayodhya in Hindu scriptures

Ramayana – one of the great Hindu epics. It is ascribed to the Hindu sage Valmiki

Ramlila – literally 'Rama's *lila* or play', this is a dramatic folk re-enactment of the life of Rama

rasgolla – a cheese-based, syrupy sweet, made from ball-shaped dumplings of cottage cheese and semolina dough, cooked in sugar syrup

sadhu – holy man

samaya – pastries made from flour, butter and spices

samsara – the repeating cycle of reincarnation within Hinduism, Buddhism, Bön, Jainism, and Taoism

shankarpali – traditional Maharashtrian snack recipe made of dough fried in oil

sharkara – brown sugar

shastika – pastries made from barley flour

shehnai – double reed oboe, common in India, made out of wood, with a metal flare at the end

Shiva – the Supreme God within Shaivism, one of the three most influential denominations in contemporary Hinduism

Sita – goddess of wealth and wife of Vishnu, Sita is the central female character of the Hindu epic *Ramayana*

smashan – cremation ground

sohan papdri – flaky Indian sweet made from sugar, chickpea flour and cardamom

subzi – a generic term for vegetables cooked with spices: perhaps the most staple dish of the Indian subcontinent

tava – cast iron griddle used for cooking flat breads

thandai – a cold drink prepared with a mixture of almonds, cardamom, saffron, milk and sugar

thumri – a devotional form of Indian classical music

yatra – pilgrimage

Notes

INTRODUCTION

p. 1 *Kashi is the whole world they say*: Diana Eck, *Banaras: City of Light*, Penguin Books, Delhi, 1983.

INSTANT MOKSHA

p. 9 *Virtue does not grow easily in Banaras*: Raja Rao, *On the Ganga Ghat*, Orient Paperbacks, Delhi, 1989.

p. 13 *A folk saying – still muttered*: Diana Eck, *Banaras: City of Light*.

SEARCHING FOR RAMA IN RAMNAGAR

p. 31 *Oh Saunaka my friend*: William Buck, *Ramayana*, University of California Press, Delhi, 1981.

p. 33 *Who is that courageous one*: http://www.valmikiramayan.net/utf8/baala/sarga1/bala_1_frame.htm.

p. 34 *Some pages in a mildewed book*: James Prinsep, *Benares Illustrated, in a Series of Drawings*, Vishwavidyalaya Prakashan, Varanasi, 1996 (1833 original).

SEX FOR SALE

p. 51 *Why do you provoke me*: Mirza Hadi Ruswa, *Umrao Jaan Ada*, M.A. Husaini and K. Singh (trans.), Disha, New Delhi, 2006 (1899 original).

p. 57 *An NGO called Guria*: see www.guria.org.

THE MICE IN THE MITHAI SHOP

p. 79 *The Indians have an unparalleled sweet tooth*: Aroona Reejsinghhani, *Indian Sweets and Desserts*, Orient Paperbacks, Delhi, 1979.

p. 81 *The poet Bedhab Banarasi eulogised the fruit*: Kunal Sinha, *A Banarasi on Varanasi*, BlueJay Books, Delhi, 2004.

THE GANGA

p. 97 *I am the shark among the fishes:* Dharmdeo Singh, *Bhagavad Gita: An Art of Living*, Llumina Press, Fort Lauderdale, 2012.

p. 97 *I come a fallen man to you*: Panditaraja Jagannatha, *Ganga Lahari: The Flow of the Ganges*, Swami Avimukteswaran and Saraswati and Boris Marjanovic (trans.), Indica Books, Varanasi, 2007.

p. 98 *The location of the city*: see Richard Lannoy, *Benares: Seen from Within*, University of Washington Press, Seattle, 1999.

THE WARP AND THE WEFT

p. 121 *The loom and the shuttle lie forgotten:* Nirmal Dass, *Songs of Kabir from the Adi Granth*, Sri Satguru Publications, Delhi, 1991.

p. 122 *I was delicate, most delicate*: Rupert Gethin, *The Foundations of Buddhism*, Oxford University Press, Oxford, 1998.

p. 126 *Julaha has come to take on some negative connotations*: 'The Julaha generally bears the character of being cowardly, pretentious, factious and bigoted; [sic] declared Crooke in his account of the tribes and castes of the Northwest provinces, published in 1896 ... the Julaha reputation for bigotry was founded, of course, on the part they took in the sectarian strife that racked different parts of India at various times in the nineteenth century', taken from Gyanendra Pandey, 'The Bigoted Julaha', *Economic and Political Weekly*, vol. 18, no. 5 (29 Jan. 1983).

p. 132 *Embroidery threads are done by women*: traditionally the weaving space was referred to as the *mardana* as opposed to the women's quarters: the *zenana*.

p. 136 *They used hammers to knock down*: see http://news.bbc.co.uk/onthisday/hi/dates/stories/december/6/newsid_3712000/3712777.stm.

THE CITY OF TEN THOUSAND WIDOWS

p. 145 *In childhood a female must be subject*: G. Bühler (trans.), *The Laws of Manu*, Clarendon Press, Oxford, 1886.

p. 151 *Turkish social anthropologist, Nur Yalman*: 'On the Purity of Women in the Castes of Ceylon and Malabar', *Journal of the Royal Anthropological Institute of Great Britain and Ireland*, vol. 93, no. 1 (Jan. 1963).

p. 154 *Asha Bhavan, or 'House of Hope'*: see www.widows-varanasi.info.

HARMONY, RHYTHM AND ORDER

p. 161 *In the East, music has been*: Osho, *The Great Pilgrimage from Here to Here*, Rebel Publishing House, Poona, 1988.

AFTERWORD

p. 183 *Are there not thousands of cities*: cited in Diana Eck, *Banaras: City of Light*.

Select Bibliography

Buck, William, *Ramayana*, University of California Press, Delhi, 1981

Bühler, G. (trans.), *The Laws of Manu*, Clarendon Press, Oxford, 1886

Coleman, Simon and Elsner, John, *Pilgrimage: Past and Present in the World's Religions*, British Museum Press, London, 1995

Coute, Pierre-Daniel and Léger, Jean Michel *Benares: Un Voyage D'Architecture*, Editions Creaphis, Paris, 1989

Dass, Nirmal, *Songs of Kabir from the Adi Granth,* Sri Satguru Publications, Delhi, 1991

Dodson, Michael S., *Banaras: Urban Forms and Cultural Histories*, Routledge, Delhi, 2012

Doron, Assa, *Caste Occupation and Politics on the Ganges: Passages of Resistance*, Ashgate Publishing, Surrey, 2008

Eck, Diana, *Banaras: City of Light*, Penguin, Delhi, 1983

Filippi, Gian Giuseppe, *Mytu: Concept of Death in Indian Traditions*, D.K. Printworld, New Delhi, 1996

Freitag, Sandria B., *Culture and Power in Banaras: Community Performance and Environment 1800–1980*, Oxford University Press, Delhi, 1995

Gethin, Rupert, *The Foundations of Buddhism*, Oxford University Press, Oxford, 1998

Greaves, E., *Kashi, The City Illustrious, or Benares*, The Indian Press, Allahabad, 1909

Jagannatha, Panditaraja. *Ganga Lahari: The Flow of the Ganges*, Swami Avimukteswaran and Saraswati and Boris Marjanovic (trans.), Indica Books, Varanasi, 2007

Kapur, Anuradha, *Actors, Pilgrims, Kings and Gods: The Ramlila of Ramnagar*, Seagull Books, Delhi, 1990

Katz, Marc, *The Children of Assi: The Transference of Religious Traditions and Communal Inclusion in Banaras*, Pilgrims Book House, Varanasi, 2007

Lannoy, Richard, *Benares: Seen from Within*, University of Washington Press, Seattle, 1999

Osho, *The Great Pilgrimage from Here to Here*, Rebel Publishing House, Poona, 1988

Prinsep, J., *Benares Illustrated, in a Series of Drawings,* Vishwavidyalaya Prakashan, Varanasi, 1996 (1833 original)

Raman, V., *The Warp and the Weft: Community and Gender Identity Among the Weavers of Benares*, Routledge, Delhi, 2010

Raja Rao, *On the Ganga Ghat*, Orient Paperbacks, Delhi, 1989

Reejsinghhani, Aroona, *Indian Sweets and Desserts*, Orient Paperbacks, Delhi, 1979

Ruswa, Mirza Hadi, *Umrao Jaan Ada,* M.A. Husaini and K. Singh (trans.), Disha, New Delhi, 2006 (1899 original)

Sherring, W., *Benares: The Sacred City of the Hindus in Ancient and Modern Times,* B.R. Publishing Corp, Delhi, 1975 (1868 original)

Singh, Dharmdeo, *Bhagavad Gita: An Art of Living*, Llumina Press, Fort Lauderdale, 2012

Sinha, Kunal, *A Banarasi on Varanasi*, BlueJay Books, Delhi, 2004

Thompson, Lewis, *Journals of an Integral Poet,* Richard Lannoy (ed.), Fourth Lloyd Productions, Virginia, 2006

Varsha, Rani, *Banaras: The Eternal City*, Prakash Book Depot, Delhi, 1996

Acknowledgements

To the many friends in Varanasi, too many to mention here, thank you for hospitality, and for opening your city to an outsider. Special thanks to: Professor Ananda Krishna, Pintu for the translation and excellent coffee, Rakesh of my favourite bookshop Harmony, for endless recommendations and kindness, Navneet Raman, Manju Sunduram, Bettina Böhme, Kashi, Pinku, Rana P.B. Singh, Atma, Sangeeta, Shivani of Aum, Jitan, Ajeet and Manju at Guria. Deepest gratitude to the phenomenal editorial team of Helen Garnons-Williams, Elizabeth Woabank and Steve Cox at Bloomsbury, and to Victoria Hobbs at A.M. Heath for getting the whole thing off the ground.

Index

abortions, 156

Adampura, 125

Aghoris, 21–7

  ascetic practices, 25–7

  solemnity, 23

Agni (god of fire), 20, 98

Akbar, Emperor, 172

Allahabad, 100, 167

  sex trade in, 61–7

Almora, 31

amrit (ambrosia), 97

Andhra Pradesh, 131

Ansaris, 126, 130, 134

arti ceremonies, 50, 54, 98, 110

Asha Bhavan ('House of Hope'),

  153–9

Assi Ghat, 3, 34–5, 37, 52, 87, 99,

  115, 168

Atharva Veda, 85

Atma (student), 147–52

Aurangzeb, Emperor, 183

Awadh, 56

Ayodhya, 31, 49

  destruction of mosque, 136–9

Baba Kinaram, 21, 25

Babur, Emperor, 136

Bahadur (guide), 123–7, 132, 134–40

Banaras Hindu University (BHU),

  53, 77, 103, 111, 147–8

Banaras Hindu University hospital,

  76

Banarasi, Bedhab, 81

Bazardiha, 141

Bengal, 100

Beniabagh, 137

Besant, Annie, 176

Bhairav temple, 14

bhajans (devotional songs), 171

bhang (cannabis resin), 80, 87

Bharatiya Janata Party (BJP), 19,
    137, 150
Bihar, 108
black magic, 53
Blavatsky, Helena, 175
boatmen, 109–14
Bofors scandal, 108
bol music, 171–2
Bollywood songs, 34, 91
Bombay, *see* Mumbai
Brahma, 54
Brahman, 12, 26–7
Brahmanism, 85, 150–2
Brahmins, 17, 19, 58, 141, 152
    *svarupa*s, 40–2, 44–5
    and Vedic chanting, 163–6
brothels, roadside, 60
Buddha, 6, 86, 98, 122, 142
buffaloes, 84, 115
bulls, 161
bureaucracy, 104, 107
Bux, Ali, 169

Calcutta, *see* Kolkata
Call of the Shehnai, The, 169
caste system, 7, 13, 18–19, 102, 122,
    135
    decline of, 184
    Muslims and, 125–6
    and widows, 151–2

chaat (street food), 28, 80
Chandauli, 23, 25
Chanhu-daro, 122
Chaukhaghat jail, 57, 157
Chauki Ghat, 185
chickens, 153
child labour, 129
children
    funerals of, 20, 28
    and *Ramlila* plays, 40–2, 44–5
    and sex trade, 54–5, 61, 65–7
China, and textile industry, 122,
    131, 134, 141
Chitrakuta, 49
Choudhary, Gupta, 14–22, 28–9
coconut water, 45
Congress Party, 108
corruption, 7, 59, 107, 147
    police and, 52, 55–6, 113
courtesans, 56–7, 172–4
cows, sacred, 83, 85
cremation ghats, 9–29, 98
crematorium, electric, 14, 28

dancing girls, 59
dargahs (Sufi shrines), 146
Dashashwamedh Ghat, 54, 137,
    145
Delhi, 52, 122, 135, 148
Devi, Girija, 174–5, 178–9, 181

Dhobis, 126

dhrupad singing, 174

dhunis (sacred fireplaces), 20

diabetes, 93

Dom Raja, 13–20, 29, 37, 98

donkeys, 44

dowry system, 55, 156–7

  dowry burnings, 156

drug-dealers, 52, 66

Durga Mandir, 43

Dussehra festival, 49

East India Company, 173

'Eight Snares of Existence', 27

elephants, 32, 46–7

Faizabad, 136

food prices, increased, 142

gaddidars (middlemen), 141

galis (lanes), 6, 123

Gandaki, river, 100

Gandhi, Mahatma, 18

Gandhi, Rajiv, 108–9, 140

Ganesh Chathurthi, 90

Ganesha, 13, 90, 139

Ganga, river, 97–119

  course of, 100–1

  fishing ban, 112–13

  pollution, 28, 102–3

  river basin and population

    density, 100

  sacred nature of, 97–9, 101–2

  see also boatmen; gotakhors

Ganga Action Plan, 108–9, 112

Ganga Canal, 100

Gangetic Plain, 100

Gaumakh, 100

gend balla (cricket), 17

Ghagra, 100

ghats, 3, 34, 58, 98, 147, 149

ghee, and cremations, 17

Girnar mountains, 25

goats, 115

Godowlia, 137

gopis (women cowherds), 174

gotakhors (river divers), 110–11

Great Exhibition, 129

Gujarat, 131

gulab jamun, 84–5

Guria (NGO), 57, 59

guru shishya tradition, 166, 178

Gwalior, 52

Haaji Mohamed, 127–32, 134, 136,

  142

Haj subsidy, 128

halwais (sweet-makers), 7, 81, 86–95

Hanuman, 94

Harappa, 122

Hari (Hindu weaver), 140–3

Haridwar, 100

Harishchandra Ghat, 13

Harsu village, 23

heroin trade, 7, 55

Hindu–Muslim relations, 135–9,
        169–70

Hinduism, 12–13, 53, 97, 102

    and widows, 150–2

    see also Ramlila plays

Hindustan Times, 91

Hirishchandra, King, 15–16

HIV, 65, 76

holy men, 54, 115, 161, 171

    see also sadhus; yogis

Home Rule Movement, 176

human trafficking, 7, 57, 60

Indus Valley Civilisation, 122

Internet, 36, 184

Jaitpura, 125

Janakpur, 49

Janakpur Mandir, 43

Jaunpur, 123

Jawaharlal (type of sweet), 94

Julahas (weavers), 125–6

Kabir, 6, 171, 186

kachori (potato pies), 80

Kali Puja festival, 137

Kamala (sex worker), 69–77

Kanpur, 61, 73, 94, 100

Kar Seva, 137

'Kashi' (the name), 7

Kashi (boatman), 35–7, 99–102,
        109–14

Kashi Vishwanath Mandir, 138

Khan, Bismillah, 167, 169–71

Khan, Rasool Baksh, 169

Khevat the boatman, 36

khoa (thickened milk), 82–4,
        90–1

Khoya Gali, 79, 82

Kolkata (Calcutta), 52, 89

Kosi, river, 100

Krishna, 85, 174

Krishna, Professor Ananda, 33–5,
        172–5

Krishnamurti, Jiddu, 3, 102, 176

Ksheer Sagar sweet shop, 87–95

Kunal (khoa maker), 83–4

kushti (unarmed combat), 117

ladoos, 87–8, 90, 94

Lal Bhagi, 126

Lanka, 49, 116

Lohta, 138, 141

Lolark Kund, 87

Lucknow, 56, 94

Ma Anandamayee Ashram, 87

Madanpura, 123, 125, 133, 137

Madhubani, 32

Mahabharata, 10

Maharashtra, 131

Mallahs, 110, 114

Mandeshwari temple, 23

mangoes, 81

Manikarnika, 10

marriages, arranged, 151

masseurs, 54

masti (love of life), 83, 124

Mazumda, Bhagwanti, 158

Mecca, 128

Mehta, Deepa, 149–50

Mela gatherings, 97

mice, 4, 86–7

milk market, 82–5

Mishra, Professor Veer Bhadra
('Mahant-ji'), 103–7, 112,
116–19

missionaries, British, 173

mithai (sweets), 81–95
and religious festivals, 81,
89–90

modak (dumplings), 90

mohallas, 6–7

moksha, 12–13, 20–1, 25, 27, 29

mongooses, 124

Mughals, 117, 131, 172

Muharram, 7

Mukul (boatman), 109–14

Mumbai (Bombay), 148, 184–5
sex trade in, 52, 70–3
musical culture, 166–82
and Muslim–Hindu relations,
169–70

Muslim–Hindu relations, 135–9,
169–70

Muslims, 123, 125
and caste system, 125–6
and Haj, 128

Naxalites, 158

New Textile Policy, 140

overpopulation, 27–9, 94

paan, 64, 83, 126

Pakistan, 29

Panchavati, 49

Pandits, 164

pani puri, 80

paropakara ('discipline of mind'),
49

Parvati, 29

Pintu (translator), 38, 41, 44–6,
48–9

police
and corruption, 52, 55–6, 113

officer assists sex workers, 72–3
and sex trade, 62, 65–8, 73–4
and torture, 84–5
poverty, endemic, 7, 65, 102, 110
among weavers, 134–5, 141–2
Prakash (priest), 163–6
Prinsep, James, 34, 172
prostitution, 7, 51–78, 149, 172–3
children and, 54–5, 61, 65–7
police and, 62, 65–8, 73–4
and stigma, 76–7
puja ceremonies, 40–1, 54
Mukut Puja, 44
Pune, 52

Qawwali (devotional music), 171
Qureshi, 126
Qutb-ud-din Aibak, 183

Raag, 167
Raj Ghat, 3, 102
Rajasthan, 131
Rama, 31, 36, 39–41, 47, 49–50, 114,
117, 136
Ramayana, 24, 32–3, 37, 39–41, 43,
48–9
Rambag, 43, 45–6
Ramlila plays, 7, 31–50, 99
rehearsals, 38–44
svarupas, 40–2, 44–5

Ramnagar, 32, 35, 37–8, 43, 45, 49,
99, 101
Ramnagar Fort, 89, 106
rasgolla, 93–4
Ravana (demon), 44, 47–50
Reori Talaab, 125
rhesus monkeys, 5, 106
Rig-Veda, 85
rishis (forest sages), 163
river fish, 116
river turtles, 112–13
Rousseau, Jean-Jacques, 78
rupee, devaluation of, 141

Saadat Khan, 56
sadhus, 13, 20–1, 27, 115, 161
see also Aghoris
Sameer (musician), 167–71
samsara, 12–13, 22, 36
Sangeeta (student), 52–7
Sankat Mochan Foundation,
107
Sankat Mochan temple, 103, 118
Saraswati, 173
Sareyan, 141
saris, 130–1
Sarnath, 153
sati, 23, 150
Satna, 32
Satya Yuga epoch, 15, 20

sex trade/sex workers, *see*
    prostitution
Shankar, Ravi, 167
shehnai music, 170–1
Shiva, 13, 25, 27, 29, 47, 54
    and *bhang*, 80, 87
    and Ganga river, 98–9, 101
Shiva Sena, 149
Shivalok, 159
Shivdaspur, 51–2, 56, 68, 74, 76
Shri Rishabh Dev, 136
Silk Route, 122
Singh, Ajeet, 57–69, 77
Sita, 36, 39, 47, 114
Son, river, 100
Sonapura, 87
Sri Lanka, 149
Sri Ramana Maharshi, 5
subzi (spiced vegetables), 80
sugar cane, 85–6
suicide, among weavers, 134, 141
Sunduram, Manju, 175–82
sweets, *see mithai*

tabla players, 171–2
tawaif culture, 56–7, 172–4
television, 36
thandai (milk drink), 80
Theosophical Society, 175
thumri musical style, 173–5, 180–1

Times of India, 156
Tughlaq Empire, 123
Tulsi Ghat, 103, 106

Uttar Pradesh, 28, 56, 100, 108

Vedic chanting, 162–6
vichikaka (brown-headed gulls),
    114–15
Victoria, Queen, 129
Vishnu, 13, 31, 184
Vishva Hindu Parishad (VHU),
    150
Vishwanath temple 54, 82, 170,
    183
Vrindavan, 31, 148, 174

Water, 149, 154
weavers, 7, 122–3
    Hindu, 134, 140–3
    Muslim, 127–33
West Bengal, 108, 158
widows, 145–7, 149–59, 161
    Hinduism and, 150–2

Yadav, Anoop Kumar, 88–95
Yadav, Khado, 4–5
Yalman, Nur, 151
Yamuna, river, 100
yogis, 1, 13, 25, 186

A NOTE ON THE TYPE

The text of this book is set in Bembo. This type was first used in 1495 by the Venetian printer Aldus Manutius for Cardinal Bembo's *De Aetna*, and was cut for Manutius by Francesco Griffo. It was one of the types used by Claude Garamond (1480–1561) as a model for his Romain de L'Université, and so it was the forerunner of what became standard European type for the following two centuries. Its modern form follows the original types and was designed for Monotype in 1929.